# The Bag
## of
# Money

# The Bag

## Of

# Money

## By *Art Burton*

# Acknowledgements

Once again, I want to thank all of you who purchased my last book and then pressured me to get out the next one. You are my inspiration and driving force. Thank you.

Bev Dauphinee, my editor, came through once again. She is a glutton for punishment as she continues to read my error-plagued copy. I never think it is error-plagued when I send it to her. When she returns it, I find out how wrong I was. As always, while following her recommendations, I couldn't resist the urge to throw in some changes on my own which she will never see until she has the published book in her hand. Any and all errors are mine. Thanks, Bev. You are a champion.

My wife, Flame, assisted with the cover design and photography. Thank you, Flame for all your help and suggestions and for putting up with those long periods when I got lost in some fictional world looking for a bag of money. Hopefully, we will soon find ours.

The turned bowl on the cover was created by master wood turner, Don Moore. Don is a true artist and can do things with a block of wood and a chisel that others can't even dream off. Thanks to Russell White for lending this bowl to me to photograph.

I always look forward to any feedback from readers, both positive—especially positive—and negative. Writing can only improve with honest criticism. Tell me in person when we meet or email me at artburton@eastlink.ca.

# ≈1≈

JOHN SLAMMED the zipper shut.

"Holy shit, Danka, did you see that?"

The dog looked at his master, gave a sharp yelp, sharing the excitement, but not knowing why. They were face to face. John, on his knees, hovered over a red and blue hockey bag with a Montreal Canadiens logo on it. Danka took a quick lick of John's cheek with his long, coarse tongue and dropped into the play position.

"I know, I know," John said. "I saw it, too."

John had sprung the lock securing the hockey bag's zipper. He wasn't sure what he had expected to find: old clothes, actual hockey gear, books. It could have been anything. But it wasn't just anything. It contained money. The bag overflowed with money. Blue, purple, green, orange, brown, a virtual salad of colours.

When he first undid the zipper, the money bulged out the top and spilled onto the ground. That's when he slammed the zipper shut. Now he picked up the money lying on the ground. There were three twenties, two tens and a five: $85. That was the spillage.

It was a cool, late spring morning and John wore a light pair of brown, leather gloves. He didn't realize it at the time, but he would be very glad of this fact later. Overhead the sun filtered through the trees, casting strange shadows on the big bag, adding an air of fancy to the situation.

With the sight of all that cash, the day suddenly became warmer. He surveyed the area around him. Perspiration beaded across his forehead. Except for Danka, he was alone. John eased the zipper open again. Slowly at first, then all the way. Money ballooned out. More bills fluttered to the ground. He scooped them up. Now his hand cradled $200.

He examined it. The bills had been around the block a few times, looked used, spendable. Bills that would not raise any suspicions regardless of where the spending took place. Again he scanned the forest around him. He was still alone. He leaned forward and looked up and down the road. Nothing.

This came as no surprise. Calling this a secondary road would be like putting a tuxedo on a busboy. Appropriately, it was known as the Back Road. It seldom carried any vehicular traffic. Joggers safely ran side-by-side down its centre.

John sat back on his haunches. He had to think. Before him was more money than he had ever seen at one time, possibly more than he had ever seen in his entire life. Like manna from heaven, it was here for the taking. Should he only take enough to pay a few bills and leave the rest? Those followers of Moses who took more manna than needed for the day were disappointed when the excess spoiled. He could fill his pockets. No one would even notice that much missing.

This money was just crammed into the bag. There was no order to it. No system. It was like a bank robber had thrown the bag to the teller and said *fill this with all your money.* But that wasn't what had happened.

Banks kept their money neat, in little rectangular packets.

This looked more like loose money scraped by the armload into the bag from a table with the denominations getting mixed together.

Drug money. They were counting it and had to make a run for it. Of course, that was what had happened.

John's imagination spun into full gear. In his mind's eye he could see the swarthy looking men hunched over a table. Colombians, that's what they would have been.

*"Putta da money into da baga,"* is how they would have talked. *"We gotta get outta here. Pedro, you hida da money in da woods."*

He looked back at the bag of money. He was getting carried away in his imagination. More than likely, the men looked exactly as he did, talked as he did. The only difference was that they owned hundreds of thousands of dollars and carried it around in a big, leather bag.

Drug dealers were the most obvious choice, the favoured choice. He wouldn't mind taking money from them. Why not? They sure as hell couldn't report him to the cops. But they were not the only possibility.

He didn't want to deprive some lonely widow of her life's savings. Some old lady who didn't believe in banks and who carried all her wealth around in a hockey bag. He laughed. Interesting scenario, but not likely the right one.

The proper thing to do would be to turn the bag over to the police and see who claimed it. They tell you that if it remains unclaimed, it will be returned to you. Maybe a small bag of money might, but a big bag of money? A big, red and blue bag of money with the Montreal Canadiens logo on it? You couldn't take that chance, and besides, who was this mysterious "they" making this claim?

If you advertise that you found a bag of money, every scum bag in the country would be trying to guess how much there was so they could claim it. They would all have a story.

The money was to pay for an important, life-saving operation at the Mayo Clinic.

The money was their life savings being used to purchase a new home, not for themselves, but for their poor mother who had spent her whole life tending to the needs of others.

They had raised the money to end poverty in the Third World. Etc., etc., etc.

No, it was drug money. Plain and simple.

Once again John surveyed the land around him. He was still alone, but he had to get into motion soon. Other dog walkers travelled these paths in great numbers. One could be along at any moment.

John fought to control all these unconnected thoughts whirling through his brain. For now, he would just move the bag to a safe place, a place where he could think. His split-entry house stood on the opposite side of this stretch of forest, a few hundred yards down the path. He would take the money there.

Under the stairs was the ideal hiding spot. It housed his hot water tank, pipes from his bathroom and entrance for his water supply from the street. No one ever looked in there but himself. Once the bag was safely ensconced in that lair, John could take his time and make some rational decisions. He picked up the bag, surprised at how heavy it was, and made his way home, cautiously looking around with every step.

Spruce bows reached out like hands to snatch at the bag, forcing John to hold it close to his body. A couple of times, the extra weight caused him to stumble over the exposed roots of large pine trees. John's house backed on this section of forested land. Development had not encroached into his back yard, yet. Maybe he would move up to something bigger, better, before it did.

Peering over the privacy fences on both sides of his property, he made sure no neighbours were watching. Would it matter if they were? After all, he was only carrying a hockey bag. This was Canada. Almost ever male person in the population carried a hockey bag at one time or another in their lifetime. John was only 35, well within the age to still be playing. He carried no excess weight on his solid frame. He fit the profile of a gentlemen's league player.

All that was academic. No one was in sight. He scurried through the gate and across his back lawn. The grass was in need of cutting. With this bag of money, he would be able to hire some kid in the neighbourhood to run the lawnmower over it once a week. Already he was spending the money and he wasn't even in his house yet. Decisions had been made.

He reached his back door, paused, then entered through the basement. His wife was shopping at Wal-Mart but he called out to her anyway. No answer. The kids were both with her. Danka bounded in beside him and ran upstairs to his water dish. John followed the dog to the split-entry's landing and made sure the front doors were locked. He peeked out through the curtain to make sure no one was watching the house. Why would they? Paranoia was setting in. He would have to watch out for that, he thought, as he returned down the steps to the rec room. The bag of money sat ominously by the door, emanating evil vibrations.

John picked up the television remote, turned on the TV and switched to the all-news station. This was as good a place to start as anywhere in his search for the owners—no he preferred losers— of the money. Finder's keepers, loser's weepers. The childhood cliché leapt uninvited to his mind.

Soldiers and civilians were dying in Afghanistan. Civil wars raged in some renamed and thus foreign to him, African countries. Fires scorched the landscape in California.

"Come on, come on. Get to the local news," he mumbled.

He dragged the bag over to the chesterfield and sat down. Slowly he undid the zipper again. The money pushed its way out through the opening. The rainbow of colours again attracted his attention. This time he noticed an array of orange and browns, fifties and hundreds, lurking in the mix, his new favourite colours. Some Americans referred to it as Monopoly money, but they were wrong. This was the real deal. Money he could spend. He started picking out some twenties, arranging them with her majesty the queen's head facing the same way. Five, ten, he counted. Soon he had fifty of them in his sweating palm. One thousand dollars and the bag looked untouched. John started to shake. He dropped the money back onto the pile of bills. There were thousands of dollars here, possibly even hundreds of thousands—no, definitely hundreds of thousands. Beads of perspiration broke out across his forehead, his heart started thumping in his chest, his hands shook uncontrollably.

Stop it, he ordered himself, holding one hand in the other. The enormity of the situation started to register. He had a big bag of money. Someone would be looking for it. Probably drug dealers. No, not would be, *were* looking for it. He thought about taking it back to where he had found it, forgetting about it and moving on with his life. That was not going to happen. He had to pay the kid who was going to mow his lawn.

At that point, the television caught his attention. Police and RCMP had conducted raids on known drug operations in various Maritime centres. Several people had been arrested, others had been detained and then released. Scenes of police cars, lights flashing on top, pulling up to houses that looked just like his flashed across the screen. The raids, a result of nine months of undercover operations, were taking place in neighbourhoods exactly like this one.

White men, not Colombians, were being arrested. Scenes of stacks of money, vials of pills, bags of weed filled the screen, money just like his. This was not absolute evidence of where the money came from, but it was a definite indicator. Only an idiot would think it came from anyplace else. John served his firm as a junior executive. He was no idiot.

He gathered up his wad of twenties, one thousand dollars, and stuffed it in his wallet. It wouldn't close properly so he halved the bundle and put one portion in his billfold and the other in his jacket pocket and zipped it shut. He checked for a bulge and found the lines of the coat looked fine.

Only ten hundred-dollar bills would have been required to make up that same one thousand dollars. No bulge, no mess. But people took notice of hundred-dollar bills. Sometimes they hesitated taking them. Sometimes they remembered who had spent them. No, the twenties were safer to use.

He then dragged the bag of money to its hiding place under the stairs. He would be able to think better without the pile of bills staring at him and it was definitely the time for serious thinking.

He wondered if there was another bag of money lying somewhere in the forest area behind his house. If there was one, there could be two. Why not? His logical mind suggested the owners of the money had filled this bag to overflowing and then put the excess in another bag, perhaps smaller or perhaps only half full.

He called Danka and went into the back yard again. The dog bounded around, trying to figure out what was going on. They had already been for their walk that day, but he was willing to go again, if necessary. John felt the lump in his pocket. It felt good. He smiled. The pair set out along the path once more, John scanning for another hockey bag, Danka checking to make sure no other dog had peed over his spots from earlier in the day. Danka knew several dogs used this same run for their daily exercise and they kept marking his territory. Freshly loaded with water, he reclaimed his domain.

As they neared the location of the earlier find, John could hear voices, excited voices. He grabbed Danka by the collar and quieted him down. They slouched down behind an outcropping of granite rocks among the exposed roots of the trees and listened.

"Keep looking, damn it, it's got to be here," said the first gruff voice.

"We have looked," another responded. "What makes you so sure this is the spot? It was dark and we were driving fast when we went through here."

"Because I used that big maple tree as a maker. I threw the bag just as we slowed by that maple. I heaved it a good one. It's got to be right around here."

"A big maple tree? A big maple tree?" a third voice said. "What about that big maple tree down there at the corner or that one up the road a hundred yards or so? There are big maple trees all along this road, you idiot. How could you use a tree as a marker when you're driving through the forest?"

There was a period of silence and then: "Maybe it was that one down there. They all look alike in the daytime."

"The Boss will have your testicles for lunch if we don't come back with his money. Spending the night in the slammer pissed him off enough, but you not coming back with the money," a pause, "well, you might be better off not even coming back. I say that as a friend."

John heard the static crackle of a walkie-talkie. A new, detached voice came from among the three men.

"A dark car just pulled on to the road. Two guys in it. Look like cops." He could barely make out the words through the electronic interference.

"Look like cops or are cops?" That voice came through loud and clear. The source was a mere twenty-five feet in front of him and heading his way. John willed his breathing to stop and his heart to be quiet. He clamped a hand around Danka's mouth. The dog struggled to get free, then sensed John's fear. He lie down quietly.

"Are cops," came the crackle. "I can see the coloured lights through their grill. Get out of there fast."

With that, the three men rushed onto the road, jumped into a parked, light grey Ford Explorer and took off in a shower of loose rocks. John waited, wondering if he should make a run for it or sit tight. Two minutes later a black Chev Impala slowly cruised by, the two occupants searching the sides of the road as they went by. One of them noticed the fresh sprayed gravel along the edge of the road. They stopped and got out, one male, one female.

"What do you think? This looks like it happened sometime today. Notice the difference in colour of these rocks compared to the ones around them. Someone took off from here in a hurry and not very long ago."

"Yeah, could be. We should give the dog master a call. Let them do a walk through in the area. See what he comes up with. With luck we might find the money and then we can nail those bastards, assuming of course, they didn't just find it themselves. "

Once again, John's heart started to pound. The police dog would start them on an odyssey with his back door as the final destination. John sat there being as quiet as possible, one hand holding Danka's mouth shut, the other fingering the wad of twenties stuffed in his pocket.

What had he been thinking? All he needed was for his dog to start barking at the cops and he would be caught red-handed. Then he came to a conclusion. If the cops were to be led to his house, that would happen whether he had the money or not. He and Danka walked this path every day. This was a lose-lose situation.

"Tell them to pick up the chairs from the interview room. Those clowns sweated in them for over four hours last night. It will give the dog a scent to look for. I can't believe we had to let them go after catching them outright last night just because there was no friggin' money in their car."

"It was either let them go or expose our undercover operatives in court," the lady cop said.

"Yeah, I know. I'd like to get my hands on the son of a bitch who tipped them off. I'd strangle whoever he is. Two minutes earlier and we'd have nailed them with the cash in the house. We're the only ones in the province who didn't score a bust."

John held his breath and waited. The sound of the blood moving from his heart to his brain pounded in his ears. Sweat dripped off his nose. Danka tried to move. John held him tighter.

One of the cops leaned on the car roof while talking on her two-way radio. The other relieved himself among the bushes. Too much coffee, John thought before his mind turned back to more practical thoughts. The wad of twenties weighed down his pocket like a bar of steel. It wouldn't be necessary to track him back to his house. He carried the evidence with him. How stupid.

The time to move had come. Both cops were still distracted. John took advantage of the opportunity and reversed his direction, slinking down the path to his house. Maybe they wouldn't come knocking after all. If they did, he had better have a story ready.

As he approached his back lawn, he noticed two more dog walkers coming from opposite directions. They too would head down the path through the woods to where the police were searching. They would disturb any smell he and Danka may have left and pollute it with their own. Their dogs would pee on the same rocks as Danka and wipe out Danka's scent. He might be safe.

He waved as they disappeared into the forest, part of the same pet-walking fraternity. None of them knew the people names of the others, only the dog's names, but they all chatted with each other on their daily hikes. He could get second-hand information about what the Mounties were up to at their next meeting. Everyone would soon be discussing the missing money. That was guaranteed.

Instead of entering his own back yard, this time he turned and continued down the path. If the police dogs did pick up his trail, it made no sense to lead them directly to his house. He would follow the path to another intersection which led to the street and the route taken by hundreds of school kids four times a day. His scent would be lost among theirs and he could safely enter his house by the front door. He had owned the money for less than half an hour and already his mind worked like that of a seasoned criminal. Once more, he thought the smartest thing to do would be to just return the money to the cops. It was, but he didn't do it. Sometimes people just don't do the smartest thing.

# ≈2≈

JOHN SLEPT poorly. He kept having dreams in which some thug kept saying he would have his testicles for lunch, interspersed with dreams of Mounties knocking on his door and leading him away in cuffs. The bag of money with the Canadiens logo on it was safely tucked under the steps covered with some old lawn chairs that needed rewebbing. John tossed and turned, slumbered and woke, then slumbered again only to face another arrest. Finally he got up and tiptoed out of the bedroom and went down to the rec room. His wife turned over and filled the vacated space but didn't wake up.

John turned on the TV. Flames lit up the California landscape. He was still on the all-news channel. Helicopter shots of mansions burning could be seen through the billowing clouds of smoke. Soot-streaked firefighters were being interviewed with the burnt-out husks of deserted homes starkly standing in the background. It was the worst fire season ever, even worse than last year. What about the local news? Had they made any progress in catching the local drug lords? He knew the answer to that question without the aid of a talking head on television. They had not. The evidence the police needed sat hidden under the steps across the hall from him.

Danka came padding into the room, sniffed at John before curling up on the floor at his feet. Even though he was as involved as John in finding and taking the money, he slept with a clear conscience, a born criminal. John envied him.

Images of police cars once again passed across the TV screen. Suburban scenes that could be his neighbourhood followed. A rebroadcast of the news show he had seen the previous afternoon. Nothing new had been added. The pictures were the same. The interviews were the same. John reached for the remote and changed the channel.

An infomercial assaulted his eyes. Man's most insidious fear was being solved by a small aerosol can of some magical substance. Baldness was being cured with a spray can of gunk that filled in those spots on the top of the head where pristine scalp shone through. Receding hairlines were being filled in with the same ease. It came in four colours: black, brown, blond and a shade of red. All four stood out like a glaring light on the victim's head. Sorry, not a victim, volunteer sufferer's head. Gullible suckers, John thought. Some people will do anything to make a buck. He clicked the remote again.

An old movie with Art Carney and George Burns came on. John remembered the plot. Three old guys had robbed a bank and then had to figure out how to use the money without being caught with their sudden new wealth. They failed. He remembered the cops warning George Burns to give it up. He would never get away with it.

John, however, would succeed. He saw no joy in just owning a bag of money. The only worthwhile thing about owning a bag of money was spending the loot.

He would not change his lifestyle. He would start paying cash for things: gas, groceries, clothes, everyday items. His mortgage, power bill, credit-card payments would continue to come out of his bank account. His credit cards would remain in his wallet until the bills were paid off. He would set up a payroll deduction for

RRSPs. It was important that his bank account not be stagnant, that it continue to have money move through it.

That was the easy part. The big problem would be to get the cash into the hands of his wife and children without them getting suspicious. Well, the children would be easy: just hold out a five-dollar bill and watch it disappear. His wife, however, was a dedicated user of her debit card. The easy way to convert her to using cold, hard cash again would be to show her the big bag of money. No, he decided, the fewer people who knew about this found loot, the better. Loose lips sink ships.

There could be no mention of this find to anyone, no close friend, no close relative, no one. He would bear the burden himself. With these thoughts churning around in his mind, he drifted off to sleep, only to be awoken by the sun shining in his eyes through the rec room windows. His watch told him it was 6:30 a.m. His neck told him he had picked a very poor posture for sleeping.

John snuck back upstairs. Marla stirred in the bed on the verge of waking. John went into the bathroom and flushed the toilet before returning to the bedroom. Marla opened her eyes and smiled at him.

"Answering nature's call?" she asked.

"Yeah," John said as he crawled back under the covers. Marla snuggled up close to him. It was Sunday morning and neither had to be out of bed anytime soon. John took her in his arms and started rubbing her back and shoulders. He moved in a little closer, their bodies in contact from breasts and chests, to bellies, to thighs. Marla wrapped a leg around John's. She frowned. There was usually some reaction by now in the part of the body that men have no control over. This morning, nothing.

"Something the matter?" Marla asked. Her hands slipped inside his pajamas and ran lightly across his bottom, pulling him a little closer. Still no reaction.

"I guess I've got some things on my mind."

Marla squirmed in closer. "That thing should be me," she said.

John tried to clear his mind of thoughts of bags of money, of testicles being served for lunch, of being arrested and led away in cuffs. He failed. He broke free from his wife's grip and crawled out of bed.

"Maybe later," he said and went back into the bathroom. It was said that people with money had different problems than mere mortals without. This was not the kind of problem John had anticipated. He sat on the toilet with the cover still down, holding his head in his hands, elbows resting on his knees and massaged his temples.

Again the enormity of his action, taking and hiding the money, swept over him. This was supposed to be a good thing. He could not let it take over and alter his life, especially in a negative way. There was a scratching at the bathroom door as fingernails lightly drummed against the door.

"Hey lover, come back to bed. We can work through this. I have my ways." This was followed by Marla's best ghoulish horror film laugh. John couldn't help but smile. He went back to bed. She did have her ways. They were able to work their way through it.

Later, as they lay luxuriating in each other's arms, they heard sounds coming from the kitchen. The kids were up and were getting their own breakfasts. Should they continue lying there doing nothing, an enjoyable nothing, and then have to face cleaning up the kitchen later or head the future work off at the pass and go out and prepare breakfast for the kids? Food sounded like a good idea to both of them. They chose to head off the impending disaster in the kitchen and enjoy a family breakfast.

The sun shone higher in the sky now and lit up the kitchen area of the house. It was too beautiful a day to be inside but what should they do?

"Let's go down to the flea market and browse around while we are deciding how to spend the rest of the day," Marla said. Summer Sunday mornings saw the local hockey rink converted into a huge open-air market. Excess sellers spilled into the parking lot.

Everything from fresh fruits and vegetables to your neighbour's junk could be purchased from the various tables lined up in row after row of pure capitalism. Price was determined solely by the market.

Used novels could be bought for as little as a quarter or as much as two dollars, depending on the deal reached between the buyer and the seller. No prices were carved in stone. At least not the prices of the items that sold. If you were unhappy with a price asked and couldn't reach a compromise, move on. The same item would probably be available on one of the hundreds of tables offering their wares. You could try again to reach your price.

"The flea market!" John said. "Yes, let's go to the flea market."

Eureka! He found the ideal venue for his newfound wealth. Cash was the most predominant medium at these places of business. Large grimy wads of cash just like his were in several pockets, both of buyers and sellers, as people came looking for bargains that could only be obtained with cash on the barrel head. No matter what the price, cash was the preferred method of exchange.

Today he would go buy, scout out what was hot, what was not. Next week he would be there selling. Regardless of his success as an entrepreneur, he could come home and give Marla a handful of cash to see her through the week. Each week he would spend a few hours standing around chatting with people, maybe sell the odd item, and then go home and circulate his new wealth. Eureka!

The weight of the world lifted from John's shoulders. He slathered sunscreen on the faces and arms of the kids, followed by a good dosing of his own face, especially across the nose and cheeks. The sun could be brutal in these wide open, paved parking lot. Marla, with her red hair and fair complexion, used a sun block instead of a sun screen. It was rated at 50 on the SPF scale. It was like walking in the shade wherever she went.

As John and family were driving past the turnoff to the Back Road on the way to the rink, they noticed an orange school bus parked on the side of the road. Many orange-coveralled people were standing around drinking coffee. They looked as if they were waiting for instructions. These men and women made up the local band of search and rescue volunteers for the area and John recognized one of his neighbours. He pulled over and rolled down the window of his van.

"Hi, Fraser, what's up?" he asked.

Fraser turned from the group of men he was with and walked over to the open window. A walkie-talkie hung from a strap around his waist, a compass dangled around his neck, folded maps could be seen poking out of a leg pocket on the coveralls.

"Hey, John," he said. "Not too sure what's going on just yet. The Mounties asked us to come out and do a search of this area of woods. They seldom tell us what we're looking for, just to report anything that looks out of place."

He looked around to see if any of his fellow searchers were within ear shot. None were. "I hear some drug money was dumped in the area. Man, would I ever like to find that. Who would know?"

"Yeah," John said. "Just kick some leaves over it and come back later and pick it up."

Again Fraser looked around in a conspiratorial manner.

"I hear the police dogs searched the area yesterday. They didn't find any loot, but it appears some suspects had been prowling around. The cops could tell that by the reaction of the dogs. The bad guys probably retrieved the money themselves. Just my luck. We're looking for clues to tie them in, I guess. But, still—" He let the thought trail off. Everybody would like to find a big bag of money.

"If you find it, let me know. I'll give you a hand carrying it out." Pause. "And of course, spending it." Everyone in the van laughed.

As they drove away, Marla and the kids discussed what they would do if they found the money. John Jr. would buy a race car, the fastest race car made, and would race it on the NASCAR circuit. Mary would buy a complete set of Barbie dolls and all kinds of clothes to dress them in. Marla would travel to exotic places. John concentrated on the driving and said nothing.

Thousands of people were already making the rounds of the tables when they arrived at the flea market. Vendors were calling out prices to anyone who showed interest in any of their wares and quickly undercutting their own prices if the person set the item down again. Bargains were to be had at many of the tables if you could come up with even a remote need for the articles displayed. Other tables had prices that would rival the most exclusive downtown shops. These sellers defended their prices in a belligerent manner that would never generate more sales for them.

"It's practically new," they said. "Never been used and I'm not giving it away."

*Right*, John thought, *and you're not selling it either, not at that price.* Experience taught him to say nothing and move on. Some people didn't grasp the concept of selling at a flea market. Everyone looked for bargains, not for something almost new, but with no warranty and at almost the full price.

"Let's start with a sausage on a bun with mustard and sauerkraut," he said to Marla.

"Get serious," she said. "We just finished breakfast."

"OK, but I think I'll have one. That's part of the reason we come to these things, the healthy food." He laughed and ordered his food from a vendor standing over a barbecue loaded with wieners and sausages.

He looked around at the various vendors and formulated a plan. He would have to convince Marla that spending his weekends being part of this business community was a good idea, an idea she could embrace with enough enthusiasm to let him do it every week. He noticed an older gentleman selling old tools with a wad of cash in his hand that anywhere else would be referred to as a flash roll. John picked up a hammer and hefted it in his hand, checking out the feel. He was a hobby woodworker so this was not out of character for him.

"Five dollars." The old man had spotted him with merchandise in one hand, showing an inkling of interest in his product.

"You're kidding," said John. "I can buy a new one for eight dollars."

"Not of that quality. They don't make them like that anymore. Look at that steel."

The old man took the hammer and pounded it against a piece of metal on the table. A sharp metal on metal sound rang out, causing heads to turn in their direction.

"Listen to that ring. That's quality. Four dollars but not a cent less. I'm losing money at that price."

John laughed. "How are you losing money?"

He pushed the last of his sausage into his mouth and wiped the mustard from his fingers on his napkin.

Marla and the kids had drifted away, looking at a table full of knick-knacks further down the line. John had to get them back to make his plan work.

"Marla, do you have four dollars?"

She turned and came back, digging in her purse as she walked. "Do you really need another hammer, John?"

John shrugged. "It's only four bucks." He unzipped his jacket pocket and pulled out one of the crumpled twenties. "Wait, I've got some money."

Now that the sale was ensured, the old man continued:

"This isn't all my own stuff. I buy it and resell it. That's how I'm losing money. You're taking the food off my table at this price." He reached out and snatched the twenty from John and placed it on the table between them.

John looked at the roll of money, then looked at Marla, then back at the roll with a "look at that" expression in his eyes. Her eyes followed his to the wad of cash.

"Looks like you can afford a few meals," she said.

The old man picked a five and a ten from the roll and handed them to John. He then fished a loonie out of his pocket and added this to the change in John's hand before adding the twenty to his own roll of cash. The roll was stuffed back into his pocket. He glanced suspiciously around with a look that conveyed, at the same time, pride of how successful he was and fear of the wrong people noticing the chunk of change he was carrying.

"The day is young. I hope to do a lot better than this."

John pocketed his change, the same kind of well-used bills that were in his bag under the steps back home, and asked: 'You do this well every week?"

"Not every week but most weeks. Depends on the weather, what else is going on, who else is here, a lot of factors and people like you who drag the price down so low that I lose money." He smiled at John.

They chatted for a few minutes longer. John picked up his hammer and dropped it in a plastic bag. He and Marla started down the line again.

"I could do this, you know," he said to Marla.

"Do what?"

"Buy stuff and resell it. This looks like easy money."

"Don't be foolish. Remember when the Harpers tried that. They ended up with a garage full of junk—no, not junk, garbage."

"Yes, that's true. I wouldn't do it that way. I'd go to yard sales on Saturday. Sell it here at the flea market on Sunday. Put anything that didn't sell out in the garbage on Monday. There would be no storing of anything." The plan formulated in his mind as he spoke. "Look at all these people here selling stuff. It's mostly the same people every time we come down here. It must work or they wouldn't keep doing it. To some of those people inside the rink it's a full-time job."

"It might work for them but I'm not going to do it. This is strictly something you're doing on your own." She capitulated much easier than he had expected.

19

John smiled at her. *I'd have it no other way,* he thought. Instead he said: "It could be fun. I'll clean up some of the junk around the house to get me started. I have all those bowls that I've turned. We definitely have more of those than we need. I'll supplement what we have with what I pick up yard-saling on Saturday. This could be a blast. And don't forget all the money I'll make. You saw that wad." He lowered his voice and looked around. "It's tax free too, I think."

And that was how John became a flea market entrepreneur.

# ≈3≈

SITTING AROUND the table in The Bull and Bear beverage room were Roger "The Boss" Johnson, Wally McIssac, Leroy Leblanc and William "Big Willie" Ettinger. Big Willie stood 6'4 and weighed 245 pounds. Even though he was hanging out in a tavern, none of it was fat. Leroy had the emaciated look of a one-time drug user even though he only disbursed the stuff to others nowadays. Wally was Mr. Average—average height, average build, average looks—who could easily get lost in a crowd. Roger stood out as The Boss. He looked the part—dark hair, chiselled chin, penetrating grey eyes, well built but not in an obvious way. He wore a light coloured suit and a dark blue tie. He could easily fit in at the board-room table of any business in the community.

The men were discussing the disappearance of last month's drug take. Leroy had thrown it away. In his defence, he had good reason to chuck it as far into the woods as he could. Two Mountie cars were hot on his tail roaring down the Back Road with Wally at the wheel doing at least 140 kph. The Back Road had only one egress and there was an excellent chance that more Mounties would be waiting for them at the next crossroad.

Not only was the money crammed into a leather hockey bag but in the bottom of the bag were several bottles of pills—ecstasy, oxy, speed, a whole pharmacy. To be caught with that cargo was a guaranteed trip to jail without passing go. Leroy had lived there before and had absolutely no desire to return.

They had a slight lead on the pursuing cop car, and Leroy decided it was in their best interest if Wally stopped for ten seconds while he, Leroy, pitched the bag of money into the woods. As they rounded a sharp corner, he noted a large maple tree and ordered the stop. The car slued all over the road in the loose gravel as it decelerated from top speed to a dead stop in a few seconds. Leroy jumped from the car and delivered the goods into the pitch black forest before the lights of their pursuers could be seen. The night was so dark, it was like throwing the bag into an abyss. Once the parcel was dispatched, they sped off into the darkness again.

The stop was all the Mounties needed to catch up to them. Twenty seconds later they pulled the two fugitives over. One police car stopped in front of them, the other taking up the rear. All four Mounties emerged with their guns drawn, two with pistols, two with shotguns levelled at the heads of the occupants of the cornered car.

Wally and Leroy offered no resistance. They had committed no crime they could be charged with other than driving on a deserted back road and that was still legal. They had, in fact, not regained their previous velocity and as a result, couldn't even be charged with speeding.

While the two suspects leaned over the front fender of their car, arms and legs spread wide apart like an open pair of scissors, the cops conducted a thorough search of the vehicle. Nothing was found. With no money and no drugs, the police couldn't hold the pair although they did take them in for extensive questioning. Leroy's instincts had been right on. He had saved everyone from imminent arrest and incarceration.

Roger Johnson and Big Willie had been nabbed back at the house. Three police cars, loaded with officers, armed with search warrants poured into the building. With the money and drugs gone, the criminals saw no need to run.

This search yielded nothing as well. Despite this lack of evidence, these two also spent a long Friday night being questioned relentlessly by various members of the drug squad. In the end, they were all sent home.

Several others had been picked up from various parts of the province at the same time. By late Monday morning, some were charged, some not, some held without bail, some putting up a small fortune to secure their freedom, others released on their own recognizance.

The news stories tantalized the readers and listeners with tales of the thousands of dollars seized, the hundreds of thousands of dollars worth of drugs, and the cache of weapons taken off the street in all four Atlantic provinces. None of these things belonged to Roger and his operatives. But if the cops didn't have it, and it wasn't where Leroy claimed he threw it, where was their money?

Big Willie, Leroy and Wally returned Saturday morning and searched the area where the money was dumped, to no avail. On Sunday, Wally had donned orange coveralls and assisted the search party as they combed the area. They had found some interesting stuff—dead cats in a bag; an old, rusty shotgun, a schoolbag full of porno magazines—but no bag of money. He listened to conversations the police held among themselves and left with the impression the money was not found the previous day either. That left only one conclusion. Someone had stolen their loot, stolen from The Boss. That person was in deep, deep trouble.

"Damn it." Roger slapped his hand on the table, causing all the bottles to shift position slightly. Others in the bar turned in his direction, saw who it was and quickly turned away. "We've got to get that money back," he said in a lower voice so that only those at his table could hear. "We have to find whoever took my money."

The others all nodded their heads in agreement.

"Well, I don't know, Boss," Big Willie slowly drawled. "This is like looking for that proverbial needle in a haystack. Anybody could have stumbled across that bag and as long as they keep their mouths shut, we'll never find them."

Leroy and Wally agreed with Big Willie but neither of them put it into words or even nodded their heads in agreement with this statement. Only Big Willy could get away with a statement like that. Neither disagreed with him either. That would have been a sure invitation to be the one assigned to find whoever had taken the money, a task that might well prove to be impossible.

It had taken two days to convince Roger that dumping the money was the smart thing to do in the first place. It was only when he had seen the piles of captured loot on Live At Five that he grudgingly agreed it was better to have it missing than in the hands of the police. But now he wanted it back and if you were tasked to find it, you had better find it.

"Why would someone be in that area on a Saturday morning?" Big Willie continued. He was not afraid to look for the needle. "The road is isolated and deserted. Leroy has no idea how well the bag was hidden from the road."

"It was dark. I was just trying to dump it," Leroy said in a whiny voice before slumping back into silence.

Big Willie scowled at him and went on. "So we don't know if someone driving by spotted it, stopped to investigate and got lucky." He stopped and let this image settle into the minds of the others. "It is unlikely anyone would walk along the road. It's in the middle of nowhere, but there are well-used paths that I noticed when I was looking for the bag. We have to see where those paths go. There may be houses close behind the woods. That could mean kids found it and, if so, we should hear about it pretty quick if we get into the neighbourhood and ask around or even just listen. Kids will be bragging about a find like that to anyone who would listen."

These were not thoughts off the top of his head. Big Willie had given the matter a great deal of consideration. Roger might think of it as his money. Big Willie also had a claim which would not be denied.

"Leroy, you go and check out the paths. Don't scare any kids you see. We don't want the cops back looking for a pervert. Make sure we were looking in the right spot. Make sure that is the right maple tree." Sarcasm dripped from his voice on the words "maple tree".

"It was the right tree," Leroy shot back. "We came around that sharp corner where we were out of sight of the chase cars and that tree stands out. It was the right tree." His voice trailed off as he noticed the smile on Big Willie's face. He was putting him on.

"Check out the amount of traffic and who uses the paths. Look inconspicuous. Borrow someone's dog if you can. No one questions a dog walker. They can go anywhere their pooch leads them. Make idle chitchat with any adults you come across. See what you can learn." Big Willie easily gave the orders. No one, including Roger, questioned his right to give them. His attention settled on Wally.

"Get into a suit and tie and grab a handful of Watch Towers from the house. Go knocking on doors and engage anyone who will listen in a discussion about all the police in the neighbourhood. Tell them the devil's work is in the air. Pretend the police are there right now before they have chance to tell you to get lost. Everyone will gossip about the cops even when they won't talk about religion. See what they know. If anybody found a lot of money, we should hear about it. Make a list of the places where the people are willing to talk. We may want to do some follow-ups if we don't learn anything today. Oh, yeah, hang onto the magazines; we're getting low on them."

When neither of the two men moved, he looked from one to the other: "Go on. Get working on this right now. You're wasting valuable time sitting here drinking beer."

Wally and Leroy almost tipped over their chairs as they scurried out of the tavern to complete their assignments.

"Think this will turn up anything?" Roger asked after the two were gone.

"Maybe. The worst-case scenario is someone is sitting on it, too afraid to act. We won't find it if that happens. We need someone spending money like it grows on trees. If that happens, someone will notice it and we have to be sure we hear about it when they do. How much do you figure we lost?"

Roger shrugged. "It was a good month. Nothing was counted yet, but I'd guess between three hundred-eighty and four hundred thousand, maybe more. Thank God we had paid our suppliers before the raid or we'd be a lot worse off. But now we have no seed money and the current climate of raids is going to make everyone cautious. They will want the money up front for the next shipment. We don't have it."

Big Willie nodded in an understanding manner. He had a nest egg stashed away. It was never his intention to live this lifestyle forever. Now might be the time to throw in the towel. If so, he would tell no one. He would just quietly disappear into the night, never to be seen again. He wasn't into long goodbyes, or deadly goodbyes either.

Meanwhile, at police headquarters in downtown Halifax, the joint task force on drug elimination was gathered to discuss the events of the previous weekend. They were going over the inventory of seized goods, coming up with the true value of the commandeered items. They had cash, drugs, guns, cars, trucks, ATVs, boats and a list of houses, the last five claimed under the Proceeds of Crime legislation.

This was a law which prevented criminals from benefiting from their life of crime and just picking up where they left off after their usually too short sentences were served. The Crown could seize anything it determined was bought with money resulting from crime. The seized goods were then auctioned off and the proceeds turned over to the government.

Except for the last part, the police were pleased with the increased power it gave them. They would, however, like to see the resulting proceeds go back to the police budgets so they could step up their efforts to stamp out this scourge on society.

Inspector Garry Holland laid down his copy of the inventory.

"Things seem to have gone pretty well. Congratulations everyone. Good job, the streets are a little bit safer this week than they were last week." Everyone nodded their approval.

This was the first meeting of the entire team since the raids. The RCMP along with forces from various cities and towns, spread over four provinces and a number of jurisdictions, had melded together to strike this mighty blow. The organization, timing and execution were spot on. The favourable results were listed on the sheets of paper in front of each of them.

"It goes without saying," Holland continued, "this was only one small, no, let's call it one large step, in the process. Two years of planning went into this endeavour and we have basked in the glory long enough." He looked up and a smile spread under his bushy, brown mustache. For the past four days, all of them had been mired in the paperwork resulting from the raids and several more days of it lay ahead of them. There had been no time to bask in any glory.

"Where do we go from here is the obvious question. I would like to turn the floor over to Sergeant Jim Mcdonald of the Major Crimes division. You all know Jim, I believe."

"Thank you, Inspector. Last Friday was a good day to be on the force. We should all be proud of our accomplishments. Our success rate was over ninety per cent. Where we were less successful, it was the results of bad information in some cases, leaked information in maybe one case and just damn poor luck in a couple of situations. There's not much we can do about that.

"Grinding this stuff through the courts is going to consume most of our time for the next several months. Many of you will feel you received a worse sentence than those you arrested. With regard to time served, you may be right." Jim noticed all the heads nodding in agreement.

"Do you know how long it took to handle the first murder case in Halifax? One week. One week from the first slap in the face to the snap of the neck from the hangman's noose."

All eyes were on Jim now. He had their complete attention.

Jim leaned forward on the podium, creating a more intimate feeling among the men. They were no longer a group of diverse units from around the province. These were men sharing an adventure story.

"Abraham Goodsides was the victim in the case. He served on the transport ship Beauford. A boatswain's mate, that would be the equivalent to a sergeant if he were on the force, someone used to giving orders not taking them." Jim noticed the look of understanding on the faces of the men. "Boatswains looked after the rigging and anchors. Goodsides was not a man to fool around with." Jim threw back his shoulders and tightened his biceps to suggest the upper body strength this work demanded. He was getting into the story.

"On this hot day in August, the harbour was bustling with shiploads of settlers arriving from England. Old Abe found himself in an argument with a seaman from the Baltimore, another transport vessel. Peter Cartcel was French who understood enough English to know when he had been insulted. He had no intention of taking any crap from an Englishman. England and France were still using Nova Scotia as a battleground for their on-again off-again war. The words escalated to a challenge to fight. Abe slapped Peter across the face." Jim's head turned sharply to one side as if he had been the one slapped.

He faced the front again and grinned. "This was 1749. Duels were still in vogue but not with Peter Cartcel. Without hesitation..."

Jim's hand went to his belt and swiftly returned with a clenched fist as if he were holding a knife.

"... Peter whipped out a four-inch knife and stabbed Goodsides in the chest."

Jim's arm shot forward to re-create the motion.

"One thrust of Cartcel's blade and Goodsides folded up on the ground, dead."

Jim paused to let the sequence of events sink in. His portrayal left a vivid picture in everyone's mind. These men were familiar with the brutality of a knife fight.

In a quieter voice, Jim continued. "The trial demonstrated equal haste. Four witnesses testified to the sequence of events leading to the demise of Abraham Goodsides. Cartcel had no lawyer or advocate to muddy the waters. The jury deliberated for a half-hour before finding the Frenchman guilty. Two days after the trial, Peter Cartcel was swinging from the gallows. The entire event took one week."

Jim smiled at his fellow officers. "Those were the good old days."

Spontaneous applause broke out in the room. A few shrill whistles echoed off the walls. Jim took a bow. He returned to the podium and straightened up some papers placed there before speaking.

"The good news in this current case is these raids were not on the low-level pushers and dealers. We were further up the food chain and the results can be seen on this list. We hit a lot of stash houses and cleaned them out." He held up a copy of the inventory. "Our successes will be felt throughout the criminal community. It will take a little longer for them to recover and we must be moving before they do."

Jim's piercing eyes made contact with everyone in the room. They all felt he was talking to them directly, and he was. "Go back to your homes and continue to harass those you arrested. With very few, very, very few exceptions, they are all back on the street even while we are still processing them. We have picked up enough information in most cases to get more warrants. Get them. Use them. Don't let the perps get reorganized. Get in their faces and stay there. Don't rely on the courts to keep these clowns off the street. You must do it yourself." Again there were murmurs of agreement from those present.

"You've got that right."

"Better believe it, brother."

"The courts, I spit on you."

Laughter rang out around the room. The sentiment rang true with all of them.

"The next phase of this operation is going to be called Enduring Success. Target the ones we picked up last Friday. Arrest them at every opportunity. Try to get them before the same judges every time so that their faces become familiar. Check the judges' schedules and time the arrests to correspond with them. This is a little extra work but, who knows, if the ugly mug shows up in front of them often enough, the message that putting them back out on the street is wrong might get through. Make sure your arrests are legitimate with all the i's dotted and t's crossed. We are going to harass them but we don't want them to have any successful harassment suits. It's no longer 1749. We have to respect the rights of these scum bags. Be careful not to offend them. But we will catch them."

"Damn right," was the sentiment that echoed throughout the room.

Jim held up his hands and turned serious. "In Halifax, we had one case go bad on us. Unfortunately it was our highest level case. We were spotted entering the neighbourhood and a phone call tipped off the dealers. We just barely missed them, in fact we caught them in a chase, but somewhere along the line, the drugs and money were dumped."

"Did you try using the canine unit?"

"Yes we did, but in retrospect, we may have done it wrong. We gave the dogs a particular scent to look for instead of letting them search out the latest scent. We're not sure if the bad guys got back to the money before we did or if some citizen came across it. What we do know is the creeps were there looking. The dog's actions showed us that much. Right now, we're hoping someone else found it and will turn it in, but it's been four days. We don't know exactly how much, but we are talking a lot of money, a lot of temptation. We have people in the neighbourhood to see what they can ferret out."

And so the meeting went on. Thoughts on what worked and what didn't and what to do the next time were exchanged. The resolve to keep fighting was firmed up to the point that a pep rally almost broke out before everyone headed back to their own jurisdictions to continue the battle of good against evil. In Halifax, they knew where their priorities lay. They set out to find the big bag of money. Look out John, here they come, and they are after you.

# ≈4≈

WHILE ALL these deliberations were taking place about his bag of money—John considered it his by now—he was blissfully oblivious. He romped around his house and workshop looking for goods to sell in his newfound business. He was excited by the prospect of being an entrepreneur, and the feeling was contagious. Even though Marla had vowed not to be a part of it, she too searched for merchandise to stock John's table. There were boxes of linens, bought but seldom used or else received as gifts and not regifted. There were bags of trinkets and knick-knacks that seemed to propagate their own offspring. There were old radios and record players left behind by technology but still working. Then John found what would be the corner stone of his business, although he didn't realize it at the time.

When he opened the closet doors in his workshop and his eyes fell on shelf after shelf of turned wooden bowls, his heart fluttered a little. Here was a unique item which would set his table apart from the hundreds that would be surrounding him. Here were items that only he could sell, made lovingly by his own hands, but with no obvious value to his family since they were stacked hidden in a cupboard out of sight.

The various grains of highly polished maple, yellow birch and cherry reflected a glint of sunlight which fell over his shoulder. People would be attracted to these items, would want to pick them up and feel the warmth of the wood, would be captured by the craftsmanship demonstrated here.

Then he gave himself a mental slap in the face. Don't get carried away: your profits are already sitting under the stairs in the blue and red hockey bag with the Canadiens logo on it. That was true. The sales items were only props in a bigger game, but this was going to be fun. He put ten of his bowls in a box to sell with the rest of the collection of superfluous treasures. He placed this box on top of the others where it sat like the crowning jewel of his accumulated obsolescence. He was ready to head into the world of capitalistic showmanship.

John arrived early at the arena parking lot entrance on Sunday morning at seven-o-five. Seven o'clock was when the venders were scheduled to arrive before selling began at eight. He wanted to get a good location. He knew the inside locations were permanently assigned to the regulars, but he hoped for a good spot outside.

He couldn't believe his eyes. Unfolding before him, like a scene from the movie Ben Hur with its ten thousand extras, was a churning mass of people. The lot was filled with row after row of tables already displaying the wares of their owners. Hundreds of people were circulating among them. He checked his watch. 7:05 a.m. The attractive young lady at the registration desk looked up at him. Despite the early hour, she was clad in a blue-flowered halter top and skimpy beige shorts. On her head was a floppy, red and blue sun hat.

"You're late but I think we can work you in."

She stood up and leaned over the table and looked to the far corner of the parking lot. John glanced into the halter top, a view which left very little to the imagination, and the image of how he usually spent his Sunday mornings flickered across his mind.

Was what he was giving up at home worth the newfound money? Marla had been sleeping peacefully when he, mouse-like, snuck out of the house at 6:50 a.m. She would be waking about now and reaching across the bed for his warm and ready body. This Sunday it wouldn't be there and if his plan worked, it wouldn't be there for several Sundays to come.

The young lady noticed the angle of his vision and cleared her throat.

"Over there," she said, pointing to the far-off corner. John looked up at her smiling face, the red rising up the back of his neck and filling his cheeks. *No, you're wrong, I was thinking of my wife back in bed.* He didn't bother to explain.

"Pick up a table at the truck and drive down this lane to the end. Turn right and drive until you find slot 653. If you come back in the future and want a closer spot, you should be here between five-thirty and six."

She settled back into her chair, everything falling back out of sight, and collected his money. "Good luck and we'd like you to stay until at least 1:30. There will be a prize draw at one o'clock for any vendors still here." She looked at the few boxes in his car and added "that could be worth more than you'll make if you sell everything."

"I didn't think the market started until eight."

"Oh, it doesn't. These are just sellers checking out each other's goods, picking up some things for resale if they think they're underpriced. Get here for this and your day could be over by now if your prices are right."

Her smile turned to the next person in line. John wasn't the only one who thought he was arriving on time to find out the reality of flea marketing.

"You're late but I think we can work you in," he heard as he climbed back into his station wagon. He took a quick glance back to see if this fellow would get his own eyeful before being reprimanded.

What had looked like so much stuff at home in his driveway now looked like a half-hearted effort compared to the half-ton and bigger truck loads around him. There were some loaded twenty-foot horse trailers and even a few motor homes. You're not in it for the money, he reminded himself. Deep in the recesses of his mind he heard a familiar voice, his voice, answer: "You could be, you could be."

John found his designated spot and drove his Atlantic blue Focus in head-first. This would give him more selling area when he opened the back and would also supply some much-needed shade. He slid the just procured table off the roof of his vehicle and snapped the metal legs into place. The crown jewels of his collection were the first things out and he set the box on the table, turned for the container of linens when he noticed someone unloading his bowls onto the table.

"Hey," he said. "What do you think you're doing?"

A deeply tanned, weather-beaten face looked up at him.

"Just helping you set up. The marks will be here soon and you want to be ready for the initial onslaught. It's like a flood gate breaking open when the clock strikes eight. If you're not prepared, you'll miss a lot of opportunities in that first hour. How much do you want for these old, beat-up bowls?"

"Beat-up bowls? They're brand new. I made them myself."

"Yeah, homemade, I thought as much." He set down the one he was examining and looked into the back of the wagon as if items made by an amateur caused him to lose interest. Then, he took a casual glance back at the table. "How much did you want for them?"

John looked at the blue dots on the bottom of the bowls. Marla, who wanted nothing to do with this enterprise, insisted he have everything priced before it went on display. People would be more willing to buy if they didn't have to inquire about the price of everything, she had knowingly informed him. Don't drop the prices until at least ten o'clock and then if things aren't moving, take twenty-five per cent off the price. At noon, cut the price in half.

For someone who wasn't interested, she had a lot of advice. John didn't want to be involved in pricing and then repricing and then repricing again. He devised this dot method. The items were divided into categories of similar value and assigned a coloured dot, blue, red, yellow, orange and so on. He had a big board with large coloured dots painted on it and a slot for him to put the corresponding value of the dot. In this way, if he wanted to lower the price of a class of goods, he simply changed the price in the slot. Voilà, the entire category dropped in value.

The blue dots were currently priced at $20 each for the initial offering. That was before he heard the description of old, beat-up bowls and the disdaining reference to homemade.

"Ten dollars," he reluctantly dropped the price in half.

"For all ten?" the prospective buyer inquired.

John's mouth dropped open. He was speechless for a couple of beats.

"No, not for all ten. Each!" He shouted the final word.

"Ooo, each, that's a little heavy. How about $75 for the works?" The man now had two bowls in his hands again, examining them closely. The early morning sun reflected off the highly polished surface, making the grain stand out even more than it had at home under the artificial lights of his workshop.

"$75. Are you crazy?" John realized he was suddenly emotionally attached to the bowls.

"Well, your only other offer was for $1 each. $75 seems pretty generous."

"$1 each? That was you who made that offer." John struggled to contain himself.

"Did you say $100 for all ten?" a voice behind him asked.

John started to turn when a hundred-dollar bill was thrust into his hands. The original bidder had had the bill rolled up in his hand all along.

"Get lost," the man said to the newcomer. "I've already bought these bowls." He piled them into the box, picked it up and moved on down the line, stopping at another table three people away.

John recognized the second bidder as the man from whom he had purchased the hammer the week before.

"I've made my first sale," he said. "How come I feel like I was just screwed without even being kissed?"

The tool salesman smiled. "You were, but by one of the best. That was Eric Sanderson. He hangs around at this end of the lot because everyone up here is new, usually only comes once and wants to get rid of their stuff in a hurry. Buys up all their good stuff if the price is right, leaves them with their junk. From what I could tell from the glimpse I got, he made a killing on those bowls. My name is Nathan Darling by the way." He held out his hand.

"John Lester. I guess I've got a lot to learn if I want to do this on a regular basis."

"I guess so. You got any more of those ten-dollar bowls?"

"Please, Nathan, if I'm going to get screwed twice in succession, let me catch my breath in between so I can enjoy the second time as much as the first."

Nathan laughed. "No, John, I wouldn't do that to you. I was just going to suggest you let me look at them and I'll help you come up with a better price. If your prices are too low, it makes it hard on the rest of us who are trying to make a living doing this."

"You do this for a living?" John asked. "You don't have a real job?"

Nathan looked affronted and then smiled again.

"This is a real job, John. I specialize in tools. Through the week, I search out buying opportunities. I clean up what I find for resale and I sell them at fair prices."

"Search out buying opportunities? You mean like 'We steal for you' opportunities?

Now Nathan was insulted.

"No, I do not. There are no hot items on my table. Aw, go to hell." He turned and started to walk away.

John realized he had crossed the line. He also realized if he was going to do this weekly, he needed coaching from someone who understood how the system worked. He might not have a better contact than this man.

"Wait, Nathan, I'm sorry. But given what just happened to me, you have to forgive me for being a skeptic. I apologize, man. I didn't mean to question your honesty."

Nathan stopped, hesitated and faced John again. His face was deep red, right up to his hairline. This was not the first time someone had implied he was selling stolen goods.

"There are crooks here right now selling their stolen merchandise. Why wouldn't there be? This is a golden opportunity for them. Thousands of people come up to them and offer to buy the stuff. No one questions where they get it. They just want a good deal themselves. The better the price, the less likely anyone is to ask the question. The buyers are complicit in the act of the theft. Just as guilty as the sellers as far as I'm concerned.

"Then, there are the majority of us. We buy what we sell and have to compete with the thieves. I run a fair business. Both the people I buy from and the people I sell to win. What did you buy from me last week? Did you feel like I ripped you off? Did you steal the stuff you're selling?"

John felt duly reprimanded.

"I'm sorry," Nathan said. "I've got to get back to my table. Good luck with your stuff." He hurried down the row of vendors and back into the central part of the flea market, the prime outside area were the regular sellers were set up.

John finished unloading his loot. With his bowls gone, there was not a whole lot of stuff left to make his table look appealing. But on the other hand, he had made a hundred bucks already and the market wasn't even officially open. He spread everything out as best he could, put on his straw sun hat and settled back to wait for the action to start.

Marla and the kids would be along later. She had reluctantly agreed to relieve him for awhile so he could look around. He checked his watch. There were still fifteen minutes before the gates opened so he walked up the aisle to see what those around had on display. Most were selling the same things he was.

These were the one-timers, folks who were just cleaning out the attic and the cellar or who were just looking for a little spare cash for whatever reason. Many were excited about the amount of money they had taken in already. Eric, it seemed, had been harvesting the prime items from all the tables. The down side, all the good stuff in this area was gone.

And then the doors to the general public were opened. A mass of humanity spread through the parking lot like water on a cement floor, going in all directions at once. Frantic buyers were picking things up, then throwing them down and grabbing something else. Rapid offers were made on items of interest. Money was thrown at the vendors as the buyers moved on, trying to see everything on the lot before anyone else did.

This went on for a half-hour, and then, the rush settled down as quickly as it had started. Now it was just a constant wave of people, leisurely strolling, leisurely examining, leisurely buying. The consensus seemed to be that the really good stuff was snapped up before 8:30; now they could enjoy themselves.

People kept asking John what he wanted for his goods. He explained the dot system to them. No one seemed to catch on.

"Blue dot. Does that mean you want $20 for this? I'll give you ten for two of them."

"Ten? That's only $5 each." John had never been very good at this negotiation racket. He usually paid what was being asked or didn't buy at all. If he was going to do this every week, there would be a steep learning curve.

"Ah, two for fifteen," he tentatively shot back.

"I'll take four." Thirty dollars was passed to John for what he had hoped was eighty dollars worth of merchandise, forty at the least and that not until after noon. It was only 9 a.m.

Then out of the corner of his eye, he spotted one of his bowls. Two ladies were cohing and aahing over it. He felt a spike of pride.

He had made that with his own hands, the design out of his own head. He tuned in to their conversation.

"He wanted $75 for it but I talked him down to fifty. Told him I wanted it as a unique wedding gift for one of my neighbours kids."

"My, my. $50. That was a steal."

"Sure was. He told me he was losing money on it but since I wanted it as a gift he would let me have it for the $50. I was prepared to pay the full seventy-five. Look at the craftsmanship. It's worth twice that much, three times if you bought it at one of those craft fairs. It's brand new. You can tell."

John felt his knees get weak. He sat back into the trunk portion of the station wagon. Eric would recover his costs by selling only two of his bowls. The other eight would be pure profit. Four hundred dollars and possibly six hundred dollars profit. He wanted to go snatch the bowl from the ladies. Take back his possession. That would be shooting at the wrong target. He was the one to blame for not doing any research on what these kinds of things sold for. He thought he had become a businessman. He had a lot to learn.

Again his mind did a shift. It was like the demon on his left shoulder was arguing with the angel on his right. You can make one hundred dollars each for them. Simply take a thousand out of the bag of money when you get home. Stop beating yourself up and get focussed.

The angel argued back. Start selling these bowls yourself and you won't need the bag of money. You can return it to the police.

Don't get stupid, the devil rebutted. That would be a lot of work to make the kind of money you already have.

Suddenly Marla was standing in front of him, snapping her fingers.

"Suffering from sunstroke already?" she asked.

John came back to the present and looked around at the crowd of buyers surging past his table. There was money to be made doing this.

"No. No, just having a meeting with my staff," he laughed. "With a company of one, these meetings can be held anywhere, anytime."

Marla examined the few things left on his table.

"I see you've sold all your bowls. There's a guy inside the rink who has a half-dozen just like yours. He's selling them for $100 each."

"$100? I thought he was selling them for $75."

"Might have been earlier, but they're priced at one hundred now. I could have sworn they were yours. What did you get for the ones you had anyway?"

John examined the question in his mind. He had to be able to show enough profit to justify the money he was going to give Marla to spend for the rest of the week. Money for groceries and anything else she might want to buy.

"$100," he said. "Must be the going price."

Good answer, the left-shouldered demon whispered in his ear. Accurate, even if not quite honest. You're catching onto this business. Have you ever considered running for office?

John looked down. He could not meet the surprised gaze of Marla's eyes.

"Go on. $1000. Let's see."

John glanced around at the people strolling up and down the row, picking things up, examining them and either putting them down or dickering over the price. He partially exposed the roll of cash in his pants pocket. Serendipitously he had brought one thousand dollars from the bag to be his profit for the day. Marla's eyes were as big as saucers on the way to becoming as big as dinner plates. Admittedly, she thought the whole flea market idea was crazy. She never believed this kind of money could be made from the junk lying around their house. She was sorry she had doubted John.

Her mouth was open in a big O. She snapped it shut and looked around to see who was looking their way. No one was paying the slightest attention to them. The table was too devoid of merchandise to cause too much interest anymore. There hadn't been that much to start with.

"Put that away," she commanded. He slid the money back into his pocket.

"There's nothing like a big bulge in the front of a man's pants to make him more attractive," she giggled. She was giddy at the sight of the wad of cash. "I can't wait to get my hands on that."

"Control yourself woman," John said. "There are children around. Look, there's even more money." He pulled out the less than two hundred dollars from his other pocket—the real profits from the morning's endeavour.

"Those pants are just full of surprises," Marla said. Her eyes were twinkling.

John grinned. "More surprises than you know. Let's blow this popsicle stand. There's no sense being greedy."

The first morning had gone better than he could have dreamed. His money-laundering plan was now in full swing.

# ≈5≈

DETECTIVE-SERGEANT Jim Mcdonald perched on the edge of his chair in the office of Inspector Gerry Holland at the six-storey, brick police headquarters building in west-end Halifax. He leaned forward.

"Not a sign of that money anywhere," he said as he shook his head. "Either it doesn't exist or it fell off the face of the Earth."

"It exists, Jim. It appears to have just been removed from circulation. That is a good thing to quote some previously popular lifestyle maven."

Jim smiled. "A damn good thing if it's true. But it would help our case a lot if we could come up with the money. It would make this waltz through the courts a lot easier. Their man is covering the bars. On the bright side, the druggies are sweating this as much as we are. We have them under surveillance in case they lead us to the loot. They are working as hard as we are to find it, harder if that's possible.

"We've gone door-to-door. So have they, only under the guise of Jo-Hos. We've hung out in coffee shops and engaged people in conversations to see if they know anything. It's the hot topic in the community. Everyone is speculating about what they would do if they found the money. None of that speculation seems to include turning the money over to us. Whoever has it must be quietly sitting on it. We will have to keep vigilant. Eventually they will start spending it, and we must be still there looking when they do."

"It may take more than simply spending to tip us off, Jim. If they don't flash it around, how will we know? It's only money, after all."

"True. What we are really hoping for is someone will start to talk about it. Brag a bit. People always brag. That's our best hope."

"Who do we think might have it and why?"

"That's part of the problem. At first blush, the location where we think it was dumped seems to be in the middle of nowhere. By road it is. But there are several paths leading through the area from adjoining subdivisions. There are joggers, dog walkers, kids playing, teens drinking, lovers doing whatever lovers do in the middle of nowhere. It's a mini city of activity. We've interviewed several of these people. All wish they had found it but as far as we can tell, none have. They're going to call us if they hear anything."

"What if we offered a reward? Would that make them more willing to call?"

Jim shook his head no. "Part of our problem is we don't really know what we're looking for. We are speculating that as soon as the perps were tipped off, they gathered up everything incriminating and bolted out the door. We have no idea how much we're talking about, whether it's both drugs and money or only one, or even what they were carrying it in. Officers on the way to the drug house spotted a car speeding away. Once we determined they were the ones we were after, we tried to have them stopped before they got out of the subdivision.

"We just missed them, but we knew which direction they were headed so we pursued their car. But by the time we caught up and pulled them over, any evidence had been dumped. We are really only guessing they took off with this evidence, but they had to stop in order for us to catch up to them." He paused and shrugged his shoulders. "Why else would they stop? Those in the car and those at the house all claim there was nothing to dump, and they are innocent. We know that's a crock but we aren't sure of what is missing."

"The proverbial needle in the haystack." Inspector Holland ironically came to the same conclusion as Big Willie.

"Exactly. It's hard to offer a reward when we don't know what we are offering it for."

"I wonder if we should tone down our inquiries. As long as we maintain a high profile in the neighbourhood, the money will stay suppressed. Keep watching but be more subtle."

Jim shifted in his chair. "That sounds good in theory but in practice, we can't afford to miss any signs of spending activity or talk of spending activity. There's a fine line between being subtle and losing contact with the case."

Inspector Holland paused to ponder what Jim had laid out for him.

"Keep a low profile in the area," he said, "but keep the druggies actively on your radar. Let's hope they lead us to what we are looking for, which is convictions of them. The proceeds of the crime are just a bonus. As long as the bad guys don't have it and as long as it's stashed in the back of someone's garage or hidden under a bed, who cares?"

Jim looked closely to see if the inspector was serious "It's drug money," he ventured. "We care."

"Whatever," the inspector said and waved his hand towards Jim. "Don't get too focused on the money. It's the criminals we're after. Let's catch them."

Jim reached down and picked up his briefcase and set it on his side of the inspector's desk. He took out a folder with a blue tab on it marked Operation Enduring Success.

"Keeping the drug dealers on a close tether is a key part of this operation, has been from the start. Not only do we hope to get them all incarcerated, but also the next generation. Here in the city, Roger Johnson had the drug scene sown up so tight, he had little, if any, competition. Nature abhors a vacuum, as you know.

This is especially true among drug users. There is a market and as long as we keep Johnson, The Boss, under close surveillance, others are rushing in to fill the gap left by him.

"We have been prepared for this from the start. Our undercover operatives are getting into the new organizations in ways that would never have been possible with Johnson. He was much too cautious. These new guys are just greedy. Our boys are quickly moving up through the ranks and we'll be ready for new raids in record time."

Jim smiled and turned the open portfolio around so Holland could see the figures and organization charts. "This is where we are already."

He slid the document across the table.

"Roger Johnson's organization is tied up in knots," Jim continued. "There is one concern. William Ettinger, Johnson's number two man, has disappeared. Somehow he slipped away from us. We know he's not behind any of this new activity because it's much too sloppy, but he could come back on the scene and take over quite easily. That would give them the level of leadership currently missing. We are watching for him."

Holland nodded his head, listening as he studied the chart in front of him. "It almost looks like we're running the drug trade now. We aren't, are we?"

"Not quite, yet. If we want civilization to be stable, we have to work like horses. If we are patient, our next raids will take out a whole new level of the operation. In fact, those raids will probably take place outside the province.

"We will never dry up the source but we may put them several months behind. The dollar value will be newspaper headline material and with luck, our operatives will still be safely ensconced in their positions ready to take on the next wave of suppliers. I hesitate to say this, but we are finally making some headway. Our secret weapon is a judge willing to interpret the Charter of Rights in our favour instead of the criminals' favour. Bless him."

# ≈6≈

JOHN WALKED into the Tim Horton's coffee shop and looked around at his fellow patrons. Most clutched a steaming mug of coffee and leaned over their tables in earnest conversation with their table mates. He spotted his quarry in one corner looking out the window at the busy scene outside as early evening traffic whizzed by on the main drag. Beside the coffee mug, a doughnut stood alone on a white saucer in front of him. He had yet to bite into the pastry so appeared to have not been here too long. The man was Nathan Darling. John had found Nathan's phone number in the local directory and arranged this meeting.

John went up to the counter where he was greeted by a smiling, blond-haired young lady in her late teens dressed in a crisply starched brown and yellow blouse. He ordered a black coffee and an apple fritter. Who would have thought you could become a multimillionaire selling coffee and doughnuts? He dropped a toonie on the counter and joined Nathan at the front of the restaurant.

Nathan's eyes illuminated into a smile which spread to his entire face. He started to stand but John put a hand on his shoulder and prevented the courteous gesture. He figured he was half of Nathan's age in physical years but not in enthusiasm. The older man's whole countenance seemed to welcome John to the table.

After some preliminary small talk about the weather, the traffic and food, John got to the reason for inviting Nathan to meet him.

"I'm thinking of doing this flea market thing on a regular basis and I guess I need some pointers to keep myself from being ripped off. You strike me as someone who knows the ropes."

Nathan nodded his head in agreement without being aware of the action. He did know the ropes.

"Eric didn't rip you off," he responded to John's implied slight on his fellow seller.

"Didn't rip me off? He sold my bowls for $100 each and he only paid me ten." John stammered. "Of course he ripped me off."

"No, he didn't," Nathan said. "How much did you ask for your bowls?"

"Well, I was going to ask for twenty, but he convinced me they were only worth ten."

"How much did you ask?"

"Ten."

Nathan smiled and held his hands out palms up in a "there you go" gesture. "He paid you what you were asking. Something he doesn't often do, I might add."

"Yeah, but he sold them for one hundred bucks each," John said.

Nathan leaned back in his chair and took a sip of his double-double. He looked right into John's hazel-coloured eyes. "Here's the rub. You were selling candy bowls or bread bowls or something like that. You got a good price for a candy bowl. Eric was selling works of art, things that could be just as easily displayed empty as full of candy. He got a fair price for works of art, good works of art I might add. You got a reasonable price for a candy bowl."

John looked confused. "I don't understand the difference. What made his works of art and mine candy bowls?"

"Ninety dollars," Nathan said. "You were asking ten bucks. That's a candy bowl. Eric asked a hundred. That's a work of art. It's all a question of perception, what the buyer thinks they are getting for the money. You have to know what it is you are selling." He reached out and placed his hand on the back of John's. "Don't worry Grasshopper, Yoda will teach you."

John laughed. "They're from two different stories."

"Ah, that shows how little you know. Yoda was actually in charge of the Shalomin monks. He just lived in a cave up in the hills instead of in the temple. Not many people knew about him. He taught the monks who taught the monks all about the Force. Go ahead, look it up, you'll see." Nathan's eyes twinkled.

"If you had bought the bowls, what were you going to sell them for?" John asked.

"I wasn't going to buy your bowls. I deal in tools, remember."

"But you offered to buy them. Then Eric snatched them away."

Nathan waggled his finger at John. "I asked if you were selling them for ten dollars each and Eric paid your full asking price. I didn't want your old bowls. Well, at least I didn't want them until I saw what Eric did with them. He was pretty to watch. He sold the first two in about ten minutes for fifty dollars each, was asking seventy-five. Made both of the buyers think they were getting the deal of the century."

"Yeah," said John. "I heard one of them. She said Eric was losing money at that price. Only five times what he paid for it."

"Well, it turns out he wasn't lying. As soon as he sold the first two and recovered his investment, he upped the price to $100 each and sold two more without even dropping the price a nickel. So, technically, he was losing money at that price.

"I don't know what happened after that, I got too busy to watch. He can afford to hold out at the higher price for awhile. Then it gets to be a nuisance to be lugging them back and forth. He may have to drop the price again. Storage becomes a question after a couple of weeks.

"If you're buying and selling, you want to be turning the product over fairly quickly. Don't scoff at the 'I'm losing money at that price' line, you'll be using it yourself in a couple of weeks. How many more of those bowls do you have?"

"I don't know exactly, a closet full and at least one in every room in the house. For a few years, making them was a great stress buster. I just made them and stored them. Never thought of selling them until I decided to get into this flea market thing. The ones I brought down last week weren't even the best of the bunch. I guess I'm still emotionally attached to the better ones."

"So at ten dollars, you weren't trying to recover your investment of time. Since it was a hobby, your time was for free, is that it?"

"At ten dollars, I wasn't going to recover my investment in wood. They are all hardwood, expensive hardwood. At one hundred dollars, I'm not sure I would recapture my time. Making those bowls to that quality is fairly labour intensive. But, yeah, on the first batch, my time was free. With crafts, you just hope to cover your costs for materials so you can keep making more."

"Well, if you're serious about doing this, you will have to rethink that policy. Your time has a value. You have to be paid for it. It's a good thing Eric got them away from you. The punters start to expect bargains like that. Makes it hard on the rest of us."

John let that thought sink in for a bit. "If I was to do this for the money, I would turn them out a lot faster than I have been. When it's a hobby, you sort of get involved with Zen and the art of sanding. You just sand because it is relaxing and clears your mind. It's therapeutic. You have to do it to understand. If you pay attention to your turning and keep your chisels sharp, you hardly have to sand at all."

Nathan nodded. He understood.

A far away look passed across John's face and he looked visibly more relaxed. Then he looked back at Nathan and the tension seeped back into his countenance as he got back to the business at hand.

"You say you do this full time. It's your only source of income?"

"That's not exactly what I said. Selling used tools is what I do full time. I have other outlets besides the Sunday flea market. I run a small shop out of my garage as well. I just don't let it dominate my life. Hours are by appointment or by chance. There's no guarantee if you drop in unannounced that I'll be there."

"And you can make a living doing this?" Working when he felt like it instead of the Monday to Friday, nine-to-five grind appealed to John now that he had an alternate source of income. If he could find other people who actually made a go of this kind of existence and could parade them by Marla, it would be easier to convince her that he should try it as well.

"I get by, but my needs tend to run to the cheap. My house is paid for. My wife has passed on and the kids are grown and living on their own. I eat a lot of macaroni and cheese or frozen dinners. This is what I do for entertainment as well as for money. It works for me." He paused and a fatherly look registered on John's senses. "It's not for everyone. There are no guarantees. You have to be prepared not to have any income at all if you want to go away or if you get sick. Oh yeah, and I have a pension coming in as a back-up source of income. That helps."

John appreciated Nathan's concern but he also had a back-up source of income. It was a big bag of money sitting under the steps in his basement. There just had to be the appearance that this could work, that he could support himself doing this.

"Sorry to hear about your wife. Has it been long?" He thought perhaps a little loneliness contributed to Nathan's willingness to meet him.

"Five years but seems like yesterday." Nathan's eyes shone a little brighter.

John allowed an appropriate moment to pass before getting back to the commercial aspect of the get-together. "Does anyone else do it full time?" he asked.

"Sure, lots of people. Eric runs over a dozen tables at the flea market. He even has a couple of full-time employees. Hires a bunch of part-timers for Saturdays and Sundays. Divides his goods up into various categories like a department store. Keeps the good stuff separated from the junk. Keeps the prices set accordingly. Isn't afraid to ask what he thinks a product is worth. Has no sentimental attachment to any of it and is willing to unload it at any price if it's not selling. Just makes you feel guilty as you buy it.

"He's like me, has no other dependants."

Nathan paused and his face crinkled into a smile as if something extremely funny had popped into his mind. "That's not quite true. He has an ex-wife to support.

"Their breakup was acrimonious. She hired a real hotshot lawyer who thought he was taking Eric to the cleaners. Eric had a six-figure income at the time and the first number wasn't a one, but I'm not sure how high it went. The Shylock came up with some sort of scheme where the more Eric made, the more his wife got. Saved him going back to court all the time to get more, which is surprising for a lawyer. I thought they lived to go back to court. He must have had some sort of payment arrangement with the wife where he received a portion of any increases. I don't know for sure. Anyway, he managed to push this revolutionary scheme through the courts. Looked like he had Eric by the balls."

Nathan shook some of the sprinkles off his doughnut and took a bite before going on.

"Eric signed the agreement, then, to everyone's surprise, he quit his job. Had no income coming in. His wife stood to get nothing. He then started this business. He's no legal whiz but he's an expert with numbers. Each year he makes enough on paper that he doesn't have to pay any taxes and everything his wife gets is taxable. She had to go out and work to live in the style she was accustomed to and the alimony was just piled onto the top of what she made. Taxed at the top rate.

"That was before they changed the rules to make the money taxable to the husband. Eric promised if they took him back to court to change the arrangement, he would be able to show no income at all on paper. She would get nothing."

Nathan sipped his coffee. "They fought him, but it turned out they had outsmarted themselves. Their agreement was ironclad; they didn't think Eric would give up his high-flying lifestyle. He fooled them; now, he's happy as a pig in shit. Enjoys what he's doing, gets twice the pleasure every time he writes an alimony cheque. Some months, if he goes on vacation, he doesn't even have to write one."

He laughed. "Sorry, what was your question?"

John joined the laughter. "I don't remember. So, where do you get the tools you sell? Who is your supplier? You must have a continuous supply to make it worthwhile every week."

"I have various sources. I go to auctions where they are selling house lots. I have contacts who let me know when people are selling their houses and moving into apartments or nursing homes. They seldom take their tools. People know I buy them so they call me. Word of mouth is a powerful advertising source. I keep supplied. Also I sell a fair amount of the bigger stuff at auctions if they expect to have the right clientele attending, men that is. I sell table saws, planers and I make up packages with a variety of tools. It never hurts to be on good terms with the auction houses. I could introduce you. If you're in the market for a new lathe, I could keep an eye open for you. Your closet can't keep you supplied forever."

"Thanks. If you have anything, I would like to take a look," said John. Nathan didn't look like the type who would take anything for this assistance but John could throw some business his way. Hell, it was only money.

Nathan continued: "If I was you, I wouldn't bother with the other junk you were selling last week. I would specialize in the wooden bowls and other things turned on your lathe. It gives your table a higher level of panache. Bring a cloth to cover the table and only put out a few models at a time. There is an eclectic clientele at this market in a variety of price spending ranges. People have an expectation of paying higher prices when your goods are properly displayed than they do when your goods are mixed in with what is commonly known as flea market items."

John thought about that for a few seconds and then nodded his head. "That makes sense."

With that, his specialty was determined. He was in the wooden bowl business, manufacturing and sales.

# ≈7≈

LEROY LEBLANC and The Boss drank a beer in the darkened corner of The Bull and Bear. They were not happy campers. Both had been hauled in for further questioning on three additional occasions. Both were aware that their movements were being monitored, almost around the clock. As they gazed around the room, there were a couple of people whose names they didn't know but whose faces were becoming all too familiar to them. These two men were having a detrimental effect on Roger's drug trade. Business was, in fact, stagnant.

With this close surveillance, Roger, a.k.a. The Boss, could not risk contacting his suppliers. His phones might be tapped, his house might be wired, his car might have GPS devices secured on it. Allowing the police to move up the ladder one level from him because of his carelessness could prove fatal.

That was only part of his problem. The other part was that the end users, the addicted unwashed and the addicted washed, as well, still wanted their fix. They had no loyalty. Anyone who could supply their habit was their main man. Business was being lost, business that might not be recovered.

His own street-level dealers were running out of product and making noises about moving to the opposition if he couldn't keep them supplied. There should be no opposition. A crackdown would follow this debacle. People would be put back in their places.

This was all just a bunch of meaningless talk, however, as long as he was being held on a short leash by the police. His lawyers had filed harassment charges but the courts threw them out. How could the wimpy courts walk all over his Charter rights? The system was going down the tubes.

"How come we keep coming before that same idiot of a judge? No one else had ever made those kinds of Charter rulings and yet every one of our appeals ends up before him. That shouldn't be happening."

Roger appreciated hard work and good organization. He would have been impressed by the efforts required to have all his cases appear before his legal nemesis, all the strings that had to be pulled, all the manoeuvring required to get more liberal judges off the bench for those brief occasions when his cases were heard. Impressed but not happy.

"Have you heard from Big Willie?" Leroy wiped a foam mustache from his upper lip. After being picked up for the second time, Big Willie had disappeared. Roger had received a postcard with a South Carolina postmark. "Enjoying the sun and the broads" the card read. It was unsigned. Roger doubted Big Willie was anywhere near the Carolinas, had enjoyed neither at the time of writing, and was enroute to an unknown destination. He was torn between cursing him for desertion and envying him for having the sense not to play the cops' game.

"Not a word," Roger said. "I'll have a serious talk with him when he gets back so don't think of following his example."

He had to keep his organization together, be ready to move on as soon as the heat was off. He picked up his glass, finished off the remaining golden draft beer and signalled the waiter for another round. The server set two more glasses in front of both of them and removed the empties. Roger threw a five and a ten dollar bill on the tray and waved him away.

"Have you learned anything about the missing money or are you still just spinning your wheels?"

"That money disappeared off the face of the Earth. No one is talking about it. No one is spending it. Our entire network is combing the neighbourhood and talking to everyone. I've had people watching the lines at the grocery store for people using large amounts of cash. Do you know how many people still pay cash for their groceries? The stores are discouraging cheques so instead of going to plastic, they have gone back to cash. There are all kinds of people out there with huge bundles of loot in their pocket. Old people, anarchists and technophobes who are afraid big brother is tracing their every move and don't want to leave a plastic trail. The cashless society is not taking over any time soon."

Leroy took a big slug of his new beer. His mustache had been replenished with a new coating of foam. His tongue shot out and made a quick windshield wiper motion across his upper lip. He cast his eyes downward, studying the cigarette burns scarring the top of the table. His voice was low, almost a mumble. "If you have any new ideas about where to look, I'm all ears."

"We had drugs in that bag as well as money, right?"

Leroy nodded without bothering to look up.

"Do we know if any of our drugs are on the street? Could this person be dealing himself? Find a couple of our sellouts and see what they are peddling and warn them at the same time about the hazards of crossing me. Those are my customers they're selling to, make sure they understand that."

Leroy did not argue with The Boss. Leroy never argued with The Boss. This time an answer was in order.

"You've never used, have you?" He asked in a low voice, so low Roger almost didn't hear him. He was looking into his beer glass.

"Used? Is that what you asked? Drugs are for losers. Of course I've never used."

Leroy looked up, stared out the window, his look far, far away. The scars tattooed on the insides of his arms started to itch. It had been years since he added to their pattern but that didn't diminish the memories any.

"Your customers, as you call them, need their fix. They don't give a shit where it comes from. They need their fix." His voice got louder as he spoke and he turned and looked Roger right in the eye. "Part of your great plan is to get people hooked, but you don't have a clue what it means when they are. Shooting up is not a choice, it's something they have to do. They need their fix. Sears, Wal-Mart, Zellers, they have no brand loyalty. They don't give a shit where it comes from. They just want a fix."

Others in the bar were looking their way. Smiles spread across the faces of the two undercover cops. The constant pressure was starting to take its toll. This assignment rated right up there with watching paint dry, but outbreaks like the one taking place now indicated it was not for nothing. Soon Roger or Leroy or both would do something stupid. They were ready.

"Quiet down," Roger said. He surveyed the room. "You're attracting attention. Sure they need their fix. I understand that. Hell, that's what puts your beer on the table." He tapped Leroy's glass as a reminder of who was paying.

"It's just that people who work for me shouldn't be dealing for someone else that fast. Where is their loyalty? I've worked hard to get where I am today. You're the one who doesn't understand. There are laws in this country, rules. Now everybody is ignoring them, those cops sitting over there are flouting them. The courts are letting them get away with it. It's just not right. This is the start of anarchy. My empire is slipping through my fingers and I can only sit here and watch it happen. Now, people I've been good to, given good jobs to, paid well, are deserting me at the drop of a hat."

"Most of them are users too, they need the access to the drugs and the money," Leroy said quietly, a little taken aback by Roger's outburst. He studied Roger closely and realized he was completely oblivious to the irony of his statements: bending the rules by the police was interfering with the operation of his criminal enterprise. He seriously thought he was being wronged.

Roger picked up his glass and swirled the remaining beer around. "Find out what they're selling and where they're getting it." Roger sat up straighter in his chair. "We're getting back in the game." He downed the rest of his beer, slid his chair back and headed for the door. Leroy drained his glass and shuffled after him to the parking lot.

Neither realized how lucky they were to have cars to go to Leroy's Explorer and Roger's Viper were to have been seized under the proceeds of crime legislation. When no drugs or money were found in their possession, the decision was made, with some reluctance, to let them keep their vehicles for now.

To do otherwise would have required some undercover operatives to reveal their identity. It was too soon for that, the cars would be confiscated in time. There was no rush.

The first watching cop turned to her partner and said, "What do you think, six beers each? Call the highway patrol boys. Give them the breathalyzer."

This would be just a nuisance stop but it would interrupt any plans the two had made, throw their already confused schedule further out of whack, and let anyone who was watching see the police were in their face. If they, the watchers, had any criminal intentions, Roger and Leroy were people to be avoided at all costs. That was a hard way to run a criminal empire, no matter how hard you worked.

# ≈8≈

SUNDAY MORNING found John displaying his wares once again at the mall flea market. He was out of bed by 5:30 a.m. and on location by shortly after six. This early hour still didn't earn him a spot right in the heart of the crowd; they were reserved by those who showed up week after week all season long. He was within spitting distance, however. If he stood on his tiptoes he could see Nathan's table and the complex run by Eric was only three rows away. On bright sunny days, Eric moved part of his enterprise into the parking lot. John was getting closer to the in-crowd.

His table was bedecked with a royal blue table cloth which hung to the ground all around. Crisp, white doilies were strategically placed on the table with a finely turned bowl placed in the centre of each. Prices ran from $150 to $300, values suggested by Nathan.

Along the front were a few snowmen turned from Nova Scotia maple with a little hook in their hats and a string attached. It was never too early to sell Christmas tree ornaments. These were priced at a mere $1.50 and their task was to get people to at least stop and look.

Hanging from the raised hatch of the Focus wagon were a series of solid looking, white ash baseball bats. He hoped there were still some people out there who preferred to hear the comforting thunk of wood hitting a ball instead of the high-pitched tink of aluminum.

At Nathan's suggestion, he had business cards printed and displayed. Not everyone carried in their pockets the kind of cash necessary to purchase his bowls, but they might be interested in contacting him later. The cards were cheap advertising.

Tucked away in the side pocket of his cargo shorts was a bundle of tens and twenties adding up to five hundred dollars. That, he figured would be a fair day's work and would more than offset his family expenses for the week.

He had to be careful not to flood too much new money into his household. There were too many people still watching. He had explained to Marla about the income tax repercussions of this additional money and persuaded her not to tell anyone how successful the business was, especially not their closest neighbour, the local gossip. She reluctantly agreed but it was obvious she wanted to tell someone about the newfound financial freedom. He convinced her to call his sister in Alberta and tell her. She was always bragging about the wages her oil field worker husband brought in and trying to talk them into coming west to join the bonanza. Marla jumped at the chance and the two talked for hours that night. He might need the extra money just to cover the phone bill. He smiled. He could cover it.

By ten a.m., he sold twenty-three snowman ornaments for a gross of $34.50. He also sold one $200 bowl and two baseball bats. They had all been made in hobby time. He had no idea of the hours involved. He did know that he had almost $270 in his pocket over and above the money taken from the big bag. If he sold another bowl, he would have to reconsider using any of the found money at all this week.

It was then that he noticed a well-dressed, older lady examining one of his more expensive bowls. She was dressed in black even on this bright, sunny, summer day and looked a little sad. John was preparing to make his pitch when she set the bowl down and asked: "Do you have any bowls with covers and perhaps a little bigger?"

"Covers? Yes, I have a few." John lifted the table covering and looked underneath. He kept his stock under the table out of the direct sun. He pulled out a box and placed it on the table.

"What exactly is it you want to use the bowl for?" he asked, trying to get some idea of which design to present to her.

The lady blushed a little and looked around to see if anyone was close.

"I want to put my husband in it."

"Sorry?" John was confused at what he heard.

"My husband. Well, more accurately his ashes. He's dead. I'm looking for something attractive I can put on the mantel."

"Oh." Thoughts of murder and intrigue dropped from John's mind.

"Your bowls look so nice but naturally, I need a cover. I wouldn't want the dust from the house to mix in with the ashes and for sure, I don't want to spill them on the carpet." She smiled at the image in her mind of her late husband blowing all around the room and settling on the cream-coloured carpet on the living room floor. Then she would have to vacuum him up.

John searched through the box for something suitable but his mind was racing a mile a minute.

"Do you need it today?" he asked.

"Oh no, dear. He's been dead for three months already. I just want something more suitable and attractive."

"What you need is an urn," John said. "I could make one especially for you in any design you want, light or dark, tall or squat."

"An urn? Yes, yes dear. That would be great. I can pay you for it. Nothing is too good for my dear, departed Henry. I do like your work." She had the cherry wood bowl in her hand.

Yes, pay me. John had no idea what he would charge for an item like this. The lady saved him the worry.

"The funeral home had some. They wanted between six hundred and a thousand dollars for them. I would have bought one, but there was nothing there I liked. Henry was such an individual kind of person, I didn't want to get just anything. What kind of wood is this?" She passed bowl to John. He noted that the price tag read $300.

"That's cherry wood. Comes from right here in Nova Scotia. I have more of it at home all properly aged."

The lady was smiling now. "This is so exciting. I get to design it myself." She took a note pad and pen from her purse and sketched a tall urn with a bulge in the centre and tapered above and below. "Henry always tended to the heavy side, liked his beer a little too much." She shaded in the centre part. "Could you make the top and bottom a little lighter and the centre the colour of this bowl?"

John studied the design. The secret of wood turning, he always said, is not to tell anyone what you're making until it is finished. That way no one ever knows if you make a mistake. Following this sketch would be more of a challenge. He reached into the box and took out a bowl made from maple.

"I could make the top and bottom with this kind of wood and the centre cheery or," he reached in and took out a bowl made from white ash, "I could make it even lighter with this kind of wood."

The lady studied her choices. She piled the three bowls one on top of the other, maple, cherry, ash. "What about this colour-scheme?"

John thought about the different textures of the woods and the challenge of turning them all at the same time. He thought about the money she was offering.

"No problem," he said.

"Oh good, Henry will be so pleased." She reached into her purse and pulled out three hundred dollar bills. Prime Minister

Borden stared at John with a severe, unsmiling face. "I'll give you this as a deposit and the rest when I pick up the completed urn. Here's my card, call me when it's ready."

John took the money. He was unsure what to do with it.

"I'll write you a receipt." He looked around for something to write on and spotted the order book purchased the previous day from Business Depot. He thought he might pick up some orders but never thought anyone would pay him in advance. He filled out the form and noted the $300 deposit and passed it over to the lady.

"Thank you, but that was not really necessary. If you can't trust someone who works with wood, who can you trust?" She stuffed the piece of paper into her purse.

It was natural to demand a deposit on custom goods. Once pointed out, John felt like a fool for being surprised at getting one. Here he was thinking he was an entrepreneur and taking lessons in basic business from a little, old widow mourning for her dead husband. He was kidding himself if he thought he knew what he was doing. On the other hand, he now had $570 in his pocket, tax free: that was a pretty good day's work.

These were hobby bowls; he could discount the time required to turn them as he had already received the value in the enjoyment of making them. Things had now changed. He was committed to making a funeral urn. He had to do it now, not when the mood struck him. Turning would now be akin to work.

John rearranged the bowls on the table. Several people dropped by, picked them up, took pleasure from their warmth and replaced them. Favourable comments were offered on the beauty of his work, on how he managed to capture the essence of the wood, on how he was a real artist. Being unable to afford the expensive wooden bowls, many were content to buy a snowman. Soon all forty of the ornaments were sold and one more bowl. As he was thinking about packing it in for the day, Eric Sanderson dropped by and picked up one of the remaining bowls. He held it up to the sun and watched the reflection make the grain shimmer.

"You were holding out on me last week," he said. "Got any more of those ten dollar bowls?" John was about to tell him to go to hell when he realized Eric was joking.

"Here I have something for you." He offered John an envelope. John hesitated before reaching out and taking it.

"What's this?"

"I realized the blue dots on the bowls last week meant you were asking $20 for them, not ten. This is the difference."

John looked in the envelope, five twenties. He gave Eric a bewildered look.

"Why?"

"I sold four of the bowls last week and the last six today for $150 each. I can afford to be generous, especially if I hope to purchase any more bowls from you. I like the way they move. I also like the way they stop people at my table to look and then as often as not buy something else. People like them. You have real talent, son. You should be making these full time. I could help you sell them."

"Why would I need your help? I seem to be doing all right here."

Eric shook his head. "You're not a closer. I've sold ten bowls in the last two weeks. How many have you sold?"

John smiled. "Twelve. Two today and ten last week."

Eric returned the smile.

"True. I guess you did beat me. These aren't really flea market items. They should be sold in a gallery or at a juried craft show. You would get a different class of people. They would pay more for them. I have the contacts to get them into those places," pause, "for a small handling fee. Give me a few of your better efforts and let's see what I can do. When I sell them, you're in money. If by some quirk of fate, I don't, I give them back and you can gloat that I didn't live up to my bragging. No sweat off your back either way." He looked at John and shrugged his shoulders with a "what have you got to lose" gesture.

Nathan was impressed with Eric, John realized, but he wasn't completely sold on him. Last week Eric ripped him off by taking all his bowls for ten bucks each when he knew they were worth a lot more. True, John had been a party to the deal; he sold them. This was an indication that Eric knew more about the business than John did. What did he have to lose? For one thing, it's not about the money, stupid. You've already got it safely stashed at home. Here's a chance to see how good your work is, see if others are willing to pay big bucks to own it. Here's the man who might be able to make this happen. He has got the biggest selling area in the flea market. He must be doing something right.

While all this was going through John's mind, Eric was content to stand and wait for an answer. He had presented his selling points, knew he was right, had nothing more to say. He waited while John convinced himself everything Eric said was true. Saw the flash in John's eye when the truth of the situation dawned on him. Smiled at that point and said: "Have we got a deal?" He extended his hand. "Let's talk my share."

# ≈9≈

DETECTIVE-SERGEANT Mcdonald stood in the parking lot of police headquarters talking to the two plainclothes cops who were assigned to follow Roger Johnson, The Boss. Despite the grey, overcast, afternoon sky, they were all laughing.

"The uniforms were waiting outside when he left. Pulled him over less than 500 yards from the pup. Johnson blew .08 right on the nose so they brought him in. Man, was he pissed off." Constable Kate Irving's smile almost broke her face it stretched so far.

Her partner, Joe Davis, nodded in agreement. The smile was contagious.

"The beauty of it now is, once he goes before a judge, our judge, we can pick him up anytime he slides behind the wheel of a car. With this DUI, he will lose his licence. One more aggravation for a man who is already aggravated to the point of explosion."

"And his little buddy, Leroy Leblanc," Kate cut in, almost dancing with the excitement of the day's events, "he has a long record of DUIs. He is going to get jail time. Oh man, the irony is too much. They sell drugs to kids like they work in a confectionery store dishing out candy and we can't touch them. They go into the local pub for a few beers and we put their ass in jail. Reminds me of Al Capone."

Now it was Mcdonald's turn to relish the moment. "This is great. Ettinger has disappeared. Leblanc will be in the can. Johnson is going to have to do his own dirty work. It won't be long before we nail his ass as well. He's not used to the hands-on stuff anymore. He's more into giving orders to others. Right now, not too many people want to be seen with him because of our open surveillance. As they say in the old country, he's been sent to Coventry. This is great, I can't help repeating it, just great."

As if in heavenly agreement, a shaft of sunlight broke through the clouds for a few seconds. Jim looked up into the bright light and equally as quick, the hole in the clouds disappeared. The message seemed to say there is light at the end of the tunnel, but you have to be quick to capitalize on it.

"You say you overheard him talking about checking up on street-level dealers to see what they were selling?" Jim asked.

Joe reached into his pocket and brought out a small cylinder the size of a golf course pencil. "This little baby is great for listening to conversations close by."

Irving interrupted: "Two box tops from Cornflakes and $1.98 and you too can own one of these." She laughed again.

Davis ignored her and continued: "Just aim this little gizmo at the speaker and it's like being at the table with him. Portable, can be used anywhere and no advance installation is required. Johnson was sending Leroy to talk to some of the street people, shake them down for information." He laughed again, shaking his head in the process. "He'll have to wait a bit for Leroy to report back. He should get at least six months, maybe a year if the judge is in a bad mood."

"OK, that should be grounds for another search warrant," Jim said. "Leave out the part about Leblanc being picked up before he could carry out the assignment. We need an expectation of finding something new. Lots of marked cars, lights flashing, make the search Saturday afternoon. Wear your uniforms just for some added show."

"The dress reds with the Stetson?" Kate asked, continuing to smile. She was enjoying this too much. She had made the initial arrest on the Friday night when they came up empty because the money had been dumped. This gave her a vested interest in the case. Turning the screws on Johnson and blocking him out of the business was a small bit of revenge. She just wanted to be around for the final arrest. If only they could come up with the missing money.

"There will be nothing to be found at the house, that's for sure. We've kept him tied up tighter than a fishing line wrapped around a submerged log. His business is dying right before his beady, little eyes."

"Sooner or later, he'll be summoned by his bosses to explain that," Jim said. "That's the meeting we want your little pencil thingy attending. Johnson is high up the food chain but he's not the Big Boss. We want to nail them both."

"Speaking of missing money, are we having any luck finding it in the search?" Kate asked.

The smile left Jim's face and was replaced with a scowl.

"None at all. We have sources at the local high schools listening in to the chit chat. No luck. In fact the subject has dropped off the radar screen there. There is no longer any speculation about what they would do if they found the loot. That was the game for the first week, a lot of what ifs. 'I'd get a hot, new car. I'd be outta this place. I'd get me some fine new threads.' Well, those weren't his actual words but that's what he meant, I think. Now it's all been forgotten. They've moved onto play other mind games.

"Our discreet inquires at the elementary school level among the teachers have turned up nothing as well. None of the students are bragging about a sudden increase in wealth at home or new PlayStations or whatever. The teachers are still listening, though.

As long as it wasn't one of them." He smiled. Anything was possible.

"We checked the multitude of used-car dealers up and down Sackville Drive to see if anyone is paying with large wads of cash. There are, but everyone can account for the source of their money. None of it appears to be a sudden, unexplained windfall. Just a lot of leg work with no results," he paused, "yet. We'll find it sooner or later. We're not giving up. You guys keep up the good work putting the pressure on Johnson. We'll talk later."

With that, Jim turned on his heel and walked across the lot to his own unmarked, black sedan. Plan B was working but it cost a ton of money in manpower to keep up the vigilance around the clock. Plan A would have been so much sweeter if only the money and drugs had not disappeared.

It had also used up a great deal of resources, and if necessary these undercover agents could be outed to appear in court. For now, they were buried too deep in the local drug organization to expose their identity. Hell, soon they would be running it if things kept up at the pace they were going. Another round of arrests was not that far off. It would be nice to close one case before opening the next one.

Jim drove to the county correctional facility, what was once known as a jail. Leroy Leblanc was still making his way through the blizzard of paperwork involved with his DUI arrest. Jim thought a little chat might be in order and radioed ahead to make sure Leblanc didn't get released on his own recognizance while awaiting an appearance before a judge. He had nothing to worry about; Judge Kendrall was clearing a spot in his calendar to slot Leroy in.

Judge Kendrall was a rarity in the judicial system these days. He was not a radical rightwinger but was not a bleeding-heart liberal either. He tried to apply common sense to the administration of justice, working within the law, of course. "The police cannot do their jobs with one hand tied behind their back," he was quoted as saying. "Today, in many cases, they seem to have both hands in shackles with a foot wedged in between them."

He still believed you were innocent until proven guilty. However, if your list of court appearances was greater than his, and he was there every day, he suspected you might not be a neophyte in the criminal system. As Dr. Phil often said "Past action is the best indicator of future action."

Judge Kendrall would err on the side of the victims, the side of the public, the side of the police in these cases. In short, if you were guilty, you would not get a free pass on some technicality. You were going to jail. His ruling might be overturned later on appeal, but you were viewing life through steel bars until that happened.

This attitude was a breath of fresh air to Sergeant Mcdonald and his fellow operatives in the world of crime fighting. Their job was to make sure there were no technicalities that could lead to a reversal. If they supported the judge, he would support them. So far it was working.

Leroy Leblanc was a prime example of what could be done. His breathalyzer reading just barely qualified him to be arrested. Most judges would fine him at worst, but it was in their purview to incarcerate him. Judge Kendrall, after reviewing all the facts, took this latter course. Everything was above board. The sentence was allowed under the statutes even if seldom used. There could be no appeal. Another high-level dealer was off the street. It didn't matter why.

Both the judge and the detective knew this form of administering justice could be a slippery slope. Neither wanted to see abuse set in and truly innocent people suffer. But for too long they had been sliding down the other side of the hill under the guise of protecting the rights of the accused. It was time to at least tilt the playing field back towards level. It was time to think about the rights of the victim for a change, especially when the accused had a history of multiple arrests.

Leroy had been waiting in the interview room for about twenty minutes before Jim opened the door and entered. Jim had watched him through the two-way glass as he sat there talking to himself, building up his defence, confirming—in his own mind anyway—his innocence. He couldn't stay seated. One minute he was up walking around, the next back in his chair and then up pacing again. He was having a major conversation with himself and by the looks of things, he had convinced himself of his innocence. It was time for Jim to set the record straight. A look of fear crossed Leroy's face when the detective entered, replaced by a look of insolence.

"What's a *major crime detective* doing on a simple drinking charge?" He asked, putting special emphasis on the *major crime* wording. He recognized Jim from the hours spent together on the previous Friday night-Saturday morning after the futile drug bust. "Let's stop pissing around. Let me pay my fine and get out of here."

Jim lowered himself into the heavy, wooden chair across the table from Leroy. The steel coffee-stained table stretched between them. Jim leaned forward to close the gap, his eyes burning with intensity.

"As you would put it, Leroy, that ain't gonna happen. You're going to do time on this one. You've climbed behind the wheel of your big SUV drunk once too often."

"I wasn't drunk and you know it. I had a few beers, that's all. No big deal. I could have drank twice that many and still not been drunk. This is all bullshit."

Jim slowly shook his head from side to side, glancing down at the table as he did so, his lips in a tight grimace. He looked up again.

"Leroy, Leroy, Leroy. You know better than that. You blew over the limit, again. How many times has that happened? You just don't seem to learn. Maybe some jail time will persuade you not to drink and drive."

"That's bull. This is the first time I've been caught in years. My lawyer will have me out of here in no time." He was back on his feet again.

Jim leaned back in his chair as if he were getting comfortable for the long haul.

"Sit down, Leroy. You haven't been taking your medication, have you?"

Leroy pushed his chair against the table, hard. "What medication? What are you talking about?"

"Come on, man. We know you've had Zanatec prescribed for you. I've got your records from the last time you were in." Jim held up a brown manila folder. "You skip your meds and you become erratic. Right now, I'd say you're manic high." Jim waited for confirmation. When none came, he continued. "You're in for a long period of depression when we stick you back inside."

The light burning in Leroy's eyes turned from a glowing ember to a lump of cold charcoal.

"You don't have anything to hold me on. My lawyers are working on getting me out right now. I'll be home long before you are today. You don't know the justice system like I do. This arrest is a joke."

"Slow down, Leroy. You're talking faster than I can listen. I don't see you going anywhere today but to a cell." Jim paused and let that sink in. "Sit down and let's talk. There might be a way around that."

Leroy stood his ground.

Jim shrugged. "Your choice, but right now, I'm your only option that doesn't include jail time." He pointed towards the chair and made a sit-down motion.

Reluctantly, Leroy lowered himself into his chair but avoided the policeman's eyes.

Jim picked up a thermos and two Styrofoam cups from the floor beside him. He poured a cup of black coffee for both of them and slid Leroy's across the table. His voice took on a more sympathetic tone. "The other night when we picked you up speeding down the Back Road, you dumped some money and drugs. Let's talk about that."

Leroy ignored the cup of coffee. "I wasn't speeding down any road. I was a passenger. There was no money. There were no drugs. If I dumped something, you would have found it. If you had found it, I wouldn't be sitting here on this trumped-up drinking and driving charge." The words tumbled from Leroy's mouth.

Now, it was Leroy's turn to grin. He leaned forward and stared Jim right in the eye. "I heard you spent all day Saturday and most of Sunday looking for it. Had the little, orange men out helping you tramp all through the woods for miles. You found nothing because there was nothing to find." This was spoken at normal speed and had a teasing quality to it.

Once again Leroy was pleased he had had the presence of mind to get rid of the goods before they were pulled over. He would be looking at serious jail time otherwise. This still didn't answer the question of where the stuff disappeared to. If the police hadn't found it and he and his friends hadn't found it, that left one big question: Who had?

Jim changed his tactics. He needed no reminders of his failure to find the evidence to put Johnson and his gang of thugs away. He leaned back in his chair and stretched his legs out in front of him. Now his voice had a quality of derision to it. "I hear you called your lawyer and he said he was too busy to come for a DUI. Told you to plead out."

This was true and Leroy was still fuming about it. It seemed the law firm retained by The Boss was swamped with work resulting from the drug raids all over the province. Their resources were spread too thin to worry about Leroy getting dinged for an alcohol-related charge. The fine would be less than the cost of a lawyer looking into it. If Leroy lost his licence in the process, tough shit, he should have kept off the road while drinking. Their job at the moment was to keep the bulk of their clients out of prison on much more serious charges. The police had done their work well in most of the cases. All the T's were crossed; all the I's were dotted. The lawyers had their work cut out for them.

"I'd call him back and tell him you're not looking at a fine. You're going to jail for as long as the law allows. I guarantee it." Jim punctuated the last line with a mocking smile.

The muscles in Leroy's neck and shoulders tightened at this news. His stress level started to climb. He had no desire to return to jail for any reason. Living a life of crime seemed to contradict this fear. Going to prison should have been part of the job description, but such was the criminal mind. He believed he would never be caught.

"I have nothing more to say to you. Leave me alone." The smile had gone from his hollow-cheeked face. He looked sullen and withdrawn. Even amid his denial that it could happen, the reality of returning to jail was setting in. The Boss would not let this happen to him, could not let this happen to him. He was a part of the inner circle and people at his level did not end up in prison on a goddamn DUI.

"Have you ever appeared before Judge Kendrall?" Jim asked. "In the days of the old west, he would have been known as a hanging judge. Are you prepared to hang for your buddy, Roger Johnson? He was picked up at the same time you were, you know. DUI just like you. Look around. Do you see him anywhere? He went home hours ago. The lawyers weren't too busy to get him out of here."

"Piss off." Leroy was running out of things to say. He should have been freed a long time ago as well. Why was he still here? He could sense the depression starting to overtake him.

"He's going to let you hang. But you can help yourself, Leroy. Fill in a few gaps for us about the operation and you can be free. I can even save your driver's licence if you cooperate."

Once again the detective was right in Leroy's face. This time with a look of sincerity. He could make it all go away. He could be the one to protect Leroy.

"I've nothing to say to you. Leave me alone." Leroy turned away from Jim's face. "Call that damn lawyer again and tell him I have to see him right now." With that, Leroy folded his arms across his chest and looked down at the table. He was through talking.

Jim wasn't. He pulled out his cellphone and called Leroy's lawyer, talked for a couple of minutes and hung up again.

"He said he's not coming in and gave me permission to talk to you."

Jim stretched the truth a little. In fact the lawyer told the sergeant to tell Leroy to plead it out. The law office was too busy to send anyone. If Leroy had done that the last time he called, he would be home by now.

Jim interpreted the statement to mean it was all right to keep talking to Leroy. They had asked him to pass on messages, after all. The dance went on for another hour, Jim promising, threatening, cajoling. Leroy denying, cursing, lying. In the end, Jim learned nothing new. Leroy, like it or not, was going to prison.

# ≈10≈

JOHN STOOD in his workshop examining his stock of dried hardwood. He was excited about this new project. Turning funeral urns had never occurred to him before, but now it made so much sense he couldn't believe he hadn't made a roomful of them. This was something everyone could use once in their lifetime. All the world was a market for this product.

He picked up a piece of cherry. The grain flowed like the ripples of a spring freshet across the face. Turning and polishing would make this into a work of art anyone would be proud to display, despite the contents. He studied the piece of wood and visualized Mrs. Collins' plans.

The old lady still grieved the loss of her husband. He could see a change take place in her as she studied the grains in the wood he had shown her at the flea market. Her mind contemplated a living, vital person, not a pile of ashes. She connected the beauty in the wood to the beauty that had been her companion for most of her adult life.

This piece of cherry wood would be a good start.

He set the piece of cherry aside and picked up a piece of sugar maple. A little lighter than the cherry, it was just as attractive.

Close examination showed him some bird's eyes staring out of the design. These two woods would complement each other well. He searched through the box of blocks and found a piece of ash the same size as the other two. It was much lighter in colour but had just as interesting a pattern hiding in its surface, waiting for a craftsman like John to bring it to the forefront for all the world to admire. He planed and sanded the edges, glued the three pieces together and set the resulting piece aside to dry.

He should let the glue dry for at least twenty-four hours.

He searched through his samples for other pieces that called out to him, declaring they were urns also. If he listened, the wood spoke to him, defining what it wanted to be. It was strange none had claimed to be an urn before because now several pieces insisted they were. He set them on the shelf and studied them. The potential existed in all of them. He just had to take away the parts of the wood that weren't an urn. What was left, would be.

He picked up one piece of maple that was just the right height but had a knot halfway up its length. It had so much promise; the waves of the grain flowed from the surface like a lake on a day with a gentle wind. Could he work the knot into the pattern? The wood insisted it was an urn so John would give it a try. He took it over to the lathe and clamped it in place. This was a solid piece of wood so there was no waiting for the glue to dry. He chose a chisel and started the lathe turning in a slow, steady speed. Chips of wood flew from the chisel as the square edges were removed to form a round cylinder.

Soon he had a long, thin strip of wood like an apple peeling curling to the floor in front of him. He stopped the lathe and studied the results of his work. Now the pattern was suggesting where hollows should be added and ridges should be left. John became oblivious to everything around him. Time passed. Wood chips piled up on the table and floor around him. An urn shape was materializing, hidden in the tree for years and now emerging in all its glory.

John stopped the lathe and admired his work. He ran his hands over the product and felt the texture of the wood. Everything looked good except the knot. The remainder of the piece was too beautiful to discard. There was lots of time to deal with the knot. He removed the spindle, attached a face plate, selected the right tool and advanced to the next stage of the work, hollowing out the cylinder. Again the world melted away as John became absorbed in the task at hand. This was love, not work.

John looked up at Marla. She stood studying him. The turning had absorbed his complete concentration making him unaware of her presence until this moment.

"Sorry," he said, "did you want me for something?"

He reached for the switch to stop the rotating piece of maple, no longer just a piece of wood but a nearly completed work of art. Grains previously unnoticed stood out, demanding the attention of the observer. Instead of a dead piece of wood, it was alive again. He pushed up his facemask and waited for Marla to speak.

"Just wondering if supper is in your plan for the evening. I called you twice and you responded both times."

"Did I?" John examined his watch. Surprise registered on his face. The afternoon had faded into evening. The missing hours were a complete blank to him. "I don't remember."

Marla ran her fingers along the gleaming length of the urn, admiring the beauty of it. She experienced a feeling of pride that she was married to the man who could make this transition appear in an inanimate object in such a short space of time.

"This is beautiful. The old man's ashes couldn't ask for a better final resting place."

John touched the wood, giving it a gentle spin to allow the light to reflect off the many facets of the ridges and grooves he had carved into it.

"This is just practice. The one I'm making for the old lady is over there with the glue drying." He glanced at his watch again and gave a harsh laugh. "I'll tackle it tomorrow."

He stopped the slow turn of the urn and brought the enemy knot to the top where Marla could observe it. "This one has a flaw."

Marla studied the area around the blemish. The grain moved out around the knot and then came back to the original path like a wave going around a rock sitting out in the ocean.

"I kind of like it," she said. "It adds character."

"Think so?" asked John. He re-evaluated his opinion but didn't change his mind. "This isn't the colour scheme the client wanted. I'll just add it to stock." He laughed at the word "client". This was no longer a hobby. He was now an artisan running his own business. In his mind he made note of the passage of one stage of his life to another.

"OK," said Marla. "But I like it. Let's eat."

Together they left the dusty workshop and made their way to the house. The afternoon was only a blur in John's mind but he had created something that would last. This was better than shuffling papers around a desk, a job he compared to pouring a glass of water into a full dishpan. It made a little splash at the moment but in seconds, no one could tell he had done it. On the other hand, this urn would be around for years to come, a testament of how he spent this one afternoon.

John slipped his arm around Marla's waist and squeezed.

"I feel good," he said. "Let's do something special tonight. We can afford it." He noticed the scowl appearing on Marla's face and added, "After we enjoy the delicious supper you've prepared, of course."

Marla laughed and gave him a gentle punch in the shoulder.

"A movie would be fun," she agreed. "There's one playing at the Empire I've been wanting to see."

We can afford it, John thought. This was the first time all day thoughts of money entered his mind. The sack of money lay untouched under the steps where it had been stashed since the first day. When he put it there, he had all kinds of plans of things to do with it, places to go, things to see, how it would change his life. The surprising thing was that it had. He was happier than he had been in years. He hadn't realized he was unhappy before. Life had been ticking along, unfolding as it should. He had a wife, kids, a job, a house, the Canadian dream, everything seemed great. It was all an illusion.

Now he had a hockey bag full of money. Everything had changed but not because of the money. Apart from the initial grab of a thousand dollars in the early excitement of discovery, much of which was still unspent, the money had served him no purpose. It was a token, a backstop, a security blanket. Everything he had done for the past three weeks, he could have done without it. This realization startled him. He had been a wimp avoiding life, taking the easy route. No more. It was time to live his dream, take some chances and do the things he enjoyed. Flip. He could hear the page turning to new challenges.

"Sure a movie will be great. It's not a chick flick, I hope."

# ≈11≈

FLIP. ROGER Johnson could hear the page turning as well. Half of his senior staff was gone. Ettinger fled the country, Leblanc in jail. Wally McIssac was not a stupid man. He did not have the organizational ability of Big Willie. He lacked the street smarts of Leroy Leblanc.

His ability was to blend in, to absorb, to find things out. To date, his abilities were failing The Boss. Wally's only task was to find out where the money was. In three weeks he was no closer than the night he stopped the car and watched Leroy throw it away.

Johnson was beginning to forget this move kept him out of jail. Now he wanted his money back; he wanted the police to leave him alone. He wanted Wally McIssac to finish his goddamn job. That much money should be easy to find in this little community.

Activity on the street returned to normal. Well, almost normal. Roger Johnson no longer ran the show. The vacuum created by police raids was being filled, not by Johnson, but by people who had worked for him and who were more than willing to move up the food chain and take his place. Three weeks had passed and to these young ingrates, the word was becoming "Roger Who?"

Oh, they would suffer. They had been fooled into thinking a minor setback for Roger was a major opportunity for them. That wasn't the worst part of it, however. Roger's suppliers were feeding the drugs which were rightly his to these upstarts, helping them to become established. People were going to pay, pay big time.

He walked over to the window and looked out. There it sat. A plain, dark blue car, two people relaxing in the front seat. They weren't even trying to hide their surveillance of him.

If only he could shake these damn cops who were stuck to him like leeches on a bare-legged kid wading along the shore of an overgrown lake in search of tadpoles. His first task was to escape from their watchful eyes.

Roger had a plan, a plan that had to be carried out right away before he appeared in court on the DUI. He knew he would lose his licence along with the fine. He had to disappear first. Once convicted, simply climbing behind the wheel of his car would be an excuse for the cops to bring him in again. More harassment. He didn't need that hassle.

He had complained to his lawyer about being picked up outside the beer joint for drinking and driving. Thinking about the conversation angered him again.

"You're guilty. I can delay it but I can't change the facts." the lawyer argued.

"I know I'm guilty," Roger fumed. "If I was innocent, I wouldn't need you. You're paid to get me off when I am guilty."

"OK, I'll work on it but there are more serious charges pending against you. They should be your main concern right now, not some DUI. You're not going to jail for that."

For Roger, not having a driver's licence would be like being in jail. The lawyer managed to delay the hearing. Roger still had a licence for now. He also had a plan.

He called Wally with instructions to meet him at the local Superstore grocery store. Once there, the two of them disappeared into the crowded aisles where, although still being observed, they could talk without being overheard. After a short whispered discussion, Roger slipped something into Wally's pocket.

Then without warning, Roger broke off the conversation and trotted down the aisle and out the door to his waiting car, illegally parked in the fire lane. He snatched the ticket off the windshield as he went by and dove behind the wheel. He crumpled the ticket and threw it on the floor in disgust. He was willing to bet this was the only ticket of its type issued this year. None of the other illegally parked cars exhibited tickets.

Wally watched Roger disappear down the aisle. Then, he slipped behind the nearby meat counter and was gone. His minder's concentration had been on the fleeing Roger Johnson running out of the store. He didn't even see Wally fade from sight.

As Roger sped out of the lot, he noticed the two plainclothesmen assigned to him jumping into their car. He laughed out loud. Escape was never his intention with this manoeuvre, it was more to release frustration over his confinement. The true plan was just starting. He pulled into the local branch of By-ways Car Rentals. He needed a clean car, one without tracking devices secured to it in some hidden location. His followers pulled up on the opposite side of the street and threw him a dirty look. Roger waved and entered the office of the rental agency.

The young clerk put down her magazine and flashed him a broad smile showing all of her pearly whites as the door closed behind him. The office consisted of a small counter supporting a computer and a printer, several tourist rack cards on a stand in the corner and a desk, chair and telephone behind the counter.

"Yes, sir. How can I be of service?" she asked.

"What's the most economical driving car on your lot?" he asked. "Not the cheapest to rent but the one giving the best gas mileage."

"That's easy," she replied. "We have a little GM Metro that gets over 60 miles to the gallon and it's also the least expensive rental. Or for something a little bigger but not quite as good on gas—"

"No," Roger interrupted. "The Metro sounds perfect."

"For just a few pennies a day more, we have the same car as a convertible. It's a beautiful day out there for driving a rag top, takes some of the sting out of having such a small car. Gives it a little more class." She laughed as she added the latter to indicate she was just having some fun with him.

Roger glanced back over his shoulder. He could see no cars meeting that description out front. "A rag top. That would be the perfect touch. Is there one here on this lot?"

Again the white teeth gleamed. "Parked right out back, filled with gas, and ready to go," she said.

Roger returned the smile, not that of a drug overlord, but the smile of an out-of-town visitor looking for some cheap reliable wheels. "Good. Let's get the paperwork done."

After the necessary discussion about insurance waivers, credit card information, and whether it would be returned to this location or to another branch, the deal was sealed. Roger was handed the keys and sent to the lot to do his pre-rental inspection. He made one quick trip around the car checking for dents and dings and waved to the clerk.

"It looks fine," he called out to her and shoe-horned himself behind the wheel. He released the seat adjustment and shot back, fully extending his legs. This isn't so bad, he thought. He looked out at the counter lady standing beside the car.

"Do you want some help with the roof?" she asked. "It's quite simple once you know how to do it.

"Sure," he said and crawled out of the car. A couple of quick releases, opening and closing of hatches and he was driving a sporty-looking little convertible. He waved to his pursuers in a follow me motion and pulled out onto the street, the three-cylinder engine purring along like a kitten. The motor was the perfect size. He knew one kilometre an hour above the limit would have him pulled over. He intended to drive less than the legal limit to maximize his mileage. He wondered how the eight-cylinder pursuer would make out with his gas guzzler.

One of the cops had the radio in his hand, no doubt informing his superiors of the change in Roger's mode of transportation. The other wheeled in behind him, making no secret that their job was to follow his every move. Roger cruised around the city for awhile with lots of starts and stops before he headed for the 101, set his cruise control at 95 clicks and let the wind ruffle his hair as it slip-streamed over the protective windshield. He was surprised to note the passenger compartment was less windy than he would have suspected. This would be an enjoyable outing.

Unlike the previous day, there were no clouds in the sky. He reached into his pocket and slipped his Ray-Bas over his eyes to protect them from the sun climbing to its zenith in the cerulean sky.

In the pocket of the door, he spotted a ball cap with the By-ways Car Rentals logo above the bill. The cap was encased in a plastic bag, indicating it was new and unused. He checked the sizing tab at the back, snapping it into the seven-and-one-eighth slot, and then adjusted the cap on his head. They think of everything. Driving a convertible with the sun beating down on an uncovered scalp could fry your brains in no time.

He checked his mirror to see how his followers were doing. Keeping their speed down on a four-lane road like this would be a challenge for them.

As they drove deeper into the Annapolis Valley, the limited-access highway turned into two lanes taking them through the backfields of large farms fronting on the secondary roads in the distance. Cows contentedly grazed in some fields, others sported row after row of carrots, corn, potatoes or other produce, all designed to feed the people of the province, signs of legitimate work, hard work, not something Roger was interested in pursuing. Perhaps poppies or marijuana might be a crop to consider.

Every other car on the road whizzed by them, some making rude gestures in the process. Roger ignored them. He had a plan.

A little over two hours into the trip, he noticed the reflected faces of his pursuers in his rear-view mirror. They were engaged in a heavy conversation. Neither looked happy. Roger figured their gas gauge should be slipping towards empty. Were they blaming each other for not filling the gas tank before the day's work began? It wouldn't have mattered; Roger was prepared to drive them into the ground. His gauge still had not reached the half-empty point. One had the radio transmitter in his hand again.

This was the make it or break it point for Roger's plan. Had they waited until it was too late to make alternate arrangements to cover him? He could only hope. The signal light of the unmarked police cruiser came on as they approached the upcoming exit. No other official looking cars were in sight.

Roger reached into his pocket and grabbed a small walkie-talkie of his own. With one hand he waved to the upset officers who were forced to give up their pursuit in search of a gas station on the secondary road. With the other he signalled Wally, who was trailing in another rental car, to pull up closer. Roger had slipped a similar walkie-talkie to Wally when they met in the store, As soon as Wally caught up, both cars pulled over to the shoulder beyond the white line.

Roger jumped into the driver's seat of Wally's car while Wally repeated the action in Roger's car. Wally was about to take off when he noticed Roger flashing his lights and waving. He waited and Roger ran up and passed him the ball cap.

"Here, wear this," he said. "It'll protect your head from the sun and makes you look like me. You should enjoy the moment while you can." Roger laughed and ran back for his new car. He was in a good mood. He dialled the car around in the road, causing the tires to squeal from the tight turn, and headed back the other way. Wally continued on towards Yarmouth. Less than a mile down the road, Roger spotted a marked cruiser screaming towards him, fast, hurrying to catch up, hurrying to cover the pursuit dropped by the city police. It was a close thing but he had pulled it off, had shaken free of his shackles.

He would love to see their reaction when they realized they were now pursuing the wrong person. Wally could make it all the way to the end of the province with ease. Several hours would lapse before it was realized they were following the wrong person.

He would have to sacrifice his contact with Wally for the time being, but Wally knew his orders. Find the damn money. At their next meeting, he would live vicariously through Wally's description of the police reaction to the lack of his presence in the little car. They would be at a loss as to how he slipped right out from under their noses. For now, more important things dominated his mind. The time had come to take back his own business.

"I'm back, you mothers. I'm back and you are about to find out why I was your boss and not the other way around." It was a menacing threat but only the birds sitting on the telephone wires along the shoulder of the road were around to hear it. As if the malevolent thought carried weight of its own, the birds all took off at once, darkening the sky with their numbers, circled in a slow arc before settling back onto the wires. Roger noticed their actions.

"You're right to keep out of my way," he murmured. "I've been jerked around for too long. People are going to pay for their disloyalty."

He sped back to the city driving ten clicks over the speed limit instead of five under. He was a free man again. In his mind, he planned the first steps of recapturing his empire. Extreme violence topped his plan. Those who deserted him would be made to be fearful for their own existence. Not only would they stop cutting into his territory, they would line up to get back into his employ. One or two bloody examples would have the remainder of them jumping through hoops to get in his good graces again. He did not have to establish a reputation for his actions. It already existed. Some just needed a wake-up call, a reminder of whom they were dealing with. Roger felt the power of leadership surge back into his body.

# ≈12≈

JOHN LESTER and Nathan Darling sipped their hot drinks at the local Tim Horton's coffee shop. Outside a bright, sunny day was drawing to a close. The high clouds formed what is known as a mackerel sky. Traces of pink flickered at the edges of the formation. Tomorrow would be another good day, weather-wise. These get-togethers had become a regular thing in the past couple of weeks and John looked forward to the meetings. Initially the discussions centred on flea market topics. What was hot, what was not. Who showed up every week, who only appeared on sunny days when the crowds were at their best. John learned a great deal about the business and was grateful for the knowledge Nathan shared with him.

Soon the topics became more personal. John learned about Nathan's early life. He had been a carpenter handyman before his wife died. His knowledge of tools was from experience and use. When he said an item had quality, it had quality. He didn't sell junk even if some of the tools were a bit rusted. The saws would cut, the hammers would pound nails without breaking, the wrenches would turn nuts without rounding off the corners. He offered no money-back guarantees, but his reputation spoke for itself.

Nathan fathered three children, two boys and a girl. Both of the boys moved out of the province to pursue their careers. Every couple of years, they returned for a visit and to show off their kids to their grandfather. The girl lived in the local area. She took it upon herself to keep an eye on her father even though he insisted he could take care of himself. He did enjoy her visits and the homemade cookies and pies she always brought along.

Along with garnering this information about Nathan, John found himself sharing his own life history. His early years, his schooling and what he did for a living. One thing wasn't shared. The stashed bag of money remained John's secret.

"Eric offered me a business deal," John said during a lull in the conversation. "He wants to sell my bowls on consignment at some craft shows as well as at the flea markets."

Nathan looked up from his cup of coffee and studied John's face. John sought advice. These comments were questions disguised as statements. Nathan set down his cup and stroked his chin as if giving the matter deep thought.

Around them, the other patrons filled their daily need for a fix of Timmies. They chatted, laughed and drank coffee. Few life-altering conversations took place at those tables. Serious decisions would be made at John and Nathan's table.

"You could do worse," Nathan said. "Eric makes money on everything he does. Don't confuse him with a patron of the arts, though. He's in it for the money."

John thought about that statement and took a bite of his fritter. He looked into Nathan's eyes. "Yeah, but can I trust him?" he asked.

Nathan shook his head. "I told you before. He did not rip you off. You did it to yourself. You allowed it to happen and it's time you took the responsibility for your inexperience and moved on."

"He gave me another $100 for the bowls," John said. "A gesture of good will."

"Eric Sanderson gave you money after a deal was closed." The surprise in Nathan's voice was real. "Maybe he has become a patron of the arts. I stand corrected."

"Well, he said he hoped to buy more bowls from me. Liked the way the bowls attracted customers to his tables."

"Ahh yes. That makes more sense. That's the Eric I know. Always working the angle. So what are you going to do?"

"I thought I'd seek out your opinion. You know the man better than I do. You have some idea if he's all talk or if he can deliver on his boasts."

Nathan answered right away. "Eric can deliver. Never have any doubt about that." He was quiet for a moment and sipped his coffee. "Your real concern is if you can trust him. From my experience, he's a man of his word. But he's also a wheeler-dealer. He will honour any deal the two of you work out. The key is to make sure the deal is favourable to you as well as to him. Honestly kid, negotiating with Eric, you're in way over your head."

For a brief flash of time, John was insulted by Nathan's stinging remark. He was no kid. Eric couldn't pull the wool over his eyes. Then he remembered the ten-dollar bowls and realized the accuracy of Nathan's statement. John needed help setting up any deal with the likes of Eric Sanderson.

"You seem to have his number," John said. "Do you have any advice to offer or, better yet, would you like to sit in while I work out a deal? I told Eric I would get back to him early this week. He's waiting for my phone call."

"That's Eric all right," Nathan chuckled. "Putting on the pressure. Putting you on a time line. 'Get back to me right away or I'll be moving onto some other deal with some other person.' And look at you. You're responding. You're jumping through his time-frame hoop."

"No, I'm not." John was on the defensive again.

"Sure you are. You want an answer from me right away so you can get back to Eric. He expects to hear from you early in the week. You won't disappoint him."

"Well, the sooner we get the ball rolling, the sooner I'll start making money."

"Right, are those your words or are they Eric's?"

"Well, they're Eric's, but he's right. I won't make any money if the bowls are sitting in my workshop."

Nathan bit into his caramel-covered doughnut. Blue, red and green sprinkles stuck to the corners of his mouth. Slowly he chewed the delicious sweet and said nothing. His tongue shot out in an experienced move as it snagged the escaping sprinkles. He took another sip of coffee. Still he said nothing.

John's impatience with the older man sparked. "What do you think? Will you help me?"

Nathan faked a startled look. "Me? You want my help?" He studied the surprised look on John's face. "I think your mind is made up already. You don't want my help, you want my blessing." John's head nodded in unconscious agreement. "You have a lot more work to do before you get that."

"More work? What do you mean? I've already got a back load of bowls made. I can make more as I need them, as they sell."

"Exactly how long does it take you to make a bowl? What does the wood cost? What does the sandpaper cost? What does the wax cost? How much electricity are you using in the process? What kind of value are you going to put on your time? How will the money you make from the bowls affect the taxes you pay on your other income? Are you going to take the bowls to Eric or is he going to pick them up? Who pays for that gas? Are you going to be expected to put in time at the craft shows? What is that time worth? Don't forget the wear and tear on your tools. Over and above all these expenses, what kind of profit margin are you looking for? Are you going to be losing money at the price you agree on?"

John was stunned by the barrage of questions. He had sort of thought about these things, but had not put a serious price on any of them except perhaps the cost of the wood. It was a price that slapped him right in the face. It came directly out of his pocket. The others were more obscure.

"I'm waiting," Nathan pushed. "If you are ready to negotiate with Eric, all these prices should be right at your finger tips. You don't have a clue what they are, do you? And that's just what comes to mind right off the top of my head. I've yet to turn my first bowl. I'm sure there are other expenses I don't know about."

He waited for John to respond. John just sat there. "Son, you gotta know about these costs before you enter any agreement with Eric Sanderson. He will hold you to the price you agree on and to the number of pieces of product you agree to supply him. Remember to him, it's just a product. He has no emotional attachment and no interest in the Zen of bowl turning."

John was too numb to answer. He was a neophyte in this world of business and he was going up against a master. His naiveté shocked him. At least he was smart enough to seek advice from Nathan, advice he badly needed it appeared.

"I guess I've got some homework to do," he agreed.

Nathan softened a little. "Now when I tell you I'm losing money at that price, you know what I mean. Let's go to your workshop and walk through the production of one bowl and see what the costs and steps to produce it are. From there we'll see how much you need to make on it and from there see how much you can hope to make. We'll hope the latter figure is greater than the former. If not, don't give up your day job."

Give up my day job? John stiffened at the thought. That option had never entered his mind.

# ≈13≈

ROGER JOHNSON had to act fast. By his reckoning he had three hours of total freedom at the outside. Less if Wally's identity was discovered before he reached Yarmouth. The option was available for Wally to keep driving until the police realized the error of their ways, but Roger figured that event would take place as soon as Wally stopped for gas. By giving Wally an apparent destination, a hotel in Yarmouth, it gave him an appearance of innocence. Perhaps the followers would wonder if they had ever been in pursuit of Roger. Why not gain his freedom and play some mind games at the same time?

Three hours was not a great deal of time. Much of it had to be invested in getting back to the city, to not only be free, but to be back in action. The return trip took much less time than the outgoing journey. In fact this was Roger's plan B. The police cruisers ran out of gas much sooner than he had anticipated, giving him time to spend the night in the city. His original scenario had the pursuit taking him much farther afield, too far to make it back before the switch was discovered. Under that plan, Roger would have headed to the other coast, the southern shore of the province. From there, he would have started his take-back operation from a distance. He much preferred to do it up close and personal. His presence would add to his threat.

The first order of business when he entered the city was to get some operational cash, some walking-around money. He pulled into his branch of the Royal Bank of Canada and rushed inside. The bank employee was all smiles and graciousness as she helped the leader of a drug ring retrieve his safe deposit box. She showed him to a little cubicle where he could conduct his business in privacy. Roger scooped a handful of cash from the box and stuffed it in his pockets. There was no time for finesse. He had other important things to do. A small makeup case was taken from the box, as well.

From the bank, Roger headed to a mid-priced downtown hotel and booked a room. He paid cash. This would serve as a temporary headquarters until he was sure of how deep the surveillance was on his other city properties. He had not escaped the watchful eye of the police just to walk right back into their gaze. A few skillful strokes of makeup, a little lightening of his hair colour, a small slither of wood in one shoe to alter his walk and Roger was no longer recognizable except to the closest scrutiny. "I'm ba-a-ck," he said to the empty room.

Fear of discovery was gone. He headed out onto the street free to walk among the general population. The local drugstore sold him a throwaway cellphone. This would be his office in a pocket.

Hiring some muscle was the next order of business. He knew exactly whom he wanted to complete the task at hand. Roger was delivering a message and it was important the communication had all the right tones, undertones and nuances in place. Roger wanted no confusion in the minds of his competition. The free ride was over; The Boss was back in charge. He entered a local dive, The Foggy Night, walked through the dimly lit room, lanterns hanging from the walls, peanut shells crunching under his feet, and pushed through the door to the back-room pool hall.

"Sorry, this place is private." A big goon blocked his way.

"Not to me it isn't, I own this fucking place," Roger said. He placed two fingers in the chest of his antagonist and pushed. The man staggered back a couple of steps but held his ground. He glared at the man who dared to lay a hand on him.

"Boss? Is that you?"

"Yeah, it's me. Get out of the way. Where are Louie and Mark?"

The bright lights of the poolroom were in contrast to the darkness of the bar he had just passed through. Roger squinted as he checked out who all were in attendance, what assets were available to him in the short term. Two men looked up from a corner table where they were playing gin rummy.

"Boss? Over here," Mark called. He waved a hand.

The threatening scowl left Roger's face, replaced with a spreading smile. These two men, although not part of his drug business, would deliver Roger's message. They had a different, more specialized line of work. Roger had called on their expertise many times in the past. The message would be delivered exactly as requested. It would be a blanket mailing to all the petty drug dealers cutting into his territory. The results would be instantaneous.

Roger pulled out a chair and joined the two men at the table.

"What's up?" asked Mark. "Are you allowed out without your keepers?" He looked over Roger's shoulder towards the door. He was only half joking.

Everyone knew of Roger's new shadow and everyone avoided him for that reason. To be caught in the net of "known associates" could cramp their own lifestyles.

"I've got some work for you two," Roger said with no formalities, no small talk. "Work to be done tonight." The three men hunched over the table as Roger went into detail about the task at hand, who, what, when and where. The how, he left up to the experts. They needed no guidance in that regard.

Others in the poolroom steered clear of the table. They did not realize The Boss was back, but Mark and Louie had their own reputation. No one wanted to appear to be interested in any of their conversations. It could prove fatal.

That phase of his comeback in place, Roger headed back to his hotel. It was time to make some money again, time to start the wheels of industry churning. The next order of business was to get some product to move. He placed a call to his suppliers. As soon as they recognized his voice, they broke off the call.

"Damn," Roger muttered as the dial tone buzzed in his ear. He redialled. The phone rang and rang and rang, unanswered. Roger sat on the edge of his bed and stared out the window at the darkening skyline as night settled in. He was persona non grata. Everyone was aware of the close scrutiny he was under, aware of the ever-present police cruisers on his street, aware his phones were most likely tapped. No one wanted to step into the glare of the spotlight with him.

He would have to go through an intermediary. Perhaps he was rushing things a little. Perhaps he should just enjoy his freedom tonight, let the message get out on the street that he was back and then make the call. In the morning, they would be much more receptive to his inquiries. In fact, if things went right, they would be trying to call him. Roger lay back on the bed and relaxed. Let the games begin.

# ≈14≈

SERGEANT MCDONALD paced around the small, confined interview room. The two detectives sat at the desk saying nothing, their heads down, a sheepish look on their faces.

"Perhaps you can explain this to me in a way I can understand," the sergeant said. "The two of you were following a goddamned three-cylinder Metro in your super-charged, eight-cylinder Ford, making no effort to be discreet, riding his ass, and you lost him?" His voice rose into a question at the end of the sentence. "You were on a limited-access highway that ran straight for mile after boring mile and you lost him?"

Constable Kate Irving looked up and followed her superior as he walked back and forth in front of her. "We ran out of gas," she said. "Well, we didn't quite run out but we would have if we hadn't stopped when we did. The exits are pretty far apart on that section of the road."

Constable Joe Davis stepped into the explanation. "There was a highway patrol car following less than five miles behind us. I radioed for assistance. He closed the gap as soon as we called him. Five minutes at the most, that's all it took him to catch up. He called us as soon as the subject car was in sight. Five minutes and there were no exits, no places for Johnson to pull off." He shrugged. "I can't explain it."

Kate Irving looked at her partner. She had nothing to add to the explanation.

"That raises the big question," continued Mcdonald. "Were you following the wrong person all along?" He tried to keep the sarcasm out of his voice, but even he could hear it creeping in. Thousands of dollars spent on round-the-clock surveillance had gone up in smoke. The success of the operation depended on keeping Roger Johnson bottled up and unable to conduct his business. Now, they had no idea where he was. They did know what he was doing, however.

Two street-level drug dealers were beaten to within an inch of their lives overnight in separate incidences in two different parts of the city. Both cases had all the ear marks of a warning to others. These were demonstration beatings. So far, neither victim had given any useful information to the cops conducting interviews. Bandages covering most of their heads prevented them from talking. Broken arms prevented them from writing. They could only nod or shake their heads and both actions were painful. The interviews were slow, to say the least. All the questions were leading by necessity and one couldn't be sure of the accuracy of the answers. Preconceived conclusions of the interviewers could be clouding the information being derived. The victims were reluctant to cooperate. They had bigger fears than the police.

"We were following the right guy. Roger Johnson was driving that little red car when it left the city. He waved to us before he got in and we never let him out of our sight until we ran low on fuel," Irving said in answer to the allegation by the sergeant.

"We pulled into Bridgetown to gas up, then right back out on the highway. It took us all of maybe ten minutes, no not even that, seven minutes. The patrol car covered for us until we caught up. Then we followed him all the way to Yarmouth. Five fucking hours cruising along the wide open highway at 95 clicks. We had old men driving farm trucks passing us, blue-haired ladies driving Toyotas lined up behind us, afraid to pass. It was a long, long trip."

She paused, shook her head and resumed. "When he got out at the hotel, I couldn't believe my eyes and neither could Joe. It was like finding yourself in a Stephen King novel, real eerie. I have no explanation.

"It was Wally McIssac and not Roger Johnson who pulled his ass out of that little, fucking car. He wore a ball cap exactly like the one we watched Johnson put on. We watched him put it on his head so we know it was Johnson wearing it. From where we sat, all we could see was that ball cap sticking above the head rest.

"We had reported the licence number of the car to HQ when we left the city; it was the same car. To be sure we checked the VIN with the rental company. There was no switch. Man I can't explain what happened. They couldn't know we'd run out of gas and even if they could, they wouldn't know when or where."

Mcdonald sat down at the table across from his two coworkers. They had been duped. They felt bad enough without him adding to their distress. Running out of gas was a rookie mistake, one they wouldn't repeat.

"Johnson was driving a Metro. Not his style of car. He planned to run you out of gas. Somehow this was all a set-up," he said. "All the time we've put into this is gone down the drain. I don't have to tell you about the time. You were the ones putting it in. Did McIssac explain how they did it?"

"No," said Davis. "He put on a big innocent act. Pretended he had no idea what we were talking about. We couldn't even hold him. He hadn't broken any laws and we were several hundred kilometres out of our jurisdiction. Big goddamn smirk on his face, he just walked away from us into the hotel where he had reservations in his own name. He claimed it was a planned trip. Left us standing there with crap all over our faces.

"There's nothing you can say, Sergeant, that will make us feel any more stupid than we feel all by ourselves. There's no way to describe the sinking feeling I felt when the wrong damn person stepped out of that damn little car. I saw it happening with my own eyes, but my mind was screaming it can't be true. This can't not be Johnson. It can't be somebody else."

Irving had nothing more to add to her partner's statement but kept nodding her head in agreement as Davis explained. She shared the gut-wrenching moment of discovery and the disappointment, the moment of total disbelief, the assault on her senses as if she were watching Doug Henning or David Copperfield perform one of their magical tricks right before her eyes. She kept expecting to see the real Roger Johnson climb out of the trunk or something and reveal the trick. Even as she sat here in the interview room, she could not offer a valid explanation of how Johnson had pulled off the impossible.

Mcdonald mulled over the explanation offered by the two constables. No apparent solution jumped out at him. In the big scheme of things, what difference did it make? It happened. Johnson was gone. It was time to rally the troops and move on. Johnson would be located again. He proved he was smart but he was still a criminal so he wasn't that smart.

"Right," he said bringing that phase of the interview to a close. "Where do we go from here? People are being beaten up in the streets and Johnson is most likely behind it. The timing cries out that it is his work. Call in your informants and find out what they know, what they suspect, and what others are doing in response. Our operation has thrown a monkey wrench into the local drug business. This could be a prelude to a turf war and we must do our best to head that off."

Irving looked down at the table and mumbled more to herself than the other two men in the room. "Why? Let the bastards kill themselves off and then pick off the survivors when it's over. It would save us a lot of jail space, time and trouble."

"Belay that thought," Mcdonald snapped at her. "It sounds good in theory right up until the first innocent child or other passerby gets killed. We don't need others to do our work for us."

Pink crept up the back of Irving's neck and spread forward into her cheeks. She looked up and faced her sergeant. The reprimand was deserved and she accepted it. "I know that, Sarge. But sometimes, you know, justice doesn't seem to be on our side."

Davis stepped in to save his partner any more embarrassment. "Can we talk to the two felons who got the shit kicked out of them last night? They may be more cooperative in the cold light of day with the drugs wearing off and every move causing them a load of pain. We could literally lean on them a little, get real close so we can hear what they're trying to tell us and maybe have a hand resting on their cracked ribs or broken arm. Sometimes that happens."

A smile crossed his face, the first smile since seeing Wally McIssac materialize in front of him in Yarmouth. He was ready to move on. He had a case to solve and sitting in the squad room wasn't going to get it done. The time to be back on the streets had arrived and he couldn't wait to get back into action. He slid his chair back and stood up. "Let's roll, Kate."

Irving looked up at her superior waiting for approval. They had screwed up in a big way and more than a brief reprimand might be in order. Under the circumstances, it wasn't their fault, but still Kate was prepared to take the blame. Johnson had disappeared on her watch and nothing could change that fact. Mcdonald understood the feeling of revulsion Irving was piling on herself. No one liked to screw up, but they had done everything by the book. Perhaps a closer eye on the gas gauge would have helped. That was picking at straws. Johnson had outsmarted them, it was that simple. Jim inclined his head towards the door and nodded.

"There are bad guys out there. Let's go get them."

Irving slapped both hands on the table. "Damn straight. Let's go get 'em."

Mcdonald watched them charge out the door, envying their youthful enthusiasm.

*Hell hath not fury like a woman scorned,* he thought. *Unless it's one who has been made to look like a fool.*

Now it was his turn to be on the receiving end of the criticism. He had to report to Inspector Holland that Operation Enduring Success had taken a bad turn, convince him the damage was repairable and ensure the supply of money to continue the campaign didn't dry up.

In the end, it always came down to money.

People got the level of protection they were willing to pay for. Crime was too lucrative, the criminals kept raising the stakes. The police had to keep doing more with less but, hey, that's why they paid him the medium bucks. He would rather walk a mile over broken glass than attend this meeting. It had to be done. Now. It was best to suck it up, take his lumps, put it behind him and move onto the real job of taking lawbreakers off the street.

He left the interview room and headed for the inspector's office. Fellow detectives gave him encouraging smiles as he walked by their desks. Everyone had heard about the sleight of hand Johnson had pulled off.

Somewhere in the future, Mcdonald would take a riding for it, but now the wounds were too open. For now, his fellow detectives offered sympathy. He knew Holland was already aware of the events of the previous day. Still, it was time to fill in all the gory, ugly details, share the pain, pass the responsibility up the chain of command.

Holland would be accountable to some other level of authority. He, too, would have to make explanations on behalf of his staff, justify the continuing operation. Mcdonald knocked on the closed door, waited for acknowledgment and went in.

# ≈15≈

"A BURIAL URN?" Nathan Darling turned the wooden object over in his hands, admiring it from all sides. "Jesus, what a gruesome thing to be making. It is pretty though if you didn't know what it was used for."

John reached out and took the urn. He allowed the light to reflect off the wavy pattern in the maple. "Everyone dies, Nath. This could be the next hot item. Cremations are on the rise and people need something to put the ashes in. I could provide it."

"You know I'm out looking for a lathe for you?" Nathan said. John nodded. "I found one at this house out in the country. The woman is selling off all her husband's tools. He ran off with some young chick and she's exacting her revenge."

"I don't know if I want to cash in on someone else's misfortune," John said. He didn't really need a new lathe. He was just trying to throw some business Nathan's way.

"Don't be stupid," Nathan admonished him. "She's selling the stuff regardless of whether you buy it or not. You're not contributing to the breakup. She's gone out and found herself a young gigolo to live with her. According to her, she comes out ahead in the deal because twenty goes into forty a lot more often than forty goes into twenty." Nathan paused and waited for John to laugh, even smile.

He did neither. His mind was on how he'd feel if Marla sold off his tools.

"Anyway," Nathan continued, "she had a whole shed full of hollowed-out pieces of wood about twelve, fifteen inches long. I asked her what they were, and she said she was using them for firewood. Now that I see your urn, I realize the man was making the same things you are, only he never bothered to finish them."

"Mine are made from wood that has been cut for a long time. It is dried out. His, no doubt, are from green wood. You make the rough shape and let them dry for a year or so and then finish them off after all the warping has taken place. I'd like to talk to him, maybe I could get some pointers."

"According to his wife, he and his young floozy fled the province for Ontario. She doesn't expect him back. His family are from there. She is the Nova Scotian. I can pick this stuff up cheap if you are interested. The breakup occurred over a year ago. The wood is probably ready to use. Shame to see it turned into firewood instead of turned into burial urns."

The last line was the clincher. The thought of all the man's hard work going up in smoke was more than John could accept. He would be running a rescue mission, not capitalizing on someone's misfortune. Besides, he concluded in his mind, the cad deserves it.

"Twenty into forty," John laughed. He caught onto the joke. "I'll go out with you and have a look at the stuff. Make sure it's not just good for firewood."

"I do all the talking," Nathan said. He had seen John negotiate. "The husband must have thought they were a hot item as well. He has hundreds of them in his shed."

Nathan picked up one of the bowls made from a cherry burl and started to examine it. "I guess that's what this meeting is all about: Will it sell is the criteria, not what is it used for. What time do you expect Eric to be here?"

"Somewhere between seven and seven-thirty. He was hard to pin down to an exact time."

"He'll be here at seven. The extra half-hour is in case something unexpected came up. He is very punctual."

"I'm still not sure about going into business with him. It's like making a deal with the devil—selling my soul."

Nathan grunted at the comment. "Don't be so melodramatic. It's about making money. Look at all this stuff. Hidden away where no one will ever see it. In the book of Matthew in the Bible, it admonishes you not to bury your talents. If you do, you will be cast into the outer darkness where there will be weeping and gnashing of teeth. You're supposed to take your talent out into the world and expand upon it."

"Yeah, yeah. I went to Sunday school. I remember the story. A man was going away and gave one servant five talents and he doubled it. Another was given two and he doubled it. The third was given only one and he hid it in the earth and returned exactly what he was given to his master. The master was upset at his lack of initiative and gave that talent to the guy who already had ten. The third guy was, what did you say, 'cast into the outer darkness.' It never seemed fair to me. The man got back his money."

"Well, you missed the whole point of the parable. Your talent is hidden here in your basement. For God's sake man, get out into the world and start using it." Nathan slammed the bowl he was holding back onto the table and turned away. A few beats of time passed. John stood there silently staring at his friend, shocked at the outburst.

"I'm sorry, Nath," he said. "I'm not hiding my talent. This is just a hobby for me, an outlet to help me relax."

Nathan turned back towards John. "No, I'm the one who should apologize. In my line of work, I go around gathering up used tools to resell, as you know. I see so much stuff laying around rusting when it could be put to good use. So much waste. It gets to me after awhile. You may think what you do is just a stress release but you should be sharing your work with the world. I mean it."

The doorbell rang, breaking the tension of the moment. Nathan looked at his watch. "6:59. That would be Eric," he said. Upstairs they could hear Danka barking.

Marla's head appeared in the doorway leading to the workshop. "There's a man at the door to see you. Says he has an appointment. Hello, Mr. Darling," she added, surprised to see there was already someone there. She was unaware of his arrival.

"Nathan, call me Nathan."

"OK, Nathan," she hesitated. "Looks like a big meeting going on. What's up?"

"Eric, the man upstairs, wants to sell some of my bowls on consignment. He's going to have a look at what I have to offer. Nath here is going to keep me from getting fleeced." John smiled at the older man who returned the smile.

"I was just telling your husband, ma'am, he's wasting his talent. He should be doing this work full-time."

"If I'm going to call you Nathan, please call me Marla. Ma'am makes me feel so, I don't know, proper, proper and old. Don't go filling John's head with wild ideas. This flea market thing is taking up enough of his time. Are you coming up or should I send the other gentleman down?"

"Send him down. This is what he's here to see." John made a sweeping gesture with his arm to encompass all the products of the many hours he spent in the workshop. "Any favourites I shouldn't sell?"

"Lot's of them but you can always make me some more." She went back up the stairs and was replaced by the presence of Eric Sanderson.

"I guess this is the right place," Eric said, his eyes taking in the wares being offered.

"This is the place," said John. His voice had a nervous halt to it. Having his work appraised for resale value was a new experience to him and he felt a little self-conscious. Up to now, he had given no thought to the opinions of others. He just did what made him feel good and when he was happy with an item, he set it aside and started on something new. This man was about to review his work with a critical, commercial eye. No emotional value would be attached to any of the work. His fears were misplaced.

"Wow," Eric said as he picked up first one piece and then another. He sounded like a kid let loose in a candy store. "You made all this?"

John swelled with pride. He had cleaned up the workshop, placed a few folded sheets over the tables and put all his best works on display under the bright fluorescent workshop lights. Everything was planned to make the bowls look their best. He had succeeded.

Eric reined in his excitement. He was here to conduct business and could not appear too enthusiastic over the merchandise offered. "This stuff is pretty good," he said masking his true opinion that it was damn good. "With a little effort, I could move some of these."

John felt deflated. These were his best items and they were only pretty good. He had expected more.

Nathan stepped up to the plate. "Who are you trying to kid?" he asked Eric. "These things will sell themselves with no effort from you. Your only concern will be to hide all the profits you make so the tax man doesn't get them," a smirk slid across his face, "or your wife."

A smile broke across Eric's face. "You're right. These are some of the best samples I've ever seen. A little more work and I should be able to sell them with ease."

"A little more work?" John was surprised. "These are finished products."

"In the amateur world, they are. But not in the professional world. You're moving up to the big leagues, my boy." He held a bowl out to John upside down. "What's this mess here on the bottom?"

"That's my personal label I put on all my work. I made the stamp from one of those kids' printing kits." As he was saying this,

John realized what Eric meant. It was a pretty cheesy rubber stamp and looked like a kid had done it. "What would you recommend instead?"

"You need a unique mark. One that nobody else uses or can easily duplicate. All your products are made of wood so you want to get a branding iron made and burn your mark into the bottom of the work. Lee Valley or someplace like that will make a custom design for you. Do you have something in mind?"

John took the bowl, studied the ink design, then put it down. "No, I'll have to give it some thought."

"Don't make it too complicated, but something with a little class. We can work on that later. You'll have to sand this mess off." Eric moved about the room examining pieces, replacing them and moving on. He came to the urn and picked it up, weighing it in his hand.

"What's this?" he asked.

"A funeral urn," Nathan cut in before John could answer. "It's for putting your ashes in after you die. Everyone should have one."

Eric mulled this over in his mind. "They might sell but that would be a different market. I'll have to think about it." Already Eric was taking charge as if this was now one of his business sidelines. He put the urn down and picked up a carousel with four little glass dishes built in.

"That's for serving condiments," John said. "It's a lazy Susan." He gave it a spin. "Set it in the centre of your table and then rotate it to get at whatever dish you want, mustard in one, relish in one, ketchup in another one, sauerkraut or whatever in the last one."

"Neat," said Eric. "That will sell." He appreciated the beauty of the objects but in the final analysis it all came down to that one question: "Will it sell?" Beauty alone could take up a small portion of his displays as long as it attracted people willing to buy something else. Otherwise the name of the game was to move the merchandise. He was not a public art gallery. He was a salesman.

"Here's the deal," Eric said to John. "I display your objects and take thirty per cent of the selling price. If it doesn't sell after a reasonable length of time, you get it back. I won't charge you for the time I invested in the failures but I get to choose what I try to sell. I have contacts at a few galleries across the country and I will put them in the trade show circuit. You will have to join the Nova Scotia Craftsman and Artists Association and your items will have to be juried. I have exclusive rights to your products unless I don't want an item. Then you can do whatever you want with it. But I get to see everything first, is that understood?"

He didn't wait for John to answer. "If I tell you to enter a competition for your work, you will enter the competition. Any questions?"

John was dumbfounded. He knew Eric was here to negotiate but this sounded more like an ultimatum than a negotiation. John struggled to grasp all the points Eric had thrown at him.

"What do you mean you have exclusive rights to my stuff? Why would I do that?" he asked when he could speak again.

"Because I am going to represent you. I am going to promote your stuff. You have to get over the low opinion you have of your work. This stuff is art. It's not flea market junk. I intend to make your name a household word in the circles that count with products of this nature. If I make that effort, I expect to be the one who shares the rewards.

"I'm also going to promote you as a person. I will expect you to show up at these events. If I can arrange gallery showings of your stuff, I expect you to be there to talk to the clients, to promote yourself. But if you're not serious about this, forget it. Go back to the flea market and peddle your wares every Sunday morning.

"But let me be honest with you, that would be a mistake."

John sought out a chair and sat down. He was overwhelmed but at the same time excited. It would be an adventure. But did he want or need the hassle? He had a big bag of money down the hall bulging at the seams. Money waiting to be spent and still sitting there untouched. Money that required no more effort than pulling back a zipper, a talent men have lots of practice at. Still, Nathan claimed he was hiding his talents, Eric was insisting he could make him a success.

"Thirty per cent seems a bit high," he said.

Eric scoffed. "Thirty per cent is an industry standard. I should be taking more because you are completely unknown and I will have to put in a lot of extra work, but I like you. Thirty per cent it is." He made it sound so final John didn't question it again.

John watched Eric drift around the room, picking up a piece, turning it in the light, putting it down and moving on. Occasionally he ran his hands over the design as if he didn't believed it came from a natural piece of wood.

"All these places you expect me to appear, I have a real job you know. I may not have the time to go to all these craft shows and galleries."

"A real job. You don't understand what I'm offering you. This is your job now. When you're not on the circuit, I expect you to be in the workshop making more products. I'm not just planning to sell these things one at a time. I'm talking of selling them in lots of ten or more, even hundreds if we interest the right people."

His gaze absorbed John's. "We're not talking a hobby here. I don't have the time to waste on someone not willing to make a real commitment. This is a career change."

He looked towards the steps.

"Get your wife down here. We have some serious decisions to make."

# ≈16≈

ROGER JOHNSON was indeed back. Not everyone in the underworld knew that right away, but the ones who counted did. The next day, in broad daylight, one high-level dealer, a Big Boss wannabe, joined the two street sellers in the hospital. He was not expected to live. The others fell in line at once. They assured Roger their only intention was to keep the business running while he was solving his problems with the authorities. They turned over their cash, less some necessary expenses incurred in his absence, to The Boss without a lot of argument. Roger noticed the necessary expenses—new cars, flashy rings, snappy clothes—but let it ride. He was back. That was all that counted.

Big Willie Ettinger was not back. This was also common knowledge on the street. The big question in everyone's mind: "Was he coming back or was the position waiting to be filled?"

The reasons for the rapid capitulation to Johnson's authority were twofold. Nobody wanted to die for the sake of money, and let's not try to kid ourselves, that was the main reason, but also The Boss's absence served as a sort of audition for the now vacant second spot. By turning over the take for Roger's missing three weeks, they not only proved their loyalty but also showed they had what it took to earn the money in the first place. Roger appreciated both of these features.

Roger had his own problems. He didn't know where Big Willie was hiding out, didn't know if he was coming back. Under the present circumstances, with every cop in town looking for Roger, he needed a strong number two man. He needed Big Willie. For now the position would stay open. For now, Louie and Mark would act as his liaisons with the rest of the organization. They were happy in their job as enforcers and had no ambitions to move up. They would be perfect place holders.

Regardless of how disappointed some of the aspiring underlings were, no one would disobey this team. Mark and Louie were crazy. The others would just bide their time and work harder to prove they could fill Big Willie's shoes.

Presenting this proof had its problems. The Boss was a ghost. Everyone knew he was back but very few got to see him. His profile was so low, he almost didn't exist. Mark and Louie carried messages to and from Roger, but personal contact was the way to make a favourable impression. Hard work was one way to move up, but it meant squat if credit didn't accompany it. The two couriers were thugs, unlikely to pass on kind words about the efforts of the people they were dealing with. Finding Roger became a passion with some of his crew. They wanted face time.

Roger, for his part, didn't want face time with anyone. Sneaking around having impromptu meetings, constantly changing disguises, moving from hotel to hotel, was a lousy way to live. It did beat the alternative by a thousand-fold. Cops parked on his doorstep, every phone call monitored, every acquaintance photographed. No, Roger could put up with the stealth for a while longer. The police action to keep him under constant surveillance cost a ton of money. Covering all his known hangouts while trying to relocate him cost a hell of a lot more. It was a war of attrition and Roger was determined to win. He was earning again, not just spending.

This very fact of the cost was being discussed in the enemy camp. Sergeant Mcdonald and Inspector Holland were having face time with each other.

"I don't want to pack this in any more than you do," the inspector was saying. "But we have to ask ourselves if the money could be better utilized in some more productive fashion."

Mcdonald paced around Holland's office. "We are being productive. Some of the intangibles are not evident on the surface but we are making huge advances. When Johnson was out of the picture, we were able to insinuate men into the operation to depths only dreamed of before. Confusion reigned and no one knew who was who in the various unrelated arms. We slipped operatives into all levels. It's just a matter of time before the raids of last month pale by the results we will obtain with the next attack. We must locate Johnson or he will foil these plans. He will realize the infiltrators are not part of his team. Damn it, we can't back off now."

Holland was reading a list of figures on his desk. His head snapped up at the last outburst.

"No one wants to back off, Sergeant. We just have to make sure our limited supply of money is being put to the best possible use."

"I'm telling you it is being well spent. We are getting results. Now we must protect those results. Do you know what will happen to any of the undercover guys who are discovered? There is a man dying in the hospital right now. He's one of them. What will happen to one of us?"

Holland got up from his desk and walked over to the window. "Of course, we can't let that happen," he said. There was a pause while he pondered his options. "We'll give it a few more days. But, Jim, you have to find him. This can't go on forever. The funding is not there."

Evident relief showed on Jim's face. He was aware of the cost of the operation, aware of the lack of money but he was also aware of the successes being made. The payoff would justify the overruns. Now if they could just find Johnson.

"Thank you, sir. We'll track him down, don't worry."

"Me worry? I've only got five years to go to my pension unless they fire me. Who wants to retire anyway?" His smile was forced and Jim knew it. "Find him son, that's all I ask."

Jim hustled out of the office and into the squad room where all eyes were on him. He gave the two-thumbs-up signal, and smiles broke out around the room. No one said anything. This called for a quiet celebration while the inspector was within earshot. They still had work to do and everyone knew they were on borrowed time.

"Davis, Irving, over here," Jim said as he entered an interview room.

The two detectives followed him in and closed the door.

"What did you learn at the hospital?" The sergeant asked without any preliminaries.

Davis sat on the edge of the table. "Not much. It was as you predicted. They were more afraid of Johnson than they were of us. All we want to do is give them three squares a day and a roof over their heads for the next five years. With Johnson, they don't even get to see those five years."

Irving nodded in agreement. "We learned the names of the people who beat them up though. At least we think we have. An EEG machine is hooked up to the head of one of them. Suffered severe concussion and maybe worse. The doctors are monitoring his brain activity. Looking to see if he has one, most likely.

"Anyway, we noticed the needles on the machine fluctuated with our questions and his attempts at answers. They still don't communicate too well. Certain names got a real reaction. There's a couple of well-known thugs named Louie Comeau and Mark Riley. When we mentioned their names the machine went wild. The doc confirmed our guess that these most likely were the perps who beat them up, but he couldn't guarantee it. Won't stand up in court but it gives us the names of someone who's been in contact with Johnson."

"Great," said the sergeant. "Not a lot but it's at least a place to start."

"There's a little hole in the wall of a bar they hang out at most of the time. It's called the Foggy Night or some such appropriate name. You can hardly see when you go inside. We thought we'd take some of this newfound money you just got us and go do some drinking there," Joe said.

Everyone smiled. Getting the additional funding was a relief to everyone; spending it wisely would be the challenge. Bar bills were hard to justify. Sitting around all afternoon in a pub and not buying anything guaranteed suspicious looks and careful scrutiny. It was a catch-22 situation.

"Johnson has to be in disguise or staying out of sight. We'll take pictures of everyone who comes in and talks to Comeau and Riley. If we don't recognize Johnson, the experts can then determine if he is in any of the photos. He may be a master of disguise, I don't know. We will need a surveillance team on the two thugs as well. If they are meeting someplace else, we want to be there."

"He got a spy camera with the same cereal box tops he used for the listening device," Irving joked. Davis was a fan of modern technology and used it well.

"More surveillance? That could be tricky," Jim said. "We only got enough money to keep the operation going, not enough to add more teams. I'll have to look over our resources and move some people around. In the meantime, it's all on your shoulders. Let's try not to lose them."

The two detectives looked at each other but said nothing. They still smarted over the trick Johnson had pulled on them. "I'll make sure the car is gassed up," said Irving after the silence stretched out for almost thirty seconds. What else could she say?

# ≈17≈

"QUIT HIS JOB? Are you out of your ever-loving mind? John can't quit his job. He has responsibilities, kids, a wife, a mortgage." Marla stormed around the workshop unable to believe what she was hearing. Trying, but not succeeding, to keep her voice at a conversational level.

"No, no, Missus," Eric held his hands up in a placating fashion in front of his face. "Think of it as a career change, not as quitting his job." Marla's reaction did not surprise him. He had been down this road before, sometimes with success, sometimes with failure. What he knew for sure was John had the talent to make a living with his turnings.

There is an intangible in the art world that cannot be learned, an eye, a feel, whatever. John had it. John's problem was not knowing how to capitalize on his skills and that's where Eric shone. Those intangibles also existed in the field of commerce.

"Career?" Marla said, her voice going up another octave. "This is his goddamned hobby. He comes down here and plays while I look after his kids." She gave up trying to contain herself. Her anger was in full flight now. "Who's going to be paying our bills while he's down here playing? You?"

She stabbed Eric in the chest with a forefinger capped with a long, but rounded fingernail. He flinched as the dart-like object penetrated his shirt. His work was cut out for him.

He started again in a calm, soothing voice. "I've been displaying some of his work at my booth at the market for the last couple of weeks. The interest is overwhelming. They fly off the table like cold drinks on a blistering hot day. You don't have to worry about paying your bills. The money will be there. More money than you have now."

"Market? The word is flea market. Don't try to dress it up. It's a flea market, a place where people go to unload their junk. I know all about it. John's been spending all his Sunday mornings there lately. Sunday mornings when he has more important things to be doing. I'm fed up with waking up to an empty bed every Sunday. I want him back there."

All her frustrations were tumbling out now. Things building up inside her but left unsaid for over a fortnight. The novelty of the extra money wore thin in a hurry. They had always had enough money to live on, to pay their bills, to put food on their table. Marla wanted nothing more. She did want John back in her bed on Sunday mornings. The confusion between the two things, extra money and quality time, was clouding her vision. A light went on over John's head as he looked at his wife. He had been so caught up in the excitement of the new facets of his own life, he had neglected her needs. He put an arm around her shoulders and hugged tight.

"I think we have to discuss this between ourselves, alone," he said.

She wrenched herself out of his grip. Her justified anger was not going to dissipate that easily. "Damn right we have to discuss this ourselves. Someone has to bring you to your senses. Someone has to get you away from these fools and their pie-in-the-sky schemes. You have responsibilities, mister." She turned to the two visitors. "Get out of here, both of you."

Danka poked his nose in the door, curious to see what all the yelling was about. He wasn't misbehaving.

John gave his shoulders a slight shrug. His embarrassment was evident. "You better leave, fellows. I'll be in touch."

Eric could see his plans going out the window. John was not going to convince Marla of anything. He stood his ground.

"We kind of sprung this on you without any advance warning, Missus. Give me five minutes to explain my plan in a little more detail to you, just to you. John, Nathan, go upstairs and make some tea or coffee or something."

Both men looked at Marla. Eric could talk all he wanted but this would be Marla's decision. She had taken control of the meeting. She looked Eric right in the eyes and calmed down a little.

"Five minutes. But you're not going to change my mind. Someone has to be the voice of reason around here."

"Five minutes. I'm not going to try to change your mind. I want you to have all the facts before you make your decision, a decision that will affect the rest of your lives regardless of what you decide. Go make some coffee." The last was directed at John. Eric would never dare to make that demand of Marla.

The five minutes stretched into ten, the ten into a half-hour and then an hour. John looked in twice, left some coffee and was sent back upstairs to the kitchen. He and Nathan could only speculate as to what was being discussed, the curiosity was killing them like the proverbial cat.

"It's been over an hour, Nath," John looked at his watch for the hundredth time as he paced around the island in his large kitchen. "What can be taking them all this time?"

Nathan sipped his third cup of tea. "I don't know but it must be good. It doesn't take an hour to say no, especially for your wife." He gave John a smile but it wasn't returned. John wanted to know what was being discussed. His thoughts were in the workshop, not in the kitchen. He continued to pace. All he could do was wait to be summoned, to be filled in. At last the announcement came. Eric and Marla entered the kitchen.

"There's a new agreement," Marla declared. She was still in charge. "For a start, no more Sunday flea markets. You've graduated from that." She gave John a smile with an unmistakable meaning as to how that time would be spent.

She looked around the room to see if anyone wanted to argue that statement. No one did. She continued: "Eric gets thirty per cent of anything that sells individually in a craft show or gallery. That is the industry norm."

Industry norm, now you're the expert, John thought but sat without interrupting.

"Anything sold in bulk, more than ten items, the price would be reduced for volume sales. The reduction comes from Eric's cut. His required work is less, John's remains the same regardless of the number of items sold."

She looked from man to man to man to see if there were any objections. No one said a word.

"For the first year, Eric will set up an account we can draw from if sales don't produce the same income we are currently making. This money will be repaid, interest free, to Eric when sales improve. This spreads the initial risk over a longer time. In return, Eric is the exclusive seller of our product. He's taking the gamble, he gets the rewards. Any questions?"

Marla surveyed the room again, once more singling each man out.

"Nathan, you are here as our advisor. Is there anything else that should be included?"

Nathan gave a start. Marla seemed to have everything in hand. He was surprised at being asked to render his opinion of the deal.

"The only thing I can suggest is we go back down to the workshop and find the real Eric Sanderson. He must be tied up in a closet somewhere. I don't know who this guy sitting here with his mouth shut is."

Everyone shared the humour. A union was forged. The transaction was made. John was now an artist, Nathan his confidant, Marla his business manager, Eric his agent. The latter two would deal with each other.

John would produce the product, Nathan would keep him sane. He would help John with the record keeping. Eric would sell it. Marla would oversee the entire operation.

The big bag of money lay under the steps, forgotten.

# ≈18≈

FORGOTTEN IS a misnomer. For some people, the missing money remained foremost on their mind. Every living, breathing second was spent trying to get it back. Its return permeated their every thought.

Prior to the night of the big bust, Roger Johnson controlled his own destiny. He controlled most, if not all, of the drug trade in the metropolitan area. There were a few freelancers, but they operated at their own peril. When, and not if, they were caught, these enterprising businessmen were dealt with in a swift and harsh manner. One which did not encourage competition.

In Metro, he could take a kilo of coke, purchased in Montreal for $40,000, cut it into bite size pieces or nose-size lines, and sell it on the street for $120,000. Not a bad day's work. On his more ambitious days, he could send to Florida and obtain five kilos for less than $100,000 US. This plan brought the added risk of getting it across the international border, not a real challenge, but a risk nonetheless and the hassle of a fluctuating Canadian dollar. But, what the hell, if you're hiding from the winter ice and snow back home, you may as well bring some product back on the return trip. He always did.

In the rest of the province, Roger was content to sell in bulk. He could turn that same $40,000 into $60,000 with little or no effort. Once again, he did not tolerate competition. Every successful businessman needed a protected territory. This was Roger's.

Even though he was back and was making money again, there were overhead expenses—cutters, mules, street sellers to pay, muscle to hire, his own gypsy-like lifestyle. It all cut into the profits. Now he had to take the drugs on consignment, so to speak. Until he could build up enough of a cushion to start paying up front again, the suppliers dictated the terms. Roger found that idea revolting. No one controlled him. Finding his missing money would put him back on top. Right now, that question sat on the top of his mind: "Who has my money?"

Another person, for whom the bag of money was the controlling factor in his life, was Wally McIssac. Unlike The Boss, Wally did nothing but look for the missing funds. This was his sole purpose in life for the last month. In his own, dull, plodding way, he knew he would find it. It was just a matter of time.

Three days a week, he still covered the surrounding subdivisions with his Jehovah Witness routine. He was getting some conversions to the faith. People were looking forward to his visits. He was a likable guy and wasn't too pushy when it came to the religion aspect of his visits. Sometimes the subject of saving their eternal damned souls never even came up. This acceptance was great, but he was not finding the money. You've got to try harder, people, harder.

Residents were losing interest in talking about the excitement of found money in the neighbourhood. Many were now discarding it as urban legend, doubting the money ever existed. Wally could not let that happen. He had to keep his watchers ever vigilant, ever on the alert for a careless word dropped in the grocery store or at a community meeting, anyplace. His task was to keep the story paramount in everyone's thinking and to keep his name right up there beside it. Wally's hope was that people would be eager to share any knowledge they stumbled across with him. After all, he replanted the seed week after week.

Three other days, he made the rounds of the local drinking establishments. Roger picked up the tab for Wally's libations in the same way Holland footed the bill for Davis and Irving. At least Roger only had to pay one bill, although Wally expected a slice of lime with his imported beer.

Wally had high hopes for these visits. He was sure anyone who found the money would feel the urge to brag about their good fortune after throwing back a few ales in the local drinking hole. It was only a matter of time before this happened. No one could hide a secret of this magnitude forever. Man has a primordial urge to brag to his fellow beings when things are going his way, when he is doing so much better than everyone else. What's the point of having this good fortune if no one else knows about it? Wally banked on this human trait.

Wally couldn't be everywhere at once; he might miss the story. A tale like that would linger among drinkers for quite a while, he hoped. He was confident someone would still be talking about it a couple of days later. That was another human trait he banked on. The need to live life vicariously through others adventures. Someone would claim to be the best friend of the finder of the money and spread the story even if the two had only been best friends for the last day and a half.

On alternate days to his spreading the word of the Gospel, Wally would make his tavern rounds. It was a tough assignment, drink beer, listen to rumours, play the slots, drink more beer. Someone had to do it. It may as well be him. As a bonus, Wally kept his winnings on his lucky days at the lottery terminals while Roger picked up his losses on his much more frequent losing days.

One day a week, Wally forgot about anything to do with money, drugs or The Boss. He needed to recharge his batteries, regain his sanity, take care of Wally. The day would start at a Chapter's book store for some light reading and coffee at $4.50 a cup. Thanks again, Roger. He would lose himself in the world of imagination—Stephen King, Tom Clancy, John Grisham, Spider Robinson, Dean Koontz, Gail Bowen—as far away from the drug scene as possible.

After spending the day taking care of his mind, the evenings would be devoted to relaxing his body in the only way Wally knew how. Again Roger picked up the tab, while Wally satisfied his needs with the ladies who strolled along Hollis Street in front of the lieutenant-governor's mansion. A royal fucking, he liked to call it. No wonder Roger couldn't raise enough of a float to put himself back in charge. Wally was spending it all.

# ≈19≈

"THEY'VE STRUCK again," Sergeant Mcdonald reported to Inspector Holland. "Twice more by the looks of things."

Worry lines showed on the inspector's face. This was not the kind of news he wanted to hear. "Twice more; this could be the start of the gang war we were hoping to avoid. What are the details?"

Jim glanced through the papers he carried in his hands. "The first one is another beating. One man is in the hospital with contusions, cuts, bruises, the like. He's a known dealer so we're pretty sure it's gang related.

"The other was a call to missing persons. It could be more serious. A mother reported her son missing, hasn't been heard from for three or four days. She says he always checks in on her a couple of times a week, buys her groceries, things like that. This week, he was a no-show. The mother's plenty worried and I quote, 'Larry is a good boy. He always takes care of his mother. Something terrible must have happened for him not to be bringing me my cigarettes. You have to find him.'"

Jim shuffled through the papers and brought another one to the top of the pile. "Larry is Lawrence Scarborough. Here's his rap sheet. Drugs, petty theft, assault. He's a Hell's Angel wannabe, drives a big Harley. Our sources identify him as one of a group of break-away dealers who tried to capitalize on Johnson's absence. I guess he didn't fall back into line. No one has seen him since last Saturday when he was bragging about becoming 'The New Boss.' He was going to be a subject of our future raids, but he dropped off the radar. Johnson beat us to him. After this much time, my guess is he is dead."

"Dead?" the inspector contemplated that thought. "I'm not sure if that's good news or bad. It serves as a warning to others to stay in line. If heeded, future violence will be reduced. But if Scarborough has any kind of organization under him, retaliation may be in order. He could be our Archduke Francis Ferdinand. It could trigger a war that will have blood cluttering up the nightly news for weeks to come." He placed the sheet of paper on his desk and looked back to see if Jim had any more to offer on the subject.

Jim thought about the historical reference. War was a possibility, but not this time.

"Our guess is his organization is weak. He was more interested in looking the part and making easy money than taking the time to build himself a good foundation of support. Those under him will simply migrate back to Johnson. They're looking for a steady paycheque and don't care where it comes from. Johnson got back into the act before anyone else could build up any real loyalty in their followers. For now, there will be a few skirmishes, but nothing serious."

"I guess that's a good thing. It's a two-edged sword. We take the top guys off the street and the fights to take their places create worse problems, more high profile at least. We can't win for trying."

"We will win." Jim looked determined. "The next generation depends on us doing our job today. It's our responsibility to make the world safer for them, for our kids, for our grandkids."

Holland nodded in agreement. "You're right, Jim. Don't misunderstand me, I never suggested giving up. We will endure the bad press coverage and do our job as we see it, not as the media sees it. Any luck in finding Johnson?" He gave him a hopeful look

"We've got some good leads. Two of my men are following the people we think are in contact with Johnson. In fact, they witnessed the beating last night. Both of them said they had never seen anything like it. Less than ten seconds, one leg and several ribs were broken, skull crushed and left like a heap of dog shit on the sidewalk."

Again Jim shuffled through his papers. "Here is their report." He scanned the papers for a second and then read:

"Constable Davis and I were following the two suspects, Louie Comeau and Mark Riley, in our vehicle. The suspects appeared to be aimlessly driving up and down the streets in west-end Halifax when, without warning, they stopped in the middle of the street. Each suspect jumped from their car carrying a baseball bat and ran to the sidewalk where two men were having a discussion. Without hesitation Comeau, whose bat was already cocked, smashed it across the knees of one of the men. The other suspect brought his bat down across the skull of the same victim. Both suspects took one body shot each before returning to their car and taking off down the street.

"The entire event took less than ten seconds from door to door. The second man on the sidewalk turned and ran at that point, too stunned to move while the beating took place.

"Drugs lay all over the street and no one dared come and gather them up. We called 911 for an ambulance and additional police units and continued our pursuit of the suspects."

"Yadda, yadda yadda," Jim flipped through a couple of pages.

"Arriving policemen gathered up the drugs from the street, and paramedics discovered more on the person of the victim while examining his injuries. They turned the additional drugs over to the arriving policemen as well. The quantity indicates the victim appeared to be dispensing drugs to street-level sellers. Charges for possession with the intention of trafficking are pending." He scanned a little further into the report but stopped reading.

Jim paused as he let the images sink in. "We're pretty sure these guys will lead us to Johnson, so we let them get away. The whole thing is captured on the in-car video. We don't think they're aware that we are tailing them. Initially we thought the hoods might be onto us when they were aimlessly driving around, but it turned out they had a destination. We can pick them up any time now."

Jim lay the folder on Holland's desk.

"Scarborough's disappearance appears unrelated. If he is really dead, outside muscle was most likely brought in to make the hit. They're pretty good at not messing in their own back yards. The beating was a warning to others that Johnson is back. The disappearance is simply removing any serious opposition."

Again Holland nodded in agreement. "That is the way they've always done it. Any investigation will lead us away from the area and not into their places of operation. How much manpower are we using to find Scarborough?"

"None," Jim said. "We left it in the hands of missing persons. They will keep us informed, but from my perspective, it would be a waste of our limited resources. A dead dealer can't tell us much no matter how high up he is on the food chain."

"We'll revisit that if a body is found," Holland said. "Murder can't go unpunished."

Jim didn't disagree. His task was to milk every last dollar allocated to him for the most value possible. Searching for a professional killer didn't meet that criteria at this time. Perhaps he didn't have bigger fish to fry—murder is serious—but at least he wanted to catch some fish and not spend all day casting his line and reeling it in empty. He let the subject drop without trying to justify his methods.

"What's the latest on the money?" Holland asked. This question eventually came up at every meeting between the two.

"No luck, yet. I've had to move some people off that search and use them to track down Johnson. We have a team following Wally McIsaac. He's Johnson's point man on the search and is giving it the old college try. We have him under loose surveillance. If he comes up with anything, we will sweep in and snatch it from his grasp. To date, he's had no luck either, but he is to be admired for his dogged determination. He spends six days a week working full time on the task.

"To save money, we don't watch him at night. We lost track of him once. That is unfortunate in a way, because that day he showed up in Yarmouth. We are still baffled about how he pulled off that little adventure. Irving is still smarting from being made a fool of. It has given her a determination to find Johnson that money can't buy. She's gone after Johnson like an angry Jesus after a sinner."

"That's good," said Holland, "but make sure she doesn't get so focused she loses sight of the big picture. Determination is good but uncontrolled passion can get you killed."

"I've reminded her partner of that. He's looking after her."

Jim continued, "We're thinking of putting the story on the Crime Stoppers promotion ad they run on TV. We were reluctant for a while. The place would have been overrun with treasure seekers but we've searched it with dogs, with ground search and rescue, our men. There's nothing there. Somebody out there knows something, this may ferret them out."

The inspector agreed. "We have nothing to lose," he said. "It's not like it's a big secret in the community. My only hesitation is the finder might have been becoming complacent, ready to start spending with the time passed. Publicity could send him underground again."

"We've considered that. On the other hand, someone may have heard something since our initial interviews and this may serve as a reminder. It's no longer the hot topic it was during the first week. Reviving the story may bring us the break we need, bring the interest level back up.

"To find this money, we will need a tip from a citizen and the tips aren't coming in any more. If somebody is out there sitting on the money, wondering what to do, this gives them a viable option. Guilt them into turning it over to us. Scare them into turning it over to us. Who cares why as long as we end up with the money?"

A concerned look came over Jim's face. The inspector took note and said, "You have concerns?"

"There is one other possibility. Our biggest fear has the finder grabbing up the money and hitting the road. He, or she, could easily set up anywhere in the country, or the world for that matter, with that kind of a nest egg." Jim shrugged his shoulders to imply it could have happened.

Holland flattened out his mustache with his thumb and forefinger, a sign he was giving the idea heavy thought. "If that happened, it's out of our control," he said. "Let's give the Crime Stoppers idea a shot. When will the first ad appear?"

Jim thought about it for a minute. "I'm not sure. It takes awhile to put the promotion together. We have to write an effective script, one that will inspire phone calls. We have to hire actors to re-create the scene. We need people who look like Leroy Leblanc and Wally McIssac. A film crew has to go on location and shoot the action then put it all together. It will be a couple of weeks, maybe more."

"That long? Get it done."

# ≈20≈

PEELINGS OF WOOD piled up on the workshop floor. John threw himself into his new job with the enthusiasm of a rookie ball player breaking into the big time. He gave two weeks notice at his old job and then took the two weeks as vacation time. He hadn't been back. His only regret was that he hadn't done this years ago.

Reaction from his fellow workers took a variety of forms. Some, the majority, suggested he had lost his sanity. Giving up a secure paycheque for what they considered a hobby could only be described as ludicrous. Some, who probably had similar dreams, gave him high-fives as he left. They considered him a hero. Then there were those who had no opinion one way or the other. John's comings and goings made no difference to them. They had their own lives to worry about. For John's part, he didn't care what any of them thought. He had made the decision and he would live with it.

The first major rift in the newfound organization came early. Eric wanted decorative bowls, things that really caught the eye of passersby. John leaned more towards the practical, things that served a purpose. Samples of each were already in stock on the closet shelves where they had been hiding for years. Eric agreed to display both, see which sold the best and John would have to respond accordingly. John was reluctant, but agreed. He hated giving up artistic control this early in the game.

In the meantime, John had a previous commitment. He had to finish the funeral urn for the flea market customer. She had already advanced him three hundred dollars. Eric thought he should get a cut. It was a product of the firm being sold. If John was spending time on this urn, he wasn't turning out a product for Eric to sell. After a great deal of acrimonious discussion, Eric settled for five per cent. Even giving up this meagre amount grated on John's nerves.

"It's not the money, it's the principle," he insisted. "You don't own all my time. I can do things on my own."

"Not true," Eric countered. "We're in business together now. I'm the exclusive agent for your wood-turning projects. I don't own your time, but I do own a share of any wood-turning products you produce. Where is Marla? She'll explain how this works."

To Eric, it was also the principle. He wanted to establish the ground rules right up front. Exclusive rights meant just that. Eric's intention was to promote John as an artist. It would cost money to get John's name out there. Money Eric put up. For his part, John would have to play by the rules. He couldn't be running little side deals which could soon blossom into another business entirely.

Eric stood firm and insisted on getting $30 from the sale. Marla sympathized with her husband but saw to it that Eric was paid. She wasn't going to let thirty bucks sidetrack the business. Principles didn't put bread on the table, and she alone seemed to grasp the real potential for the success of this team. Their individual talents naturally complemented each other. John was the artist; Eric had the right connections and the drive to make this venture succeed. Bowls, urns, whatever, locked up in a closet in the basement did not produce a single nickel of profit, no matter how good they were.

Thus it was, while John put the finishing touches on the urn, Eric showed up with a photographer and a reporter. The newspaper planned a promotional section for the upcoming craft show at Exhibition Park. They were doing filler pieces on the various contributors, and Eric saw to it that John was among the featured artists. Pictures were taken of John at work, his finished products, and the urn he was working on. Eric had purchased ad space in the tabloid to get this much extended coverage. Building an image required this extra effort. Serendipity would jump in and play a part, but Eric had laid the ground work with his investment.

The reporter had never seen a lathe in action. The evolution of a plain block of wood into a quality work of art right before her eyes intrigued her. The grains in the wood popped out with just a gentle touch of John's chisel. When John applied the thin layer of beeswax, the whole piece took on a life of its own, enthralling the young lady. Her enthusiasm bubbled over.

"I've got to come back," she insisted. "This has full-page feature written all over it. I want to get pictures of every step along the way. I've seen funeral urns before but I never gave any thought about how they came into being. This is amazing."

Eric stepped in and offered a bowl to her. "The bowls are even more amazing to watch coming to life," he suggested. These were the items he planned to push. He would promote them over the urns. She took the bowl, surprised at its lightness.

"It's so thin and fragile," she said. "You make it with those big, clunky tools from a solid block of wood?" She turned it over in her hands and studied the new logo branded into the bottom.

"My trademark," John said. He was still shy about the new symbol, a stickman standing over a machine that could be a lathe. The design was simple but effective.

"I like it," the reporter said. "It captures the essence of what you do."

Eric smiled. He chose the design from the many Marla had created.

"We can arrange for you to follow one item from start to finish," Eric said. He didn't want the reporter's initial enthusiasm to get lost along the way. He wanted a firm commitment for a return time. "What's best for you, later this week or next week?" Ever the closer, he intended to seal the deal.

The reporter took a little, red date book from her pocket and flipped through the pages. "This week I'm tied up with the show stories. It'll have to be next week. I'll book space in an upcoming Lifestyle section. We may even get the cover. These would look great in colour."

Eric consulted his calendar. They agreed on a time and date.

Thank you, Jesus, Eric whispered to himself. Free publicity like this was more than he dreamed of when he bought the promotional ad. John would need a haircut, a hairstyle would be better. Eric would look after that. He would work through Marla. John would balk if he thought it was Eric's idea. Eric didn't need the hassle.

# ≈21≈

"I SAW YOUR picture in the newspaper," Mrs. Collins said. "You looked so intense as you worked on your wood machine."

The first official funeral urn was being delivered. Intense, John liked to think of himself as looking relaxed when he was turning. Added responsibilities added extra layers of concentration, he figured. Or maybe the camera captured his true essence.

John handed the cardboard box to Mrs. Collins and waited for her to open it. Eric managed to come up with an appropriate plain white container that was almost exactly the right size for the urn. A copy of the new logo was burned into the top surface of the box. Mrs. Collins hesitated.

"This is it," she said. "I hope it looks as good as the one in the picture in the newspaper."

John smiled. "It will. It's the same one."

This bit of news pleased Mrs. Collins even more. She bunched her hands into little fists at chest height and shook them with excitement. "I showed the picture to my neighbours," she said. "I told them you were making an urn for Henry." She lowered her voice and leaned towards John in a conspiratorial manner. "I think they were jealous. Wait until they hear that picture is Henry's urn."

She placed the box on the table and gently lifted the lid. Light blue tissue paper cushioned the urn from the sides, and she peeled away the layers, allowing the light from the afternoon sun to drift through the kitchen window and reflect on the warm brown colours inside.

"Oh, it is beautiful," she said. "Look at this, Henry. It's so beautiful."

John looked around the room to see whom the old lady was talking to. They were alone. Then he remembered the day at the flea market. Henry would be Mrs. Collins' late husband. He wondered if Henry talked back. He shuddered slightly at the thought.

Mrs. Collins gingerly picked the urn from the box and admired it from all sides; the three layers of wood—ash, cherry and maple—all reacted to the light in different ways, making the urn seem to be a living, moving entity.

"This is your new home, Henry," she whispered, a tear coming to her eye which she made no attempt to hide. John watched, moved by the sight. Mrs. Collins was not talking about a receptacle for Henry's ashes. She could visualize a place to store a lifetime worth of memories.

Fleeting images passed through her mind from their first fateful meeting fifty-five years previous to the last agonizing days of Henry's life as he succumbed to a long, courageous battle with cancer.

Courageous battle, what a joke. The insidious disease took over Henry's vibrant body and riddled it full of holes leaving him a dried, withered husk of eighty-seven pounds before destroying his lungs and taking his last breath.

John looked away. He could feel himself tearing up as well. When he first accepted this commission, money dominated his thoughts. Justifying his participation at the flea market to Maria had been the goal. Now, as he saw the reaction of Mrs. Collins to his work, he realized he had accomplished much more than making himself a few dollars. He had brought acceptance and closure to this lady's battle with the passing of her husband. Henry now had a suitable final resting place, a place where he could be proud to spend eternity.

"I hope this is what you were expecting," he said, more to break the silence hanging in the air than to look for an answer to the question. Mrs. Collins happiness with the finished product exuded from every pore of her existence.

She came back from her reverie and stared at John for a long second as if wondering why he was there. Then her eyes brightened. She dabbed away the tear running down her frail, white cheek. "It's perfect," she said. "Absolutely perfect. Let's put Henry in it right away. He's been waiting for three months for his new home. I know he will love it, too."

With that, she turned and carried the urn into the living room and placed it on her fireplace mantel. John obediently followed behind her. She took down a plain white box with a red rose on top of it and looked at John with a bit of embarrassment. "Henry's been living in the box supplied by the funeral home all these months. He didn't want to move from there until we found the right vessel for him. Henry was set in his ways and hated the hassle of moving. This is what he was waiting for."

John crossed the room, plucked the urn from the mantel and helped her remove the tight-fitting lid. It was designed to be spill-proof. The lid would not come off if the urn accidentally tipped over. As a result, it took a fair amount of strength to open the container. John held the urn with both hands while Mrs. Collins shakily tilted the box to dump the contents into it. John looked down at the cream-coloured carpet on the floor. He looked back at Mrs. Collins' shaky hands.

"Perhaps we should do this at the table and place a sheet of paper underneath while we are pouring," he suggested.

Mrs. Collins stopped. "Yes, we should. Henry was just anxious to get into his new home. You have to wait a minute longer, dear," she said to the box.

John carried the urn to the kitchen while Mrs. Collins trailed along behind him with the box of ashes. The box was bigger than John had anticipated. He hoped all of Henry would find space in his new home. It was going to be close.

Mrs. Collins had given John the dimensions of the box when she made the initial purchase. He had done the math. Converting the volume of a square box into the volume of a round cylinder required calculations he hadn't used since high school. He silently prayed he had used the right formulas. He had hollowed out the inside using those specifications, now he was concerned the urn might not be big enough. *Too late now*, he thought and poured.

With the vessel secure on the table, the transfer of ashes went a little smoother. Very little of Henry escaped. The spread out newspaper captured the errant ashes that tumbled off the rim onto the table. John folded the paper into a vee and a slight tap brought the last bits of Henry's remains safely into their new home. He fit with a little room to spare. John replaced the lid with an audible sigh of relief.

He gave his arms a shake to relax the tense muscles. The moment had been more traumatic than he had realized. What would they have done with excess Henry if John's calculations had been wrong?

An awkward moment of silence followed. Both had been caught up in the assignment of Henry's new home, had shared a special passing of time together.

Things changed. They had to settle up the bill. Financial considerations seemed out of place under the circumstances but Mrs. Collins was first to return to the present. Her purse was sitting on the side counter. She opened it and took out an envelope and passed it to John.

"I was only planning on a six hundred dollar urn," she said. "I'm so pleased you brought the more expensive one but I'll have to go to the bank and get you the rest of your money."

John looked in the envelope at the three one hundred dollar bills. He hadn't even considered what he was going to charge. The initial deposit was more than he had ever been paid for any of his products. He could feel his face flushing.

He realized this was why he needed Eric. Eric was comfortable collecting money; John wasn't. Eric had declared six hundred dollars to be the value of the finished urn when he negotiated his five per cent cut. John still had to put on the finishing touches at that point. Now Mrs. Collins wanted to pay him even more.

"Six hundred dollars is the price," he assured her. "Nothing more is required."

"On no, dear, I've looked at a lot of funeral containers in the last three months. This one is definitely worth more than six hundred dollars. It's in the thousand dollar range, maybe more."

One thousand dollars. The mere words sent a chill through John. Someone was willing to pay one thousand dollars for his work. The thought overwhelmed him. He couldn't accept that much money from this sweet, little old lady in front of him. They had just shared a moment together giving her poor departed husband a new home. They had a special bond.

He looked around at his surroundings. Mrs. Collins wasn't struggling to get by, but she was by no means wealthy. Her judgment was clouded by the need to do the best for her late husband. Price was not a consideration.

"Let's call it a business opening special," he said. "This is my first funeral urn and I want you to have it for no additional money." He passed back the envelope. "You inspired me to make a change in my life, and it would take away from the experience to have you pay me. Let's call it a 'Henry Collins Special.'"

The old lady was moved by the offer, but she always paid her own way. "I'll tell you what," she said, "you take this money, we call it a Henry Collins Special, and you retire that design. Only my

Henry will have an urn exactly like this." She beamed at her suggestion.

John gave the idea a little thought before agreeing. "It's a deal," he said. He never made two things exactly alike anyway. Henry could have his unique resting place.

He reached out to shake her hand. She looked at the hand, looked at him, stepped inside the outstretched arm and game him a warm hug.

John smiled to himself. Eric Sanderson never sealed a deal like this.

# ≈22≈

ROGER JOHNSON stirred in the queen-sized bed, pulling the soft, blue blanket up around his neck. An internal battle was taking place between the increasingly urgent pleas of his bladder to seek relief and the sheer warmth and comfort of the Posturepedic mattress which insisted he stay put.

He opened one eye and looked around the dimly lit room. The decor was hotel blah. A 27" TV stared back from the foot of the bed, a small sink to its left and an air conditioner gently humming beneath the curtained window to his right. A nondescript still life of flowers by some unknown artist hung on the wall above his head.

The bladder won out. Johnson threw back the blanket and hustled off to the bathroom to the left of the door to the room.

Once relieved, he walked back into the room, went over to the windows and peeked through the curtain. Where was he this morning? As a steady flow of money started coming in, the quality of the rooms increased, but it was still a different place almost every night. Sources told him both of his houses were still staked out twenty-four hours a day by the police. They couldn't continue this expensive surveillance for much longer. Not even The Boss demanded that kind of expenditure.

He could see morning traffic starting to build. He checked his watch. Seven-thirty a.m. He had slept late. Even though most of his business dealings were late night affairs, by nature he preferred to awaken early, a self-proclaimed morning person.

Crawling out of bed early allowed him time to relax, read his newspaper with a coffee and lay out his plans for the day. Some of his custom had to take place in the nine-to-five world among legitimate commercial operations. Last night he had done the laundry, turned drug money into acceptable currency. Now this currency had to be invested to produce even more acceptable currency.

The new proceeds of crime acts made doing the laundry more important than ever. Anything purchased with money traced back to his drug operations could be seized and sold by the Crown. In the unlikely event he was ever caught, convicted and jailed, he wanted his recently acquired belongings waiting for him on his release. Ensuring that demanded he jump through some extra hoops. Big Willie had been the master of this task but Roger knew his way around the washing machine as well.

He ran several small discount stores in the more depressed areas of Metro. By shopping at his stores, the citizens of these areas were able to afford things they could normally only dream about owning. They flocked to his establishments and laid down their hard-earned cash. Most never questioned the cheap prices. The few who did assumed the merchandise came from liquidation sales—companies going out of business, ends of lines and the like.

Johnson accepted their cash, threw in multiplier and wrote himself dividend cheques of much greater value than the money actually earned. All cash sales and slick accounting made it possible. Some of the stores were becoming so popular they were almost breaking even—almost, but not quite. The losses incurred were a cheap way to legitimize his drug earnings.

In a way, this money laundering gave him a chance to give back to his community. These were the roots he had come from. He knew how hard it was to get by on minimum-wage jobs. He also recruited low-level soldiers from these neighbourhoods. Having the ability to purchase nice things in his store, planted the seed in them to aspire to even nicer things. If they came and worked for him, he could show them how to rise up in society.

Even though Roger wanted to be paying cash upfront for his drug buys, it was important to keep these business concerns propped up. He had to be patient. He had to spread the money coming in around to keep all the irons in the fire at least warm, if not hot.

Last night, the meetings had been with men who ran these discount stores. They knew where the money came from to set up the various operations, but they themselves had clean hands. Roger demanded they stick to legitimate things in all their dealings. They were happy to comply. None wanted to see a jail sentence in their future.

Now they were putting added pressure on Roger. They wanted to open another location. Business was good. He agreed to think about it when things returned to normal.

Today, his task was to spread some of this clean money around to totally legitimate businesses which were unaware of where his investment capital flowed from. The final step, the pressing and folding part of the laundry process. He wanted to avoid losing another sack of cash. To do this he spread it out.

Roger called down to the kitchen and ordered a room-service breakfast. This was one of the advantages of moving up the food chain of hotels in the area. Breakfast set the tone for the rest of the day. It could not be enjoyed if you were constantly looking over your shoulder, worrying about who might identify you.

In the privacy of his own room, he could take his time and leisurely spread the packet of strawberry jam on his toast. He could take the other slice of toast and dip it in the yellow yoke from his over-easy fried eggs and savour every bite. He enjoyed his coffee black and liked to actually take the time to experience the harsh taste of a full-bodied beverage.

While he waited for this food, he stepped into the shower to wash yesterday's man away. The hot, stinging water swept the black hair colouring down the drain. His olive complexion turned back to pinkish white. Yesterday, Roger was a Middle Eastern businessman. Who would he be today? For a couple of relaxing moments, he forgot about the concern and let the water wash over him, allowing his mind to go blank, to search for Nirvana.

A rap on the door brought him back to the present. Breakfast. He turned off the water and yelled to the food server.

"Just leave it outside the door. I'll take care of you later."

Stiffed again, thought the young man who delivered the food. He had heard the "I'll take care of you later" line too many times to believe it. The old morning shower trick; he should have waited until the water was turned off before knocking. He left the cart and walked back to the elevator. To his amazement, an envelope was waiting for him in housekeeping before he left for the day, a generous tip inside.

Roger Johnson did not welsh on his debts. He expected good service and was prepared to make sure he got it.

Roger finished savouring his breakfast and donned his image of the day. He travelled with two suitcases; one carried clothes, one carried a theatrical makeup kit. He had become quite adept at applying the magic pastes and lotions. Today, he would be an overweight, balding, red-faced country bumpkin with money to invest.

He had two appointments with investment bankers. Men full of suggestions with one thing in common, they got a cut of the action. Commission it was called in the legitimate world, skimming off the top was the term in Roger's other life. Often he wondered who the real criminals were. No matter, they made his money that much harder to trace back to its source. That was the object of the exercise, another cost of doing business.

He checked the stranger in the mirror one more time. He recognized the cool, calculating eyes, but nothing else. "Let's go play hide and seek with my money," he said and walked out the door.

# ≈23≈

"I HAVE GOOD news and I have bad news. Which do you want to hear first?"

Eric and John were sitting in the new reception-studio Eric had created in a struggling strip mall along Sackville Drive. Once John had quit his day job, Eric had stepped up in a big way by renting this downtown location. It was a small, simple room with a laminate floor of light maple and sky-blue paint on the walls. Samples of John's work were displayed on various shelves and pedestals around the room, each with its own lighting source.

A backroom housed a slightly-used, but still state-of-the-art lathe and all the trimmings that allowed John to fully function at this location. John had dreamed of owning such a machine. He had never thought his hobby could justify the expense.

Nathan showed some surprise at the money invested. He couldn't be sure if Eric had great faith in John's ability, if this was simply another business opportunity for his friend, or if Eric wanted to use this as another way to hide money from his money-grabbing wife and her shyster lawyer. He never expressed these thoughts to either John or Eric.

Eric brought clients interested in bulk purchases to this studio to sample the various offerings available. Great pains were taken to make everything look its absolute best. The display could be seen from the sidewalk through the large picture windows. Interested passers-by were encouraged to make an appointment for actual viewing.

In that way only serious buyers took up any of Eric's valuable time. Marla occasionally took down that sign and unlocked the doors to customers when she made the five-minute journey to bring John his lunch. This resulted in a few off-the-cuff sales.

John hated that good news, bad news cliché. He had heard it much too often in his last life before he became an artisan. He thought those days were over. No one ever wanted to hear the bad news, but reluctantly they opted to hear it first. He was no exception.

"What's the bad news?" he asked.

Eric smiled. He had just won a bet with himself. Eric always chose to hear the good news first. There was enough bad news in the world. It could wait.

He placed the muffin that Marla had brought in with their coffee on the plate provided. Nuts and raisins. He'd have to be careful at these meetings. Marla's baking could become addictive and Eric was always conscious of his weight.

"The funeral urns you were making against my advice," he said. "I took them around to some crematoriums to see if there was any interest."

"And?" John encouraged Eric to continue.

"They're too small."

"Too small, that can't be. They're the same size as the one I made for Mrs. Collins. Henry fit in there with room to spare. I watched her pour him in, helped in fact."

Eric held up his hands in supplication. "Don't shoot the messenger, John. That is what they told me. They're too small by about a third."

John rubbed his hands through his hair and tried to figure out where he had gone wrong. "I'll have to check the insides. Maybe I didn't hollow them out as much as I should have. Henry fit in his as if it was made for him." He chuckled. "I guess it was made to his exact specifications."

"Perhaps, that's the problem," Eric said. "How big a man was this Henry dude?"

John thought about that for a minute before answering. "I don't know. Mrs. Collins gave me the measurements for the size of the container. I did the math and made one that size, filled it with sand and used that as my guide to how big the urn should be. She rambled on about their life together. Said Henry tended to be on the heavy side but I guess that's a relative expression. She was as skinny as a rake, herself."

"It's all academic anyway." Eric said. "The funeral home people said they are too small. What else can we use them for?"

"Henry fit in his." John wasn't about to give up. He spent hours turning out funeral urns and was proud of the results. "These are made from blanks Nathan provided from the country lady. There were a whole bunch of them this size. I went with them first because they were the same size as Henry's. I thought the others were too big. He must have thought he had a market for them. We may just have to find the right customers.

"Henry's funeral was handled by Snow's Funeral Home. I saw it on the bottom of the box as we poured out the ashes. They may remember him."

He snatched up the phone and dialled 411. In minutes he was connected to the sonorous voice of the funeral director.

"Yes, I remember Henry," came the reply to John's inquiry. "Three, four months ago. Such a sad story. He died from cancer, you know. There was hardly anything left of him when he died. You could easily pick up the remains in one hand and move him around. One of the worse cases I've ever seen and believe me, I've seen a lot."

"So he wasn't a typical case?" John asked, already knowing the answer.

"No, he was the extreme case," the funeral director answered. "The body became consumed by the disease, but the mind refused to give up and die. He looked totally emaciated by the time we received him."

"Thanks," John said and broke off the connection. "Did you hear?" he asked Eric.

Eric bit into his muffin again. "Yes," Eric said after he swallowed the bite. "His voice carried right into the room."

At that moment Marla walked into the room with some fresh coffee from the nearby Tim Horton's. She observed the long faces.

"What's up?" she asked.

Eric looked at John but said nothing. He had been opposed to making the urns right from the start and had told Marla as much. Nathan should have used the stuff as firewood.

"My funeral urns are all too small," John said. "It turns out Henry wasn't your standard run-of-the-mill size-40 corpse. I've got about a dozen of them finished. What a waste of time."

He walked across the room and picked up the one Eric had chosen to display. It was made from a solid piece of yellow birch with just a touch of spalting in it. The black lines formed an intricate pattern around the container in contrast to the honey-coloured wood.

"This is too nice to discard. There has to be a use for it." He dejectedly returned it to the shelf.

"Of course there's a use for it," said Marla, ever the practical one. "You need to find something smaller than a human being, that's all." She refreshed Eric's cup from the coffee urn and poured one for herself. As manager, she now joined the meeting.

"Very funny." John scowled at her. He was in no mood for humour. "What do you suggest?"

Marla picked up the urn. She held it up to the light coming in the studio window and stroked the wood.

"Anyone would be happy to make this the final resting place for their pet," she said. "Dogs, cats, whatever. There's a market for them, I'm sure. If not, that's what we are paying Eric for. He can create one." She smiled at Eric. He winced. Making the rounds of crematoriums was bad enough, now she wanted him to do pet cemeteries.

John was skeptical. "No one will pay the amount we would have to charge to make this worthwhile. There are hours and hours of time in each one of those." The early, rough work performed by the original owner was the easy part. John had imparted life into each piece of wood.

Marla looked at her husband and placed a hand on his upper arm. "My poor naive, out-of-touch little boy," she said. "People will pay much more for their pets than you can imagine. If you want to be crass and look at only the money side, this will be much more lucrative than human urns."

John flinched at the suggestion. It wasn't about the money, he told himself. There had to be at least a half-million sitting in a bag under his steps at home. He had never dared to count it. He feared he might get caught with thousands of dollars spread all around the room. As each day passed, he thought less and less about this alternate source of income.

Eric's ears perked up at this suggestion. "Do you really think so?"

"I don't think so, I know so. A pet lives with you for fifteen or twenty years; they are a member of the family. Their death is as traumatic as the death of a human loved one. We have the same feelings for Danka as we do for the kids. Sometimes, I think, we love him more. He always listens to what we say, never gets mad and stomps out of a room. People will pay, especially for something like this."

She hoisted the urn in the air in front of his face. "Are you man enough to admit you were wrong, if this turns out to be the case?"

Eric uttered his deep chortle of a laugh. "When it comes to making money, I have no ego. Dollars talk. Not only will I accept that you are right, I pray that you are right. That brings me to the good news, if you are still interested."

"Oh yeah," John said. "What's the good news?" He was still getting over the shock of finding out all the urns he had made were the wrong size. Another part of the learning curve. He should have done some research first.

"Everyone I showed the urns to loved them. Increase the size and they will be more than happy to buy them from us. It turns out I may have been wrong. But let's look into this pet thing first. If Marla is right, it might be the way to go. They take less wood, less time and might bring in more money. Now that I think about it, I've seen the seventy-dollar coats for dogs in the stores. Coats that would cost twenty bucks for a kid."

Marla nodded her head but was not really listening. She still had the urn in her hands. "We could customize these," she said. "We have the branding gear for putting our logo on the bottom. Can the brand be applied to a round surface?" She looked at John.

"I don't know. I guess so. Why?"

"I was thinking. If we get some images of the various dog breeds, German shepherd, collie, poodle, the common ones, we could burn it on the front of the urn. One poodle looks pretty much like every other one. Make each one unique, just for that breed of pet. What do you think?"

"Good idea," said Eric. "After the initial investment of moulds, that would be an extra that is pure profit, almost."

John gave Eric a withering glare. He was thinking of the look on Mrs. Collins' face as she placed the remains of her husband in the urn, the tears in her eyes.

"There's more to this than money, you know. People are dealing with the loss of a loved one."

"What?" Eric snapped. "Right, money isn't everything. You keep that thought firmly in mind when you write your next mortgage cheque or buy your weekly groceries. It will be foremost in my mind when I'm out selling them and making a living for you."

John blushed. "Money isn't everything. That's all I'm saying."

Marla intervened. "What do you think of the branding idea, John? Can you do it?"

He looked at his wife, thankful she was the one who dealt with Eric on the financial end of the business. "I'll experiment, but it shouldn't be a problem. I'll burn the image in before I put the wax on and the image will be softened a little. I don't know. Let me try some things."

Marla turned to Eric, taking control of the meeting. "See if you can find some outlets to sell them and what kind of price we are talking about. It's only a good idea if we can turn a profit."

Eric nodded. Marla talked his language. Someone in the family understood which side of the bread had to be buttered.

"I'll get back to you," he said and got up and left.

Marla wrapped her arms around her husband. John was still smarting from Eric's money comments. "Don't worry honey, this will work out for the best. You are going to make a lot of people happy, help them through their grief."

John hugged back. I hope so, he thought.

# ≈24≈

JOE DAVIS gently kicked Kate Irving under the table. For the last four hours, they had been alternating between this dingy bar and the equally dingy cafe across the street. There was a limit to how long you could sit in a bar and nurse one beer without arousing suspicion. Both cops were dressed in heavy work shirts, blue jeans and Kodiak work boots. Under their arms Joe carried a yellow hard hat, Kate a pink one. Construction was taking place down the street and this was the common uniform in both establishments. In one corner, a small, fuzzy television showed an all-news channel. No one appeared to be watching.

"What?" Irving had been semi dozing with her eyes open, a talent developed from long years of practice. She casually glanced around the room to see what had piqued her partner's interest. Nothing jumped out at her. She gave Joe an inquisitive look and shrugged.

"Over there at the end of the bar, near the poolroom door," Joe indicated without actually pointing. "The balding, middle-aged salesman type; he seems lost in a dive like this."

Kate's eyes drifted in the direction indicated. The other bar stools were occupied by men and women dressed like themselves soothing their aching muscles after a long day on the job; professional drinkers who spent all day propping up a bar somewhere, their red noses and fleshy jowls a testament to their dedication; and some obvious low-lifes who either sold drugs on the street or supported the sellers with their purchases. There were no Mr. or Mrs. Middle Class white-collar representatives present. None, that is, except for the man at the end of the bar.

"Could be lost," Kate offered. "Or selling something to the bar owner. Glasses, soap, peanuts." She looked at the mess of shells on the floor.

"Or he could be The Boss," offered Joe. "His clothes are out of place but he looks as if he fits in quite well. His attitude is 'Don't mess with me, I've had a bad day.' He appeared quite at home when he walked in a minute or two ago."

Indeed, Roger Johnson had had a bad day. His paranoia was in full operation. Two uniformed policemen were waiting for him in the lobby of his hotel when he came down that morning. He ducked back into the elevator and returned to his room before they spotted him and spent the next hour trying to figure out how they found him. He then took the fire escape chart hanging on the door of his room and plotted an escape which avoided the main lobby.

Unknown to Roger, one of the two cops planned to meet his sister who was visiting from Alberta. He had no idea of the disruption he caused in Roger's life. The sister landed in town the night before on business. They arranged to have breakfast together and agreed to meet later in the day when both wrapped up their respective work.

Roger's first appointment of the day was with an investment broker, a man he had been dealing with for three years. This would be a test of Roger's disguise.

Rain had been falling when he left the hotel through the service entrance. Now he had to worry about his makeup as well. It claimed to be waterproof. Was it?

Someone else sat in the broker's chair when Roger entered the office. His man had called in sick that morning and his appointments were being looked after by a senior staffer. They assured Roger the replacement broker knew his way around the investment world, had over twenty years of experience with the company, and could look after Roger's needs. Roger politely declined and left the building.

From there he briskly walked up to Spring Garden Road, entered the Garden Mall, took the escalator to the second floor, hurried along the full length of the upper corridor and exited on Dresden Row. He crossed the street and entered a small restaurant where he took the window table and watched to see who followed him out the door. Two coffees and a Danish later, he had spotted no one suspicious.

That didn't allay his fears. The cops at the hotel weren't following him; they were waiting for him. The alternate broker was already in the office when he arrived there. Somehow the police had figured out his itinerary for the day.

As he watched the steady rain falling from the steel grey sky, Roger relaxed a little. He recognized the paranoia. No one could possibly know his schedule. It was all in his head. He made it up as he went along. The coincidences freaked him out. Since escaping the constant surveillance, he had been pushing too hard, trying to do too many things at once and recover his empire too fast. He had to accept the fact that the world did not revolve around him. Besides leading to delusions of persecution, this could lead to amateur mistakes. He had to force himself to relax a little and take his time.

As that thought settled over him, a cop car pulled up out front, windshield wipers slapping away the falling rain. Roger bolted for the rear door of the restaurant. This is crazy, he kept telling himself, but nonetheless, he continued to run. No one followed him on his excursion through the kitchen and out the back door, but his day was ruined.

He knew he could not function and perform to the best of his ability while running scared. He needed a rest. He had to relax and take stock of how his plan to retake his empire was coming together. Today would be a holiday.

Still looking around at everyone on the street as if they were all following him, he made his way back to his hotel. There were no cops in the lobby. He went to his room, turned on the TV, sat in the maroon, upholstered easy chair provided and closed his eyes and thought of nothing.

When he awoke, Judge Judy was barking at some poor slob not to interrupt her when she was talking. He was not the only one having a bad day, it seemed. Outside of a stiff neck from his unusual sleeping position, he felt refreshed. He went into the bathroom and checked his makeup. He was still a stranger. The rain had not altered it or made it run.

He looked at his watch. His stomach was telling him he was hungry. The day was pretty well shot. He debated between ordering room service and going out to eat. The inserts in his cheeks which filled out his face to match his heavier body made eating in public awkward. He could take them out, eat in his room and enjoy the meal or he could put up with the uncomfortable chewing action and eat in the presence of other people. He realized being alone all the time was encouraging his paranoia. Despite that he ordered room service.

The sun peeked through the clouds by the time he finished eating. A glorious sunset lit up the western sky. He grabbed a tan overcoat and headed for the elevator. The holiday had ended.

The elevator doors slid open to reveal a uniformed policeman. Roger was shocked. This couldn't be. His first instinct was to turn and run. Instead, he held his ground. The cop spoke to a tall, attractive blond woman and she laughed. They paid no attention to him as he climbed aboard.

"We'll head out to my place where I will get out of this monkey suit and then you can treat me to a fancy supper," the cop suggested to his companion. "That is if your expense account is up to it. Otherwise, I grill a mean barbecued steak and baked potato."

"We'll decide when we get to your place," the blond responded. "I've had a long day and might just want to relax with a stiff drink first. A shot of Crown Royal on the rocks will clear my head."

"No problem there," the cop said. "I still pour the best shot in the family."

The two shared a laugh. This statement carried a history which Roger would never know about, or care about for that matter. He was just relieved to see this was a simple family reunion and not more aggravation for him.

And that is how Roger Johnson ended up sitting at the bar of a dark, little dive under the observation of two undercover police officers.

Davis got up from his chair and approached the bar. The little camera he was so proud of was tucked inside the curled fingers of his hand. He walked by the suspect. Click, click, click, he rattled off three quick pictures before going into the washroom.

He looked around at the filth and decided against exposing any parts of his body to this atmosphere no matter how urgently he had to relieve himself. After a suitable pause, he returned to his seat in the darkened corner of the bar, taking three more shots from a different angle on the return trip.

A smile at Kate Irving indicated his success.

The businessman said a few words to the bartender who went over to the poolroom door, opened it and looked in. He gave a quick nod and returned to his position behind the bar. The businessman downed his beer and walked out into the darkness of the street. The street light was burned out or broken, most likely the latter, and the only illumination came from the dim neon sign over the bar.

Kate and Joe debated whether to follow or keep waiting for their initial subjects, Mark and Louie. Events made the decision for them. The two thugs exited the poolroom and followed the stranger into the street. Joe took up a position by the window where he could observe what was taking place on the sidewalk. Kate drifted out onto the street and crossed the road where her view was unimpeded. Quietly, she called for backup. Two people could not follow three suspects if they decided to separate.

The three hoods stood in the dimly lit street having an animated discussion. The businessman appeared upset about something and the two thugs were listening. It was obvious they disagreed with what was being said but their attitudes suggested they were the supplicants. Contradictory to the general appearance, the businessman had to be Roger Johnson. No country bumpkin would be ordering these two hoods around in their own neighbourhood.

Joe left his position by the window and staggered out to the sidewalk. He stood there for a few seconds, swaying as if he may have had too much to drink and couldn't remember where he was going. Then he turned and lurched towards the three men. They picked up his approach in their peripheral vision, stopped arguing and stepped aside to let him pass.

Click, click, click. Joe continued down the street. He had three perfect pictures of the standard shoulder-to-shoulder picket fence photo-op. This may tie Roger to Mark and Louie when they were charged with assault for the beatings they had been dishing out around the city. Every little bit helped.

Joe stepped into the doorway of a deserted H&R Block tax office. It was the wrong time of the year for them to have any customers. He took out his mini microphone and aimed it back down the street.

"Listen man, if the cops found you, it's not because of anything we've done," Louie explained to Roger. The tone of his voice suggested he was repeating this statement for the fifth or sixth time. Roger wasn't listening. Once again his delusions of persecution were in full flight. His feelings of relaxation from the afternoon had deserted him. He was sure the police were following him and equally sure these two men were the cause.

"You're the only people I have contact with. It has to be you." Roger was emphatic.

"We don't need this shit," said Mark. "You're not paying us enough to listen to this crap. Come on Louie, let's go back inside and get a drink. We're through with you, man. We don't need your money, and we sure as hell don't need you."

He turned to walk back to the bar. Roger grabbed his arm. In the blink of an eye Roger was on the wet sidewalk staring up into the cold, green eyes of Mark Riley. "Don't ever touch me again," Mark said. "You may call yourself 'The Boss' but you're a two-bit drug dealer to me. Louie says we didn't give you up, we didn't give you up. Got it?"

It was a rhetorical question. The dynamics of the group had taken an abrupt change. Roger lay on the sidewalk, more a look of surprise on his face than one of fear. He kept his mouth shut. Roger dominated others with fear of what he would do to them. Mark and Louie had no fear.

Mark straightened up, adjusted his jacket and went back inside the bar, leaving Roger lying on the concrete. Louie glared down at Roger for a few seconds before turning and following Mark.

Joe had dropped his mike and yanked his camera out of his pocket. Everything happened so fast he wasn't sure if he managed to get any good pictures of the altercation or not. One thing was certain, there was disunity in the ranks.

Roger got to his feet and brushed off his clothes. He could feel the dampness on his butt from the rain-soaked sidewalk. He rearranged his body weight to make sure the lumps were in all the right places.

Grabbing Mark was a stupid thing to do, a mistake he would not repeat. For now, he still needed their help. He swallowed his pride and re-entered the bar himself. He only employed the best available resources. For now, that was Mark and Louie. He had some big-time sucking-up to do, but he could do that if he had to. Roger never lost sight of the bottom line.

Joe crossed the street and walked down to where Kate stood. The stagger was gone. He was sober again

"What do you think?" he asked

"It's Johnson, no doubt about it. I wonder what the argument was about."

Joe smiled and produced his mini mike. "If you saved your cereal box tops, you would know." He waved the mike in Kate's face.

"I guess I've got to get me one of those. You'd think the department would supply them. It would make our job a hell of a lot easier."

"There's dissension in the ranks. Johnson thinks we are on to him and that Mark and Louie are the reason. He's right, but he must be psychic since we just found out. He claims they are the only ones he is in contact with. They must be filling in for Willie Ettinger and Leroy Leblanc. Johnson must be getting desperate for help he can trust. Those two clowns combined don't have the brains of Big Willie."

"We don't need the two thugs anymore, let's pick them up right now while Johnson is present. Charge them with the assault we witnessed. We'll pretend we don't know who Johnson is and keep him under secret watch instead of overt surveillance."

She looked up and down the street to see if anyone paid any attention to them. "If he thinks he can be right there in the same room with us and we don't recognize him, it will have to make him over-confident.

"He's in such a hurry to re-establish himself, he's making mistakes all over the place. This will make him even more careless. Grabbing them will send Johnson to the shallow end of the brain pool for his next round of help. It will help rebuild our case faster and who knows, the way he's working so hard, there might be another bag of money to seize."

"Good idea, Kate. Do you think we should get the photos checked out by the whiz kids back at headquarters first just to make sure it's him."

"Nah, it's him. Didn't they as much as say so when they put him down onto the sidewalk? Let's make our move now. Shatter the nexus if they haven't already done so."

"OK, but I'm not taking them on without a couple of carloads of backup. We've seen these two at work and I don't want to diminish your abilities, but I don't think we could take them in alive by ourselves. At least not take them in and maintain our charming, good looks."

Kate glanced through the window at the crowded bar. "Suppose if we went in with our guns blazing, we'd get any support from anybody else?"

"We need eyes on every side of our head and a pair of guns each. Let's just call in the troops."

Kate agreed. The call for backup went out across the airwaves.

# ≈25≈

FIFTEEN MINUTES later a dark-coloured van pulled up and parked down the street from the Foggy Night. Several men clad in black body armour, carrying automatic rifles, jumped out and lined up along the sidewalk.

"The cavalry has arrived," said Kate Irving. She and Joe walked down the street and identified themselves to the man who appeared to be in charge. They outlined the layout of the rooms inside the bar and described the intended arrestees and where they should be sitting.

"They'll be easy to spot," Joe said. "They're the ones with the most attitude. There's a guard on the door of the poolroom, a big guy, and he carries a gun in the back of his pants. Gives him a little class carrying it that way, he thinks. Blow his ass off if he tries to draw it out in a hurry. These two guys aren't going to go down easy so be prepared to use necessary force right from the get-go."

The sergeant in charge of the Emergency Response Team smiled and looked back at his men. "That's the only way we operate, my son. Just keep out of the way."

The rain that had given way to the sun at the end of the day started to fall again in a wet drizzle.

"One other thing," Kate explained. "There's a fat guy in the room dressed in a suit. Looks out of place, like a salesman or something. He may be sitting with the two we're after. We don't want him hurt or arrested no matter what he says or does. He's under surveillance and hopefully will lead us to bigger and better things. With luck he'll be content to get out of the way and stay there."

"He had better," the ERT officer said. "We will take him down if he gets in the way. It's the only way we operate. Sorry, but that changes for nobody. Our own safety is our number one priority."

"OK," Kate said. "But be gentle." She wiped the accumulating moisture from her face and tried to dry her hands on her equally wet slacks. "Go get 'em. We'll be right behind you."

Three members of the squad deployed to the back of the building in case anyone attempted to escape out the back door. The bulk of the force rushed into the bar and headed straight for the poolroom door. Everyone scurried out of their way, some even stumbling to the floor. Those who were slow in reacting were shoved to the side without slowing the pace of the advancing men.

The two dark-clad figures in the lead carried a three-foot battering ram. They didn't break stride as the poolroom door collapsed on the floor with a thundering crash, freezing everyone inside where they sat. Mark and Louie were in cuffs on the floor before they could set down their beer. Their glasses ended up in foamy puddles around them.

"What the fuck is this all about?" Mark managed to stammer as he was hauled to his feet.

Joe stepped through the door. The action was over. No one was hurt. "You're under arrest for assault with a weapon," he said. "What have you got to say for yourself?"

"Nothin'," Mark said. "Aren't you supposed to advise me of my rights, that I can keep silent?"

"You're watching too much American TV. You can sing like a canary for all I care," Joe said. "We don't need a confession. We've got you cold on video."

He looked around the room at the others, pausing at Johnson and then moving his gaze to the person beside him.

Roger Johnson moved back against the wall with the pool players, saying nothing. Sweat poured down his back under the extra padding. He couldn't believe his luck. He would have to call a lawyer before Mark and Louie reached police headquarters. He wanted the lawyer to make sure there was no singing of any sort. He didn't want them plea-bargaining their way out of jail and him into it.

"You have to Mirandize them. You've violated their Fifth Amendment rights," the young punk beside Johnson said. He pulled down his shirt sleeves, stuck out his chest and flashed a know-it-all look at everyone in the room. "I know the law."

Joe walked over and looked him straight in the face. "Is that right, counsellor? I'll have my partner, Lennie Briscoe, do that at once." Smiles flickered on the faces of the ERT members. The others in the room remained stone-faced. It looked like a clear violation to them.

*Please keep your mouth shut and be quiet.* Roger tried to transmit the telepathic message to the man beside him. Let these guys do their job and get the hell out of here.

Joe looked over at Roger. "What do you think, sir?" he asked. "Is the counsellor right?" He could see Roger squirming under his gaze and fought back the desire to smile.

"No, he watches too much TV," Roger agreed but said nothing more. He averted his eyes from Joe and looked down at the floor.

Kate was enjoying the by-play but didn't want to push things any further. "Let's move them out," she said to the sergeant.

The bartender stood in the doorway wiping his hands on a dingy towel. "Who's gonna pay for my door?" he asked, staring at the cop with the sergeant's stripes.

Joe turned and took in the fat man and headed towards him. "Send the city a bill," he said. "We'll have the fire inspector deliver you a cheque."

As he arrived at the doorway, he suddenly reached behind the bouncer and pulled the pistol out of his belt and pointed it towards the ceiling. "You've got a permit to carry this, I assume."

At the sight of the gun, one of the ERT members immediately had his automatic weapon aimed at the man's head six inches from his face. His assignment was to watch for that particular weapon. Joe's action had surprised him, but not enough to prevent him from reacting.

The bouncer fell back against the wall. A dark spot appeared in the front of his pants and worked its way down the inside of the leg to form a puddle on the floor between his feet. The hole in the end of the muzzle was like staring into a large black mug. He could visualize the bullets lined up in the magazine.

"He hangs to the left," Joe said. No smiles appeared this time. An exposed gun in the room kept everyone on full alert. "Cuff him, and take him in too."

Joe's gaze swept the room. "Anyone else carrying concealed weapons?" he asked. Heads shook in the negative all around the room. "Do we have time to search everyone?"

Kate approached Joe, their faces inches apart. She reached up and took the gun from his hand, ejected the magazine and cleared the chamber. "You're having way too much fun with this," she whispered. "Let's get out of here."

Once more Joe looked in the direction of the uncomfortable Johnson, then back at his partner. "Make that bastard sweat a little," he said in an equally low whisper. "Make him pay for leading us all across the province in a wild goose chase."

The remaining members of the force relaxed their grips on their weapons ever so slightly and stood down. They waited for orders to search the room. If that was going to happen, they were more than willing.

"Let's get these guys in jail for the night," Joe said and everyone shuffled out through the small doorway, walking over the downed door and into the comparative darkness of the main bar, a little brighter than usual as light from the poolroom spilled into the gloom. The previously full bar was now at less than a quarter capacity. Several patrons suddenly remembered an appointment somewhere other than this bar. The remainder, mostly construction workers, wanted to see what was going on and were craning their necks to see though the door.

Two cops escorting Mark and Louie to the paddy wagon parked outside had left. Before shoving the thugs into the back of the wagon, they read them their rights, the shortened Canadian version. They could remain silent and they could retain legal counsel if they could afford it. Otherwise, they could try to work out a deal with Legal Aid.

# ≈26≈

"DON'T SAY A word until you hear the complete idea."

Excitement danced across Eric's face. Marla, John and Nathan sat in the studio listening expectantly to the latest machination from Eric's money-scheming mind. Marla opened herself to listen. Nathan expressed more curiosity than anything else. Worry lines crossed John's brows. *What now?* he thought.

Eric picked up a funeral urn from the display rack. It was one of the cheaper ones made from white ash. The company targeted all sectors of the death market from the least expensive to the most. When it came to taking money, Eric believed in being an equal opportunity money gatherer.

"Look at this urn," he said. He held it in their faces, giving them no choice. "Four hundred dollars, right? Add two inches to the base and leave it square instead of turned and I can add at least one hundred dollars to its value. Right now, this urn would most likely be buried instead of displayed on a mantle or something."

Unconsciously everyone nodded in agreement. The company produced two kinds of burial units: those actually buried in the ground and those used to hold the loved one's remains while being put on display in the house. The latter drew the heavier prices. They also required the most work and the better quality woods, although the higher cost did not accurately reflect the extras involved. People were just willing to pay more for them. Eric gladly accepted the payments.

At John's insistence, they also carried a line that made no profit for those with little or no means to make the more expensive purchases. Prices ranged from what you could afford going right down the line to free. If John had studied law, this would be his pro bono work.

Eric produced a two-inch, highly polished base almost from thin air. He had it setting on the shelf beside him ready for this demonstration and used a little prestidigitation to produce it. He placed the ash container on top of this base. Randomness played no part in this marriage; the two pieces blended perfectly.

"Looks good?" His gaze covered all three members of his captive audience. No one objected to this observation.

"Hardly worth a hundred bucks," Nathan volunteered when the others remained silent. John's look suggested agreement. Marla held her own counsel. She knew there had to be more.

Eric rotated the base one hundred eighty degrees. A small clock embedded in the wood came into view. "What do you think?" he asked.

Surprise showed on everyone's face. Marla reacted first.

"Not bad," she said. "Now it serves a utilitarian function as well as a decorative function."

John grunted. "It's pretty utilitarian as a final resting place," he said. The more fine work he produced, the more he exhibited the traits of a temperamental artist.

Marla looked at her husband. "Of course that's true," she said. "Utilitarian may not have been the best word. Now it has added features that the living can take advantage of as well as the dead."

She supported his newfound passion. She understood John believed the urns were more than a money-making scheme. Still, they were running a business here. Food on their table came from the sale of these products. He should never have been allowed to deliver the first urn to Mrs. Collins unattended. That almost spiritual experience influenced every thought he had about the burial containers. It showed in the quality of his work.

"I'm just a simple carpenter, not a designer," Nathan said, "but you could have done a better,job of centering the clock on the base." A wider gap existed at the bottom than the top.

Eric's smile brightened. "You're right, Nathan. There's more." Secretly, he had hoped John would make that observation, but accepted Nathan as his straight man.

The presentation came in three parts. He set the unit back on the shelf and reached into his pocket, producing a small brass plaque. He peeled the protective cover off the sticky tape attached to it and stuck it on the base in the space below the clock, then presented it as proudly as if it were an Olympic gold medal.

Marla leaned in and read the writing engraved on the piece of metal aloud.

"Thy time was the time of love – *Ezekiel 16:8*," she read.

"Nice." Surprise showed in her voice. Such a moving sentiment coming from Eric seemed out of character. She would have expected something more along the lines of *spend it now, you can't take it with you* or even the blunt and to the point: *time is money.*

Eric reached into his pocket again and withdrew two more plaques. He read the statements: "The Lord will deliver him in time of trouble – *Psalm 41*." He paused and then read the other one: "It is time to seek the Lord – *Hosea 10:12*." He handed them to John who quietly reread them and passed them to Nathan. Neither made any comment. They shared Marla's surprise.

"These sayings came from the Bible but expressions relating to time or to death abound out there," Eric said. He was trying to get a feel for the others' reactions. "Time, you no longer have a hold over me or I bide my time waiting for you."

A large turned clock on the wall loudly ticked off the seconds.

"I like it," John finally said after a long pause. "No offence Eric, but did you really come up with this idea?"

"None taken," Eric replied, "and yes I did. You have the wrong opinion of me John. I'm not the evil money-grabbing villain from a Charles Dickens novel you portray me as. I'm a little more practical than you, that's all. I've always had to work for everything I've got and that allows me to seize an opportunity when I see it. This is not a bad thing."

Although to everyone in the room, Eric seemed to epitomize the rich, successful businessman, things had not always been that way. There were nine kids in his family with Eric being the oldest boy. He had two older sisters. Their father had been a "seasonal employee" and was only gainfully employed part of the year. How much that part consisted of depended on the current rules in effect for the unemployment insurance requirements. That was back when it was UI, insuring you against unemployment, instead of the current EI, presumably insuring you against employment. This would have been more accurate in Eric's father's case.

Most men at the fish-processing plant where he worked accumulated seniority which allowed them to start work sooner after a layoff and stay longer as the existing work diminished, eventually leading to full-time employment for the lucky few. For Eric's father, it allowed him to work the exact number of weeks required for the maximum UI and not a week more. The rest of the year he spent sitting around drinking and making babies. He insisted he was a skilled fish cutter and wouldn't compromise his ethics by taking work in another field. His skill at the avocation of baby making kept Eric's mother tied to the house and working like a slave.

Early in life Eric learned that if he wanted any spending money, he would have to get out and earn it himself. This he did, starting as a paper boy when he was big enough to carry the heavy bundle of papers door to door, moving up to a carry-out boy in a local grocery chain and finally starting his own lawn mowing-snow shovelling business when he started university. He learned early to always be on the lookout for a money-making opportunity and he learned well.

After graduation, he entered the business world. His work ethic helped him move rapidly up the corporate ladder to become chief financial officer for his company before his acrimonious divorce and strange alimony terms set him free to pursue his own interests.

These interests now included John, Marla and wood turning. He not only thought outside the box, he lived outside the box and had no restrictions on his entrepreneurial endeavours as long as a financial gain showed at the end of the day.

Eric kept all this close to his chest. None of his partners needed this information. He did not need a Freudian analysis of why he did what he did. His business associates only needed to know that his plans created wealth most of the time. They were invited along for the ride if they wanted to come and wanted to contribute.

"How long will the clocks stay running?" asked Nathan. He had a practical streak as well. "A dead clock on a burial urn doesn't strike me as too appealing."

"The readouts are LED," Eric explained. "They use very little power. The NiCad batteries should last at least five years and are easy to change. The clocks fit snugly but the flip of a screwdriver will bring them out and the battery is easier to change than the battery in your watch."

John picked up the base and examined it. The slot appeared to be made with a drill press. It would add a few seconds to the manufacturing time once the machine was set up. He studied the piece of ash. It must have come from his supply. The match was perfect. Eric must have somehow taken the same piece of wood that was used to make the urn.

Squaring and finishing the base to the same quality as the urn itself would take more time. John was a wood turner not a finish carpenter. He wondered if Eric had done it himself or hired someone. Nathan reached for the base and John passed it to him.

"I could make these," he said. He had read John's mind. "I do more than sell carpentry tools. I know my way around a saw and a sander."

John looked at his friend. "Yes, you could." The idea appealed to John. The whole concept took on a new meaning for him.

"Eric, this is a wonderful plan. Not just because it will make us more money, but with a clock on the urn, people will be drawn to look at it. It will keep the departed one alive in everyone's thoughts. Even if your motives are financially driven, the results are a positive thing. Will we have any trouble getting a supply of the clocks?"

"Thank you," Eric said and added after a slight pause, "I think." Praise from John was hard for him to earn. "I have a good source that can get us all we will need, at least in the short term."

He did not elaborate. A box in his warehouse at home contained a thousand good-quality clocks. He had tried to sell them at the flea market, but was unable to garner anywhere near a break-even price. Time pieces had become too cheap. He needed a more novel approach to move them and providence offered this chance.

John didn't need this knowledge, either. It would only dampen his enthusiasm for the idea and return Eric to the ranks of a scheming money grabber. Seeing the reaction of the others, Eric thought, *I did come up with a good idea, better than I realized.*

"*Time is on my side – M. Jagger,*" Marla said.

John scowled at her.

"What?" she asked. There's a big world out there. Everyone doesn't share your tastes. We have to appeal to everyone. Shakespeare was only a contemporary playwright in his day. Now we've elevated him to the point where only golden words spewed from his pen. " She turned to Eric and asked: "Is there a practical limit to how much we can put on one of those shields?"

"The type has to be big enough to read and every letter makes it more expensive but you could put four lines on there, I'd say."

Nathan shook his head in disagreement. "There is no limit if you have something worth saying," he said. "Just because Eric presented us with a two-inch block doesn't mean that is the definitive size. You could have a block six inches deep if the message warranted it. The client would have to decide if it was worth the expense, not us. Did you have some other ideas?"

"Don Quixote had a line that might work. *'There is no remembrance which time does not obliterate, nor pain which death does not end.'*"

"My wife quotes Cervantes?" John expressed his surprise. Marla curled up her nose at him and made a face.

"My husband knows the author of Don Quixote?" she mimicked. Both of them impressed Eric. When he wasn't making money, he read voraciously. You never really know people, he thought to himself.

"As a warning to others, we might want to quote Robert Herrick," he said: *"Gather ye rosebuds while ye may, Old Time is still a flying."*

Marla interrupted: *"And the same flower that smiles today, Tomorrow will be dying."*

Again she scrunched up her face. "There might be a place for that but, I don't know, you'd have to let someone suggest it to you rather than the other way around. It's advice to virgins to put out, you know?"

"No," Eric said, "it's classical literature."

"Men were horny in those days, too," Marla answered. "Nothing has changed."

"Napoleon Bonaparte had a line about time," Nathan said. Everyone was getting into the swing of things, he may as well have a go as well.

*"'Go, sir, gallop, and don't forget that the world was made in six days. You can ask me for anything you like except time.'* A bit wordy but it makes you think."

Heads nodded all around.

"*There is no sorrow which length of time does not diminish and soften,*" John added.

He was thinking of Mrs. Collins and the acceptance of Henry's death that evolved from the first time he met her until the last. "Cicero or one of those old guys gets credit for the line. I would have to look it up. We seem to be stuck with the idea that time has to be mentioned in the line because it is sitting under a clock. This is really only the epitaph on a headstone. People could say whatever they wanted." He turned and faced Eric. "Can we make these things ourselves or would we have to farm them out?"

A trace of a grin flickered across Eric's face. "Now you're thinking like a businessman. As it happens, I have the gear to make them myself. Something I acquired a few years back when I was buying and reselling trophies. A little patience, an eye for type styles and the ability to spell correctly are the prerequisites. That last ability can't be overstressed. There is no correction fluid, no eraser, no backup key. If you screw up, you throw it away and start at the beginning again with a new plaque."

"That leaves John out. His spelling is atrocious," Marla said. "I, on the other hand, am a grade six spelling bee champion." Another production worker was added to the payroll albeit in a dual role, executive and tradesperson.

# ≈27≈

"THE EMERGENCY Response Team. Don't you think that was a little over the top?"

Detective-Sergeant Mcdonald sat on the corner of his desk talking to his two officers, Kate Irving and Joe Davis. Being a sergeant of detectives didn't quite rate him a real office, but he did have a light blue, five-foot padded partition around two sides of his desk. The other two sides were real walls. The door was an opening where the two floating sides didn't meet.

He had a corner office with a window overlooking Windsor Street, a pizza parlour and a barber shop. It beat sitting out in the pit with everyone else.

Three containers of Chinese food took up one corner of the desk. Chicken fried rice filled one. Vegetables occupied the second. The third spilled sweet and sour chicken balls onto their plates. Jim had sprung for the takeout meal delivered from the Chinese restaurant just up the street. All three dug in with gusto, their mood upbeat.

Joe laughed. "Maybe a little. We checked first. They weren't doing anything at the time and were willing to have some real-life practice." He wiped sauce from his chin.

"And," Kate interjected, "Joe was worried about getting his pretty face messed up."

"Yeah, that too," Joe agreed. "Really, they were glad to help. The sergeant likes to keep them sharp and active. And man, I give them top marks. You should have seen them in action."

Kate turned serious. "The effect it had on the people in the back room of that bar justified the cost. Roger Johnson stood right there and watched. The pictures Joe took passed inspection. Despite the clever disguise, the forensic boys definitively identified the eyes, not that we had any doubt."

Kate speared a broccoli shoot and held it up to her mouth, then gestured with her fork. "He's under observation again. That in itself justifies everything we did."

Kate popped the broccoli into her mouth and chewed. "These two thugs, Mark and Louie, were the most feared men in the business. They never knew what hit them. The ERT boys had them on the floor and in cuffs before they realized we were even in the room. It put the fear of God into everyone watching. No thinking person will be lining up to take their place with The Boss. That only leaves the dumb ones. They make mistakes. We cash in on dumb mistakes."

The pleased look on Kate's face wiped out the memory of the dejected look she had displayed after the classic car chase.

Jim nodded. "Sounds good. Where is Johnson now?"

"Staying in a hotel uptown. Doesn't know we are on to him again. Ron Smith was called in before the bust went down. He took over the surveillance and we left with the prisoners. Johnson thinks he walked away clean. With his organization breaking up under him, we need him involved in the day-to-day action, to get his hands dirty again. That will make it harder for some high-priced mouthpiece to get him off when we bring him in."

Kate loaded a fork with rice and looked up at Jim. "We will bring him in, soon. That bastard's ass is mine." Kate said the last with a determination in her voice that could not be denied.

"I understand the interviews with the two thugs were unproductive." Jim said. He didn't want his officers too emotionally involved in their cases, but he let Kate's remark slide.

"That sums it up," Joe said. "They almost had a lawyer waiting for them when we brought them in. Same one Johnson uses. He was dressed up in a tux and wasn't happy to be there. I think he was dragged from some function where he was being a pillar of the community. Johnson must have told him to handle this personally and not send some flunky from his office. He's afraid Mark and Louie know too much and are not really committed to him."

Kate continued. " I agree. They'll make bail and be back on the street today or tomorrow at the latest. I get the impression they are freelancers, not part of Johnson's organization. I don't think they'll be working for him again for awhile. There was some sort of falling out before we grabbed them. Having to spend a night or two in jail will exacerbate the feelings between them."

Jim pondered this information. "Let's not take any chances. I'll get Judge Kendrall working on this right away. Let's get them locked up and denied bail or at least threaten to lock them up and see what shakes out. If they land in jail, it will at least create the perception on the streets that we are winning. If they give up Johnson, we'll throw him in jail instead."

"They'll go to jail before they give him up," Joe said. "It's not loyalty to Johnson. They have reputations to maintain. Being imprisoned doesn't bother them. They'll have food and shelter and they will be nobody's wives. They have no fear of that. It will be their own little kingdom within hours. Even the guards are intimidated by them."

"Good enough," said Jim. "If they want to be kings, let's crown them." He cleaned up the last of his Chinese food and dumped the paper plate in the garbage beside his desk. "Do you think they are responsible for all the recent beatings?"

"No doubt about it. The only one we will make stick is the one Joe and I witnessed and caught on videotape. No one else will testify against them. Following them was a lucky break for us."

Jim walked around his desk, sat down and pulled open a drawer. He brought out a file folder with a red tab on the upper edge.

"The expenses for Operation Enduring Success for last month." He threw the folder across the desk towards Kate. She picked it up, glanced through it and passed it to Joe.

"Big numbers, no denying that, but a lot of them are inaccurate. The biggest expense is salaries. We are going to be paid regardless of what case we are working on. No one is suggesting the police force is overmanned, are they?"

"No," Jim said, "just overpaid." He smiled.

"Let them be involved in one takedown like we had last night with Mark and Louie and our salaries would never be mentioned again."

"True," Jim said. "I agree. Inspector Holland agrees. Even the elusive people above him agree. Everyone agrees until budget time and then someone has to pay the bills. No one remembers the takedown. They remember the cost of the van to get the ERT there, the cost of the gas, the cost of the beer you drank during the surveillance." He took the report from Joe and flipped back and forth through the pages. "Here it is. 'Beer – The Bull and Bear - $6.00. Another $3.00 for a spritzer.'"

"For Christ's sake, is that in there?" Joe asked. "That is when we took Leroy Leblanc off the street. Roger Johnson will be fined $800 or more. Are those figures in there?" Joe kicked the garbage can beside the desk. Not hard. Just enough to show his disgust. "Police work ain't cheap. But neither is the alternative—anarchy."

Jim held out his hand in front of himself, palms angled towards the floor, moving up and down a couple of inches. "Calm down, everybody. Calm down. I was going to say I thought the figures looked pretty good considering what we've accomplished. That's not the official word, mind you, but it's what I think. Every penny still has to be pinched until it screams uncle, but keep up the good work. The data we're acquiring, along with the information from last month, will soon lead to more raids. It will catch everyone off guard. No one expects two major raids in a two or three month span. Hang in there guys and keep on truckin'."

He pointed to the partially filled food containers. "Take this food with you. It's paid for and not on any expense sheet. Enjoy it."

The detectives had been encouraged, now they were being dismissed. They all had work to do.

# ≈28≈

PHASE TWO OF Eric Sanderson's plan was in effect. Not only were John's bowls on display at the Exhibition Park Craft Show, so was John. Along one end of the great hall, John's bowls were on static display. In front of them, John demonstrated his skill on an operational lathe. To give Eric his credit, it was one of the more popular demonstrations at the show. People were amazed to watch the layers of wood peel off to reveal the item hiding underneath. The two rows of chairs set up in front of his lathe carried a constantly changing wave of people. As soon as one couple got up to leave, another slid into the spot

John had a few bowls, started at home, that he put the finishing touches on in front of the crowd. Once added to the display to be sold, some member of the crowd snapped them up almost immediately. The desire to say "I saw that being made" drove these sales. Little did the buyer realize John performed the bulk of the work long before anyone arrived at the show in the privacy of his own workshop. Between the bowls, he turned out toy tops or souvenir-sized baseball bats to give to the kids in the crowd. Free items never fail to attract a crowd.

Eric put in the same long hours as John, manning the cash register, his smile and charm offsetting John's seriousness and intensity. They made a great team. For every ten or so free bats or tops they gave away, a parent walked away with a bowl safely wrapped in a custom-made box with the new logo on it. The cost of the toys was less than a buck each. The bowls sold for $200 and up. Running out of product before the end of the show was Eric's biggest fear.

Consequently, on day two of the show, funeral urns became part to their display. Eric balked at the idea at first. John accused him of being in denial about the reality of death. At John's age, death seemed an obscure concept. At Eric's age, the reality hovered much closer. The show's clientele had a mixed reaction. Although sales in the urns were not what you could call brisk, several older people, mostly women, examined them closely and took business cards away with them.

The clever verses on the bases generated lots of comment. Eric's view started to soften. Opportunity for profit seemed to be looming on the horizon. There could be lots of future sales being generated. After all, who wanted to parade around a craft show carrying their eternal resting place in a shopping bag?

Funeral urns were not the strangest thing being sold at the show, although they ranked up there near the top. The event filled three buildings at Exhibition Park. A committee juried all the products, keeping the standards high. The most prominent items for sale by far were various types of designer clothing. They ran the gamut from kids wear that any child would be happy to be seen in to adult creations that rivalled any Halloween costume and everything in between.

Scattered among these items were original paintings, from both the abstract and realism schools of art; leather work of every description; food items from various cultures, John's personal favourite; hand-stitched quilts, which again showed how beauty is in the eye of the beholder; candles, scented with every imaginable odour: sea breeze, cinnamon, apple, lavender; and assorted pottery, trinkets and hangings.

Mrs. Collins arrived on day two, walked past all of the above and came right up to the wood-turning booth.

Eric cringed when he realized who had entered their domain. He had never met Mrs. Collins, but he had definitely heard all about her, her late husband Henry and the urn. He had heard more about the urn than he ever wanted to hear. Now the batty old woman invaded his space.

His concerns were misguided. The men couldn't have hired a better company spokesperson. She ignored Eric. He returned the favour, although in his mind he schemed up a plan to move her on.

To John she said: "Henry loves his new home. He's so pleased there."

She turned to the people in the chairs behind her. "This nice man created a lovely resting place for my Henry." Everyone turned to listen. Mrs. Collins did have a commanding presence and a voice that required you to listen.

"Henry's been dead for four months now," she continued, "and was unhappy until Mr. Lester turned a beautiful urn home for him. Last week's newspaper carried a picture of it." A few heads nodded.

Eric watched John react like a thermometer dipped in hot water. The red started at his neckline and climbed to the top of his head. Eric figured it probably started at the tips of his toes if the truth be known.

"The last couple of days have been the best since Henry's passing. He keeps telling me how happy he is." The crowd responded to the little widow. Smiles crossed their faces as they shared her joy.

She turned and thanked John over and over. John's solemn face cracked into a wide smile and at the same time his eyes got misty. He came out from behind the lathe and gave the old lady a long hug. The crowd, pleased with his presentation before, now loved his human side. Sales spiked.

As Mrs. Collins toddled off, John turned to Eric and whispered: "That's what I was trying to tell you. It's not just about the money."

Eric returned the smile and nodded in agreement. He suddenly loved Mrs. Collins as well.

"I understand now," he said as he rang up another $250 sale. "You were right all along." He reached out to another customer. "An excellent choice, ma'am. You can feel the warmth and texture of the wood in that bowl." Cha-ching. Another sale.

John and Eric's little show drew good, constant crowds, but a demonstration at the opposite end of the hall outdrew them. A lady, advanced in years, dressed in long, rich textured, purple robes was telling the future by reading tea leaves and coffee grounds. She charged twenty bucks for one of her sessions which took about five minutes, slightly more if her subject was demonstrative and entertaining—good work if you could get it. She went under the name of Madam Ruth.

Reading tea leaves could be described as mostly art. Building and maintaining a crowd of prospective buyers combined art and science. Madam Ruth excelled at both.

The customer would be invited to sit and drink most of a cup of tea while they chatted. They would then turn their cup up-side-down on the saucer, spin it three times and pass it back to Madam Ruth who would study it for several seconds.

Her demeanour would become serious and she would intone: "Look here," as she stared deeply into a near-empty cup at the remaining tea leaves. She would point to what might be described as an image of a bird. "This bird indicates a trip in your future." The crowd would lean in to see what Madam Ruth saw. An overhead camera displayed the inside of the cup on a small TV screen. Heads nodded. They could see it.

"Yes, yes," the eager respondent would tell her. "I'm going to Toronto to visit some old friends."

"A long trip," Madam Ruth would continue as if not hearing the other person. "Use caution and be careful of your money." Good advice anytime.

"Why?" Concern instantly filled the person's face.

"See over here." She indicated three leaves shaped like an axe. "Beware of those around you. These specks on the edges of the cup, people on the periphery of your circle of friends are some who might take advantage."

Madame Ruth looked up with a knowing smile. "But if you are cautious, you will thwart them. Forewarned is forearmed."

"Oh thank you, thank you. I will be on the alert." Already it was twenty dollars well spent. Others searched their purses to see how their funds were holding up. Several twenties materialized throughout the crowd. The owners eagerly edged forward.

The show's brochure advertised the booth as selling home-made, locally flavoured teas—blueberry, maple, strawberry, whatever. These little packets moved well at five dollars a container. The aroma of fresh brewed tea filled the air, having a calming effect on everybody watching.

The booth maintained a staff of three who brewed, served the free samples and sold the teas. They owned the business; they hired the fortune teller to bring in the customers.

The tea tasted good, the quality high and the price fair if you bothered to stop and try it. Madam Ruth provided that service. She stopped the ever-moving crowd of buyers and got them to look at the products on display. Everyone came out a winner.

The sellers in the two booths on either side didn't complain either. On the right, one of the many people selling tole painting displayed their craft. On the left, canvas bags with sail boats or other nautical scenes stitched into them covered the walls. Both items moved briskly.

John had spotted Madam Ruth watching him demonstrating his skills and wondered what her specialty was. If it was clothes design, her styles were certainly unique. But at this show when it came to self-described fashion designers, anything was possible.

Some beautiful lingerie turned out to be evening wear in this new age, some silky looking evening wear turned out to be pajamas. It was more than John could figure out.

Madam Ruth wore an ankle-length, flowing gown of purple silk with gold floral designs running though it. On her head, she sported a pink scarf-like creation with a large, sparkly jewelled pin in the front. Crimson, high-buttoned boots could be seen on her feet as she walked along the hallways. Spotting her in a crowd offered no challenge.

During one of his breaks, John drifted up to her end of the action. As he approached, a customer climbed out of the fortune-telling chair, an amazed look on her face.

Madam Ruth zeroed in on John in the crowd like an owl on a field mouse. She invited him to join her. He blushed and declined. She leaned towards him and in a low, mysterious voice said: "I have an important message for you. I think you should sit down."

*Nice come on*, John thought and started to walk away. She grasped him tightly by the arm and stared intently into his eyes. "Please," she said. "No charge."

The attack took John by surprise. He pulled back on his arm, but continued engaging the wild woman's eyes. Common sense told him to get back to his own table. He hesitated. Her eyes displayed a sense of urgency. Curiosity won out. John sat down.

Madam Ruth offered him a tiny cup of tea, the leaves swirling through the liquid. To his surprise, he enjoyed the taste. She seemed to become calmer, and they chatted about his display as he drank.

"Don't drink it all," she instructed him as he approached the bottom of the cup. "Turn it over into the saucer and give it three spins."

John complied.

"Now turn it upright with the handle facing you."

The friendly look on the woman's face dissolved into one of complete seriousness. She leaned towards John while staring into the cup as if consulting the Muses. Her gaze slowly returned to his face. Her eyes took on a burning quality that repelled John slightly. She took his hand in hers.

"You have recently found something of immense value," she started.

John sat bolt upright. She had his complete attention. She lowered her voice so only John could hear her warning. "You must return it. Trouble will overwhelm you if you don't."

Others leaned in to hear what she was saying. She waved them back. "Please, only for this man's ears. Stay back," she commanded.

Some looked perturbed, others accepted it. Everyone moved back. Her look left no room for argument.

Her concentration returned to John. "Does this make any sense to you?" she asked.

John was flustered. "Yes. No." He shook his hand free. Words eluded him How could this woman know about the money?

She reached out and placed her hand on his again. He could feel the heat it generated and once more pulled his hand back. Fear washed through John's mind.

"I don't know what this refers to," she said, "but I feel very strongly that you must return whatever you found. You have to decide yourself."

Then, as if a light had been turned off, the intensity left her face. Her features went slack and then her bright smile returned.

"I hope this has been of some help to you," she said. She seemed unaware of the message she had transmitted a few seconds earlier. Shaken, John got to his feet. He held the back of the chair, unable to trust his ability to walk away.

"Thank you," he said, for no reason he could fathom. Thanks was the last thing on his mind for what had just transpired. Then he pushed through the crowd and returned to his own booth. The others, curiosity written all over their faces, made a path for him to escape.

All the way back the message bounced around in his mind. Had this crazy woman really told him to return the money or experience dire consequences? Had the extreme pace of the last two days finally caught up to him causing hallucinations to take over his mind? That had to be it. Madam Ruth could not know about the bag of money hidden under his step.

He stopped in front of his lathe and looked up at Eric.

"I've got to get out of here," he told him. "I've got to go home right now."

Eric's face was flush with the show's success. The show had generated sales beyond even his imagination. He was about to object when he looked down at John's terrified demeanour.

"Oh my God, what's wrong? Has something happened to Marla?" His thoughts immediately went to the worst-case scenario. He jumped down from the small raised platform behind the lathe and put an arm across John's shoulders. John's ashen face sent a shiver through his own body.

John shook off the arm. "No. No, I just have to get out of here." Without another word, he turned and ran to the nearest exit. Eric started to follow, stopped and looked around for some one to explain what had taken place. No one had noticed the brief confrontation. They were picking up bowls, admiring them and looking for someone to take their money. Confused as he was, Eric automatically reached out to accept the funds.

Marla stood waiting in the doorway of the house for John to exit his car. He had been sitting there for at least thirty seconds.

"Honey, what's wrong?" she asked, starting down the steps.

"Eric called and told me you rushed away from the craft show without any explanation, and that you looked as though something had badly scared you. He's concerned."

John got out and looked up at her. He tried a smile, failed and tried again. All the way home his mind had been racing. He had to figure out where the fortune teller got her information. Not from the bottom of a teacup, that was certain. John would never buy into that scenario. He had given no thought as to what he would do when he got home, what he would say to Marla. If he had been thinking clearly, he would have expected Eric to call her. Eric must be worried about his investment running off like that.

"I'm OK," was the best he could come up with.

"OK? That's not what Eric thinks. You've scared him badly. What is going on?"

"I don't know, Marla. Maybe it's just the stress and pressure of performing like a trained seal for the last two days. You know, I'm used to working all by myself with no one watching. It just all caught up to me."

Doubts about the reality of the message formed in his mind. Could this psychic know about the money? Impossible, he told himself for the hundredth time. Maybe he simply exaggerated what she said. Read into things that were in his mind, but not hers. Blew the warning way out of proportion.

Marla approached the side of the car, her arms out in front of her. "Come here, big boy," she said. "Eric told me you are doing a wonderful job. Everything is selling like hot cakes."

"Right, everything is selling," John said as he folded her into his arms, relishing the comfort and familiar warmth. Then he stepped back. "That's all Eric is interested in. I have to keep pouring out this stuff. He wants it faster and faster but I refuse to give up on doing it right. I'm not going to sacrifice the quality."

He felt guilty lying to Marla but she was buying the story. This small lie was better than the big one hiding under the steps in the basement, a lie by omission.

"Eric understands that," Marla said. "Quality is what sets your work apart from everyone else's. He wants you to maintain it as much as you do. You're just tired. Come in and lie down for a while. I'll call Eric and tell him everything is all right."

John descended the stairs and into the rec room where he lay on the couch. He consciously avoided looking towards the room holding the bag of money.

Marla called Eric, reassured him, and then joined John in the rec room. She slid her hands under his head and massaged his neck and shoulders. The tension eased out of his body. He forgot about Madam Ruth and her piercing eyes, her psychic knowledge.

John rolled over on his side and nestled his face into Marla's belly. He put his arms around her. Soon his breathing slowed, became more regular and deeper. Little noises came from him, more purring than snoring. He drifted off to sleep.

Marla settled back, resting her head on the top of the chesterfield. Her fingers idly rubbed John's shoulder. Soon, she joined him in the land of nod.

John began to twitch and his eyes jolted open. Once again someone was going to have his testicles for lunch. The bad dreams had returned after an absence of over a month. For a second he felt as if he was suffocating. Sweat ran down his face. Drool came from the lower corner of his mouth, leaving a wet spot on Marla's blouse.

He realized what impeded his breathing. Marla had slid down in the seat and her breast was up against John's mouth and nose. The bad dream left his thoughts at once. He blew into the opening of the blouse. Marla squirmed a little but didn't wake up. John leaned forward and kissed. Marla leaned in to him, then sat up with a start. Her eyes were open but consciousness hadn't fully returned. She looked down at John and smiled.

"What are you up to?" she asked.

"Right about here," John said and kissed her again.

Marla leaned forward and blew in his ear. One thing led to another when suddenly the back door slammed open and one of the kids yelled, "Mom? Dad? Is anyone home?"

A scurrying of activity followed as they both rearranged their clothes.

"Down here," John said, his voice husky. "What do you want?"

"Nothing," came the reply and the door slammed shut again.

John looked up at Marla. "I'm not through with you. We'll finish this later."

"Damn right we will," she said and walked over to the wet bar, adjusting her bra and pulling her blouse down as she went. She ran a glass of cold water and brought it to her lips. She looked out at the kids playing in the backyard.

"How'd we ever manage to have more than one?" She passed John the glass. His face was still flushed.

"I don't know," he said, then drifted back into the rec room and sat down. Already his thoughts were returning to the threat in his dream and the mysterious words of the fortune teller. He sat down and put his head in his hands. What kind of trouble could the bag of money bring him? It was safely hidden away. He could think of two kinds. One with the police, one with their adversaries. Neither boded well for him. What was he to do?

# ≈29≈

ONCE AGAIN Roger Johnson found himself repacking his suitcases. He showed no enthusiasm for the task. He liked this hotel. The food was good, the bed was comfortable and it was close to the action. Still, it was time to move on.

He had escaped a bullet the night before while witnessing the arrest of Mark and Louie. Those damn detectives looked him right in the face, conversed with him, scared the shit out of him. He could see all his efforts to shake their surveillance spiralling down the drain.

That stupid jail house lawyer, arguing for the rights of the accused, took most of their attention, it was true. But still, his disguise stood up. He felt a sense of pride in that.

Now, some unfinished business demanded his attention. Larry Scarborough's body lay in a shallow grave just off a woods road outside the city.

Everyone in the underworld of the drug culture in the metro area heard of his disappearance. Everyone had their own idea of what happened to Larry and despite their willingness to share their views, no one knew for sure.

Some speculated Larry took his short-term drug profits and ran. They gave Larry far too much credit for intelligence. Greed drove Larry's decisions.

Others figured Larry used his head to stop a bullet or some similar stupid, but fatal action. That view recognized how The Boss took care of any competition that didn't know when to back down. He hadn't became The Boss by making idle threats.

Some of the younger kids on the street had heard the stories but discounted them as legend building. The older men in the trade not only knew the names of people who had disappeared, they had been personal friends with some of them. In their opinion, Larry's fate was a fait accompli.

Roger faced a conundrum. Should he let these diverse rumours continue to circulate or should he set the record straight? A few minor holdouts still sold drugs without giving Roger his cut. Mostly, they confined themselves to one corner of one city block and serviced a few regular junkies, long-term customers.

They didn't shop around for more business. They had no visions of expanding their operations. Their take would hardly qualify as pocket change for Roger. Many had paid their way through college dealing drugs and still maintained a minor customer base carried over from the old days.

In the past, Roger ignored these two-bit operators. Now, his goal demanded he re-establish himself as cock-of-the-walk. He couldn't tolerate any competition. What he really needed to do was find the son-of-a-bitch who stole his bag of money. The example he would make of that cocksucker would send shivers through every wannabe hood throughout the city. Until that happened, he had to continue his current course of action.

Revelations about the whereabouts of Larry Scarborough's body would snap these independents in line in a hurry. No one wanted to die for pocket change. They would trade the needs of their drug-dependent friends for their own safety in the wink of an eye if they thought a serious threat to their own lives existed. The discovery of Larry Scarborough's body would meet the criteria of a serious threat.

The downside of having Larry discovered would be increased police activity. Everything had to have a downside, Roger thought. He believed the police had written Larry off as dead. To them, Larry would be just another drug scumbag who had found his maker. No big deal. As long as no body came to the forefront, the authorities could ignore Larry.

They could tell his mother the search continued, but so far nothing had come to light. All that would change once a body rolled into view. The police would have no choice other than to actively investigate the death. The media would be looking for daily updates, would want to know the details of the investigation, would want to see results.

Roger felt no threat from an investigation. He had clean hands, well almost clean. He had made one phone call once he sprang himself free of police surveillance, a phone call that would never be traced. He had opted not to hire Mark and Louie for this job, although they would have taken on the task with no hesitation and done it as well as anyone else.

He wanted distance between himself and the triggerman. A call from a payphone in Halifax to a payphone in Montreal arranged the takeout. The recipient of that call hired the killer or killers. Roger didn't know who or how many, although stories said there were two. He didn't know their names; they didn't know his. These degrees of separation protected everyone. No one could plea bargain the other's freedom away.

Without being present at the time, Roger knew what took place. The two men—at least Roger FedExed enough cash to cover two return air tickets—flew in to the Stanfield International Airport, stole a car from the long-term parking lot and drove into the city. With an address supplied by Roger, they showed up at the stash house where Larry held his drugs and money.

Roger had heard several versions about how it all went down. Although the details varied in minor points, the general thrust remained consistent.

Two men splintered the cheap door with one solid kick. Larry lacked the experience to have heavy-duty deadbolts installed with reinforced frames. Once inside, one thug pointed a gun at Larry's head while the other aimed a Mac-10 at everyone else in the room.

Larry's gang held no heroes. The others sat on their hands and said nothing while the two men frog-marched Larry out the door, never to be seen again. No one called the police. No one offered any assistance. Definitely no one followed the trio to see which way they were going. The entire seizure, in and out, took less than a minute.

The rest of the story came to Roger from Montreal. On the way back to the airport, the car pulled off onto a side road at Exit 5 on Highway 102. Larry apparently offered his kidnappers more money than they could imagine. Roger had no idea where those funds would come from. Larry pleaded for his sorry, crime-infested life and vowed to give up any activities competing with The Boss and to get out of town forever. These men had no idea what boss Larry referred to and didn't really care.

One of the imports drew his pistol. Pop, pop. He put two bullets into Lawrence Scarborough's head.

Roger could only imagine the rest of that scene. The sound would have echoed throughout the forest but no one would be around to hear it. Cars zooming by on the nearby highway at 120 kilometres per hour moved too fast for the noise to register on the driver's consciousness.

The second shot only provided insurance. The first bullet had accomplished its intended task. The killers scraped back a layer of humus just off the path, deep enough for the body to be almost level with the surface. Laid Larry in it, face up, hands folded across his chest, eyes closed, looking peaceful. The removed leaves were sprinkled back over the body and they were finished.

They had stashed Larry out of sight for a while but discovery would not take too long. Proper burials were not in their job description.

From there, they whisked back to the airport in the stolen car. As luck would have it, another car occupied the parking space they had recently vacated, but they found one in the next row. They left the new parking ticket on the dash. The returning vacationer might or might not notice the different spot. He would notice his parking bill came to considerably less than anticipated, but you could be sure he wouldn't complain to the attendant about that. At most, he would regret not having brought back another bottle of duty-free booze with the money left over from his trip. The car and crime would never be married together.

Thus, Roger's current dilemma. The decomposing body demanded some sort of attention. Should he let the body be discovered on its own, which would happen soon? Tip off someone about the body, which allowed Roger to control the timing? Or properly dispose of it, delaying the discovery for years, if not forever?

This added one more worry he had to deal with in his hectic schedule. With Mark and Louie in jail, he needed some people to do the street work for him. Someone had to distribute the drugs and collect the money, all the money. No one held back on Mark and Louie. Although Roger claimed to be back in charge, a few still tested his control over the entire city. They held back a little of the revenue for themselves. Roger knew who they were. He would deal with them later.

For now, he had to decide about Larry. It could no longer be put off or the decision would be made for him. No decision became, in itself, a decision.

At the moment, Roger had more police problems than he wanted to deal with. Even though he couldn't be tied to the murder, the authorities would try their best to pin it on him. They would intensify their efforts to track him down. As a result, hiding the body seemed the most logical choice.

The big question in Roger's mind now: Who could he trust?

It was true, the yellow pages contained a number of ads for people whose business advertised the disposition of the dead. They tended to want death certificates, however, and would question two bullet holes in the side of the head. Funeral homes were out.

Roger needed someone who wouldn't be repulsed by a slightly ripe, dead body, for whom discretion was a way of life and who would be willing to leave the country immediately after getting rid of the body, at least for a little while. Roger knew only one person who fit the job description. Big Willie. Where are you, Willie, when I need you the most?

Willie already knew where the other bodies were buried. One more wouldn't make any difference. The challenge was to find him, persuade him to come home and do the deed. Unlike so many others, money wouldn't work with Willie.

His tastes were simple, he wasn't a spendthrift. No flashy rings reflected from his hands, no $3,000 dollar suits covered his body, and no expensive alligator shoes anchored his shadow to the sidewalk. While others snorted their generous profits up their noses, reinvesting in the company so to speak, Willie squirrelled his money away in mutual funds and money markets.

Wherever he ended up, the source of his next meal didn't concern him. At times, Roger envied this talent. Now, he wished he had more leverage over Willie. He would have to rely on friendship, if he could locate Willie at all. What were friends for if not to use?

The last postcard arrived from the Carolinas shortly after Willie disappeared. Willie didn't want Roger to worry about him. Roger knew Willie owned real estate across the country and in the States. He pondered the choices his friend would have and thought back to his descriptions of each property. Not the physical descriptions, the emotional descriptions. Roger decided Largo, Florida, would be a good starting place. Willie rented out a house down there. Had he become a landlord in residence? Roger hoped so.

# ≈30≈

"HI, REMEMBER ME?"

John didn't have to remember. Eric had reminded him several times about the interview. John had been awaiting the arrival of this person with not a little trepidation and now she stood before him dressed in a dark business suit with white blouse, plunging at the neckline, skirt at mid-thigh.

"I'm Rhonda Dubinkski from the Herald. This is my photographer, Edward Collinchuck." She indicated the man holding the large camera standing behind her. His dress was more casual, slacks and a sweater with a collared shirt showing in the V-neck. "We have an appointment," she added.

"Of course I remember you," John said, shaking her hand. "You did that excellent article for the craft show. I've received several favourable comments about your work."

His attention turned to the photographer.

Collinchuck reached out to shake John's hand. "Call me Ted," he said. He had the firm grip of a man used to handling heavy cameras in awkward positions. John recognized the name from the caption under various pictures he had seen in the daily paper. He also recalled that Ted had won various Atlantic Journalism

Awards for his work. Unlike the unknown photographer who had accompanied Rhonda the last time, this was the A team. The newspaper was taking this assignment seriously. Just what John needed, extra pressure.

"Hi, Ted." John shook the outstretched hand.

He swung the door open all the way and stood back. "I have to admit I'm a little nervous about all this attention. I have a few things set up in the studio and a piece ready to start from scratch. It will only be a simple bowl. I'm sure you don't want to spend all day here." He let his natural smile come through and she responded to it.

"Just relax," she said. "We don't bite. Your work fascinated me the other day when I was here. I'll spend as much time as it takes to get the full story. I saw you at the craft show over the weekend, but you were too busy to disturb. I watched the lady who raved on about her husband's burial urn. Money can't buy that kind of endorsement. You'll have to fill me in on the details."

Colour filled John's face. He recalled getting emotional in Mrs. Collins' presence. Now he discovered others were watching.

Rhonda continued: "Her reaction to your work must have made you feel good. She seemed so pleased. It must make the job much more worthwhile when you have satisfied customers like her come up to you in public to praise your work."

John had never thought of it in those words before, but Mrs. Collins had made him feel good about himself. The feeling vanished forever with his tea-leaf reading by Madam Ruth. If only he had stuck to his own end of the exhibition hall and tended to his own business.

"Mrs. Collins is a special kind of lady. She has a way of taking over a situation." He laughed as he thought back to the way the old lady had so freely told the crowd about talking to her dead husband and his new home. John envied her free spirit. He relaxed a little more.

He led the duo into his studio where Eric had set up what he considered were John's most photogenic works. John believed he had better pieces and Eric agreed with him. But, Eric pointed out, some of the products had to be seen in real life, to be held, to be touched, to be appreciated. Others would look good in two dimensions on a newspaper page. He aimed for the best visual effect. "Trust me," were his final words. At Marla's urging, John went with Eric's instincts.

Ted started snapping pictures as soon as he entered the room. Contorting his body into pretzel-like shapes to capture the exact angle for the shot. Shooting from above, from below, up close, back a ways, individually and in groups, he photographed the entire collection.

"This is great stuff," he said. "Stands up well for the camera. The contrasts and colours will look good in the paper." Once again, John was forced to admit to himself, Eric had come through.

Rhonda nodded in agreement. Having Ted assigned to the story would ensure the visual effect would be stunning. Writing an equally captivating story would challenge her creative talents.

"Your work is beautiful," she said, "but let's see the artistic process in action. Can you work and talk at the same time?"

John looked thoughtful. Artistic process? He never thought of his turning in those terms.

"I don't know," he said. "I always work alone. I've been told I do talk to myself a lot so I guess we'll have to give it a try." He forced a weak smile.

They left the studio and entered the workshop. Marla had swept the floor clear of any shavings from previous jobs, every tool hung properly in its place, and selected pieces of raw product were displayed along one wall. Everyone worked to make this interview a success.

"This is where it all happens," John said. His comfort level rose in the safe confines of this room. In here, he felt the master of his domain.

"If we have lots of time, then maybe I will start with a pair of candlesticks." He took control of the interview. He picked up a piece of maple about fourteen inches long and an inch and a half square.

"It's your show," Rhonda assured him. Ted moved in and snapped a few pictures of the stick of wood.

And so the day went. There were two six-inch candlesticks lurking in the piece of maple. John found a plate in a piece of yellow birch and he made a ring stand with a cover that came off to reveal a secret hiding place for more rings. The last item he gave to Rhonda over her protests that she couldn't accept gifts. John insisted the piece claimed to be hers. It spoke to him. He could both talk to and listen to the wood.

Ted documented every step of the process on film and Rhonda scribbled copious notes. Explanations came easily to John as he got involved in his work. He discovered he could talk and turn at the same time. It was as easy as walking and chewing gum. The morning whizzed by in a flash.

As things wound down, the two men stepped out of Rhonda's hearing range while she perused her notes.

Ted admired his newly acquired plate. He had watched as the object released itself from a piece of spalted maple. Black lines flowed through it like contour lines on a map. Ted was proud to own it.

"I could have told you it wasn't a bowl when you started," he said.

John laughed. In the short span of the morning, the two had developed a rapport that went beyond photographer-subject.

"It almost was, but not quite. You should have warned me. It would have saved a lot of time if I had cut it in two to start with. There would have been a lot less shavings to deal with and you could have had a pair of plates."

"I'm glad I didn't," Ted said. "It gave me a chance to see the creative process in action. I could barely discern when it turned from a bowl to a low-sided dish to a plate. Rhonda didn't even realize you screwed up. She thought you planned on a plate right from the start."

John reached out and took the dish. "That's the way it goes sometimes. Spalted wood cracks easily. There are times you should be giving your full concentration to what you are doing and not talking at the same time.

"It's like life. You never know from one minute to the next what is going to develop. Sometimes you have to keep your mouth shut. If you don't, you have to be prepared for the consequences, adapt to what happens and move on."

"That's deep," Ted said. "I thought it was just a plate." He smiled.

"Yeah, that too." He handed the plate back to Ted. "Sometimes it is just a plate." His smile showed he took no offence from Ted's remark. Ted had intended none.

The studio door swung open and Marla walked in with a foil-covered tray.

"I brought lunch," she said. She folded back the foil to reveal an assortment of sandwiches. "Coffee's in the car."

John retrieved two insulated serving urns. One held coffee, the other tea.

Rhonda joined them and said to Marla: "Your husband has such talent. You must be proud of him."

"Oh yeah, I'm proud, really proud." She laughed. "I never thought him setting out on his own would be so much work for me, though. Have a sandwich."

Ted bit in to a ham and tomato sandwich, wiped the mayonnaise from the corner of his mouth and said: "Isn't this the area where the drug money disappeared a while back? I took some pictures in the woods of the searchers and then of the typical suburban neighbourhood. I'm sure it was around here."

"This is the place," John said. "I've got the money stashed in my basement." Everyone shared the joke.

The whole interview process had been cathartic for John. Talking freely about his newly found vocation allowed him to expel any fears he may have had about his resolution to leave his old life behind. Rhonda's penetrating questions forced him to confront, explain and understand the entire decision-making process. Doing this with a stranger allowed him to speak more freely than he ever had with Marla or even Nathan.

He felt more relaxed than he had in days, months even, in fact, ever since the day he had stashed the red and blue hockey bag under the steps in his basement. The time had come to take care of that item. He didn't need it anyway.

# ≈31≈

JOHN, MARLA, Nathan and Eric sat around the table at Ming Sou Garden Restaurant. Chinese figurines hung from the velvet-covered walls. Bright red rice-paper pagoda lamps hung from the ceiling and provided the dim lighting. Deep maroon leather covered the seats in the booth. Everything reeked money. Eric was paying. The drink orders had been placed and now everyone studied the menu deciding what they wanted to eat.

"Are we ordering individually or are we going to order bulk dishes and share them around?" Marla asked. Her gaze circled the table taking in all three men, demanding an answer. None came. "Hello, everybody. That was a question."

All three reacted as if someone had flipped a switch with variations of the same answer.

"Doesn't matter to me," Nathan said.

"Either way," Eric responded.

"You decide," John said.

"OK, I will," Marla fumed. Men, sometimes they were so useless. "We will get two kinds of rice, one with meat, one with vegetables, a chow mein, sweet and sour chicken and a beef and broccoli." She looked around the table. "Any objections?"

Eric looked at John and Nathan. None of them believed the matter presented any option of additional discussion. They remained silent.

"Good," Marla said. She signalled the waitress. A young lady clad in a tight, red silk wrap appeared and deftly took the order. She looked at the others to see if they had anything to add, accepted their silence, smiled brightly and whisked off to the kitchen. Almost immediately she returned with their drink order.

Eric took a sip of his whisky, cleared his throat to get everyone's attention and said: "It's crunch time folks. We have to decide if we are in the wood turning-business or if we're just playing around with a fun type hobby."

Eric had arranged this get-together. His voice carried a heavy degree of seriousness.

"We'd damn well better be serious," John said. "I've quit my day job."

Marla studied Eric. Eric knew John had resigned so the question must carry some overtones not immediately obvious. "I thought things were going quite well," she said. "Sales are good. Your contingency fund is untouched." She looked at John and Nathan before returning her gaze to Eric. "Everyone seems dedicated and is making the required effort. You're not losing interest, are you?" Her voice contained a challenge. Her eyes sparked.

Eric leaned back in his chair as if physically threatened. "No. No, not at all," he said. He leaned forward again. "In fact, I'm prepared to take us to the next level. But if I do, we all have to be prepared to work."

Now it was John's turn to become defensive. "What next level?" he asked. "I've been putting in my hours every day, a lot more hours than I ever put in at my office job. You've found a way to add hours to the week so I can work even longer?" He forced a smile. "I knew if anyone could do that, it would be you."

As chief wood turner in a wood-turning business, he figured he contributed more than his share; not that he objected. He looked forward to going to this newfound job everyday. Marla, in fact, had to limit his hours or he would never be out of the workshop.

Eric took a bigger shot of his drink. The intensity of the others had caught him off guard. He had never questioned their dedication.

"No, the next level is guaranteed sales. Right now, John, you just make stuff on a whim, so to speak. Whatever you make, I try to sell. Honestly, your work is so good that it almost sells itself. We practically cleared our stockpile at the Exhibition sale." This brought smiles all around. Eric continued: "But, if you don't produce something, no one notices because there is no quota system."

John slammed his whisky and ice down on the table, slopping a little onto the covering, two ice cubes escaping and skittering across the floor. "You want to put me on a quota system? This is supposed to be art I'm producing. I'm not an assembly line worker." Other heads in the restaurant turned towards them.

Marla placed a calming hand on John's arm and squeezed. Nathan wiped up the spilled drink with his white, linen napkin.

"Guaranteed sales?" Marla asked. "How guaranteed?"

"Ten funeral urns a week, every week. The full-meal deal. Everyone's involved. We need the bases on them with the clocks. A variety of brass plaques with different sayings plus the option of custom-made plaques. That's two a day, five days a week." He paused to let all that sink in before continuing.

"That's the minimum amount we would have to produce. Make them as artistic as you want. There are no restrictions on the design. If these move well, there could be more. The rest of the time, you're free to make anything you want. Are we ready to move to the next level?" It was more of a battle cry than a question.

Silence followed. Each person weighed the personal ramifications of their required commitment. Each person had a different level of involvement in the finished product, but all would be called upon to work on a regular basis. This would be a team effort.

Marla spoke first. "How good is the money? This commitment has to be worthwhile." She tried to sound practical, but the excitement in her voice rang through. Eric counted her as a yes.

"Good question," he said. "It's very good." He paused to let that sink in. "Having said that, a rider is attached. Anything not up to the standard of the demonstration unit will be returned and replaced. That means not only are we going to be producing ten a week, all ten are going to be up to our top standards."

John waved that objection away with a brush of his hand through the air.

"That's not a problem. I wouldn't let something inferior leave the shop anyway."

Eric smiled. Two yeses.

"But," John continued, "ten a week, I don't know. As long as we have these pre-turned ones that Nathan found, I can do it. To start from scratch, ten might be too many."

Now Nathan stepped into the discussion. "Any new ones are going to have to be pre-turned anyway," he said. "In those numbers, green wood is our only option to maximize our profits. We have enough seasoned wood on hand to go for a little over a year. I could start rough turning next year's supply now and John could perform his magic next year."

Eric had his unanimous support. He raised his glass. "Of course, there will be things to overcome, but let's drink to success."

"Success," the others said and took a bonding drink.

At that point, the waitress and a helper arrived with the trays of food. The steaming rice filled two large metal bowls. The remaining three dishes crowded the table with an arresting variety of fragrances and colours. Each person drew from the closest container and passed it on. Soon all four plates were filled to overflowing with an appetizing variety of food.

The serving dishes still looked untouched. Martha signalled the waitress again. "Could we get all this to go?" Her arm swept across the table.

"No problem," the girls said. This was the accepted procedure in this place of business. Everyone ordered more than they could eat.

Quiet ensued for a few minutes while everyone satisfied their initial hunger, intensified by the quality of the food on their plates. Finally, John broke the silence.

"No offence, Nath, but you're talking a lot of hours on your feet. If I'm turning out ten a week, so are you, and you have to do the bases as well."

Nathan cut a chicken ball in half, dunked it into the red sweet-and-sour sauce and popped it into his mouth. "I think I can handle it, young fella," he said. He chewed thoughtfully for a few seconds, then shrugged. "If not, the option is always there to hire someone else. Let's wait and see."

Eric stirred the chow mein around on his plate. He looked at John and seemed to hesitate. "Maybe it's time to start searching out other turners, anyway," he said, his voice low. He waited for John's objection.

John washed down a bite of broccoli with a drink of water. "I know a couple who do quality work that I could live with," he said. "If this takes off, we could bring them in, at least on consignment. Most turners are pretty independent."

Not taking on the challenge never occurred to anybody. Now they had to work out the steps required to make it happen. One by one problems were raised, discussed and overcome. The unit became a little tighter with the challenge. Eric was surprised, but pleased with John's new attitude. Somehow, he had changed, and for the better.

"I have one more question," Marla said after the dishes were cleared from the table and after-dinner drinks were served along with the fortune cookies. "Where are we selling this many urns?"

Eric beamed. His turn to brag had come. "New York City," he said. "I told you my contacts are far-reaching."

"Good old U.S.A." Marla swirled the wine in her glass and looked pensive before continuing. "In that case, I have an additional rider to include in the contract."

"Oh?" Eric was proud of the deal he had worked out. "What's that?"

"We want to be paid in Canadian funds."

"Canadian funds?" Confusion showed on Eric's face. "Why?"

Marla pointed at him with her drink glass. "Our economy is going to outperform theirs. The value of the Canadian dollar is going to go up." She downed the drink. "We are not going to take the loss. If they balk at that, ask them if they have no faith in their own economy. Tell them we are willing to bet on ours, surely they should be willing to bet on their own."

Eric didn't reply right away. "Canadian dollars? That may work," he finally said. "But they are businessmen first and American nationalists second; they might not want to take the chance on their own government's handling of the economy. From what I've seen, I sure as hell wouldn't. The glory days of Bill Clinton are long gone."

"Neither do we," said Marla. "Canadian funds converted to whatever they offered in current U.S. dollars." It was not open to discussion.

John sat quietly with his own thoughts racing through his mind. With this contract, his new company would be a success for some time to come. Hard work would be involved but that didn't concern him. Something else did. The bag of money sitting under his steps back home could become an albatross around his neck if it was discovered. He must get it into the hands of the police, somehow.

To date, the money remained virtually untouched. It served as a cushion to give him a soft landing if something went wrong with this new life he was carving out for himself. He was doing something he enjoyed. Marla had blossomed with the founding of the company. She had thrown herself into it heart and soul, and she didn't even know there was a cushion to fall back on.

Decision time. The money would go back. A slow smile spread across his face. How sweet it would be to catch the bad guys at the same time, he thought. He knew they still actively searched for it. The supposed Jehovah Witness who showed up at his door every week couldn't be any more obvious in his intentions. John would work on this. It had to be done right.

As he came out of his reverie, all the others stared at him.

"What?" he said.

"You look like the cat that ate the canary," Marla said. "What's that silly, little smirk all about?"

John smiled. "No, this smile is about the canary who catches the cat." He didn't elaborate.

# ≈32≈

DETECTIVES KATE Irving and Joe Davis leaned against their unmarked police car parked beside Highway 102. Overhead black clouds threatened to dump rain on them at any moment. Kate looked up at the sky. "Does it always rain out here at the airport?"

"It seems like it," Joe answered. "I think they looked for the wettest, foggiest part of the province to build it. The weatherman says it's going to clear later this afternoon."

A marked SUV pulled up and parked behind them. K9 Unit covered half the front door above the police logo. The dog master crawled out and walked up to the two detectives. They shook hands and turned their attention to a rutted, side road used a few years back for hauling out cord after cord of pulp wood from the forest. Now it sat idle and mostly unused. The road backed on an industrial park, but a buffer of trees kept the buildings out of sight. A short distance in it turned and ran parallel to the main road.

"This is the place?" Constable David Ferguson, the dog master, asked.

Kate nodded her agreement and motioned towards the left-hand side of the road with her head. "Somewhere in that area is the best we can figure. We stayed out here so as not to contaminate the area with our scents. The killers were most likely the last people in the area. The road looks pretty overgrown with weeds. I don't know if forensics can find vehicle tracks or not."

"Yeah," Joe added, "sometimes after these all-night shifts we smell like a dead body." He laughed. The other two did not. "Lighten up, fellows. We're looking for a dead drug dealer. One of the bad guys. Don't pretend you care about him. Think of all the misery he has brought to so many other people. His days of inflicting this damage are over. He will never do it again. Good riddance."

Joe didn't fake any remorse over this fellow human being's death. He spent his life cleaning up the messes caused by their type. The guy distributed misery when he was alive. Dying didn't turn him into a saint. Joe frowned on hypocrisy.

"That's true," Kate said, "but who is going to bring his mother her cigarettes?" She recalled the line from the missing person's report. "Even he wasn't all bad. He loved his mother."

She forced a smile. She couldn't argue with Joe on this. The loss of the person they sought caused no drain on society, quite the contrary in fact. Openly crossing The Boss should earn him a Darwin Award.

"How do we know he's out there?" Ferguson asked. He still hadn't taken the dog from his car. He wanted a few more details before he started the search. So far, no one had told him anything.

Why was the person dead? Was it accidental, homicide, self-inflicted or natural causes? What were the chances of live people still being out there carrying guns ready to shoot anyone who came into the area? Little things like that which could affect his search pattern.

Kate and Joe exchanged glances. How much information could they reveal without compromising the operation? "We've got a suspect under observation on another matter," Kate explained. "In the process, we monitored a cellphone call suggesting we would find the remains of Larry Scarborough, a wannabe drug lord, in this area. He's been dead since last Saturday as near as we can figure. We believe the killers deviated from their rush to the airport long enough to dump Larry somewhere out here in the bushes. There shouldn't be any problems. They're long gone."

Joe watched the cars zooming by on the way out of the city. Hopefully passers-by assumed he had been pulled over by the police SUV and not that they witnessed a secret meeting between two branches of the police department.

"We want to quietly find the body, do our investigation and keep it all on the Q.T. ," Joe added. "We have reason to believe someone else is coming to do a better job of hiding the body. We want to find it first without disturbing the scene, confirm the identity, and lie in wait for this guy."

Ferguson nodded his understanding "If someone left a corpse lying around for a week, I can probably find it without the dog. It should be pretty ripe by now."

"Yeah, we figured that, too," Kate said. "We don't know how well it is hidden and we don't want to mess up the crime scene too badly. The chances of finding the actual killers are slim but you never know when something might come up in a later case. We want to document as much as we can without causing much fuss for now. We want to avoid the media. Can you find him?"

Kate issued the last challenge more to get the dog master moving than to express any doubt in his ability. The cops were on a tight time schedule if all of their plans were to play out as planned. Each phase of the plan operated on a need-to-know basis, and the dog master only needed to find the body. After that, his part in the game was over. Get moving, Kate urged in her mind.

Ferguson grunted as if the question deserved no answer. Finding a week-old body would be child's play for his dog. In this quiet rural setting, it would literally be a walk in the park. He opened the back hatch of his vehicle. A big, black and brown German shepherd sat on the flat surface. His fur had a high gloss shine from constant grooming. The brown eyes expressed an excitement suggesting his anxiousness to get to work. The dog agreed with the detectives. "Let's get this show on the road." There was no actual movement, but you could feel the pent-up tension in the dog's muscles. Ferguson pointed to the ground.

"Out, Bosco."

The big dog sprang from the wagon and sat beside his master, the dog's eyes on the cop's eyes, waiting for further instructions, almost straining on an invisible leash.

"Search." Ferguson issued the command. Bosco shot down the road, nose in the air, going from one side to the other seeking a smell that was beyond human capability to detect. His speed suggested he had already picked up the scent. Now, he simply had to pinpoint the exact location. The three human cops struggled to keep up as best they could. Bosco had taken over command of the operation.

Three hundred yards down the road, three football fields from the main road between Halifax and Truro where thousands of cars passed daily, the dog abruptly stopped, came back a few steps and and sat down. His fellow lawmen caught up, slightly out of breath.

"He has detected a cadaver," the dog master explained.

"No shit," Joe said. The crisp fresh air now had an overlay of an odour that could only be one thing. Decomposing flesh. The smell was all too familiar to Joe.

Ferguson scowled at him. His own nose agreed with Joe's. "It's close by." His attention returned to Bosco. He snapped a leash to his collar. "Search."

This time, nose to the ground and more slowly, the dog left the path and sniffed a few feet into the woods and stopped. He started to dig at a pile of leaves. Ferguson yanked the leash, and Bosco sat down again, giving his handler a "take it easy" look.

Ferguson reached down and affectionately ruffled the dog's fur. "Good job, boy. Good job." He looked at the detectives. "There's your corpse." Evident pride filled his voice. He had promised quick results and Bosco came through with flying colours.

A small mound of leaves piled in the telltale shape of a shallow grave marked the current whereabouts of Larry Scarborough. The setting was tranquil, masking the violence that had so recently taken place at or near this spot. A canopy of hardwood trees offered constant shade. It no longer took the sensitive nose of a dog to locate the body; all three could do the job themselves.

Kate reached into her pocket and came out with a photograph.

"Let's make sure we have the right DB," she said. "In this area you never know for sure. I've been out here before playing this same game with the same results." She slipped a pair of blue nitrile gloves onto her hands. She brushed a few leaves away from what she hoped would be the head end of the body. She wanted as little disruption as possible.

"Oh Christ." She fought back an urge to vomit. She had guessed correctly. Larry appeared to be sleeping, except for the two black holes in his forehead and the hundreds of tiny, white maggots crawling over his exposed flesh. She held up the picture.

"Close enough," she said and looked at the others for confirmation.

Joe shuddered and then nodded. "Cover him up again."

He turned to Ferguson. "Good job. We expected nothing less when we called for you." He gave the handler a pat on the back. "Can I congratulate your partner or would that be unwise?"

"Let's just say I would prefer you don't. I'll let him know what a good job he did for you." Ferguson knelt beside the dog and ruffled his thick fur again. "The detectives thank you for doing such a good job, fellow." He rubbed him under his chin. Bosco looked at Joe and gave one short, crisp bark. *"You're welcome."*

Kate laughed. "Smart dog. Can he find the brass for us?" Kate referred to the empty bullet casings. Finding the casings would let the cops know if the killing happened in this spot, what kind of weapon killed Scarborough and would also assist in the unlikely possibility of matching any gun found in the future. Although Kate wanted the area left as undisturbed as possible for when the forensic team came out, and it was up to forensics to find the casings, her curiosity trumped procedure. It came with being a cop.

The three stepped back out of the area. Ferguson commanded the dog: "Bosco, find the bullets."

Bosco sniffed the air for a few seconds, then lowered his head to the ground and walked ten feet from the scene of the body. Again he sat down.

"Here you go," Ferguson said. He stuck a pencil in the open end of one of the casings, noting its exact location, and held it up. "Twenty-two calibre," he said. "No overkill. Just a straightforward execution. Kicked out to the right. I'd say they buried him almost where he landed when they shot him." He replaced the casing where he found it. The experts would re-create the scene.

This satisfied Kate. They located the correct body. They verified the crime scene location. They could probably say with reasonable certainty that a professional hit man pulled the trigger. She placed a call to Sergeant Mcdonald and reported their findings.

Capturing the person coming to claim the body would be their next task. The initial part of the information derived from monitoring Roger Johnson's cellphone, proved accurate.

Everything had come together so quickly that morning. Kate and Joe were dragged from their beds early at the urgent request of Inspector Holland. The fact they had worked until three a.m. impressed no one.

A hurried meeting took place in Inspector Holland's office. Present besides the two detectives were Jim Mcdonald, Inspector Holland and a young cop who turned out to be a technical wizard. The latter presented details of the vital, overheard message to those present.

Cellphone call messages circulate freely in the ether waiting for anyone with the right equipment to intercept them. Roger's calls had been monitored constantly since the detectives reacquired touch with him. The throwaway phone prevented the calls from being traced to Roger but they were available to overhear and tape. The police did both. Roger would become acquainted with this aspect of the technology when he went to court.

All the calls in Roger's vicinity had been intercepted, analyzed and rejected until the technicians singled out Roger's messages. Once they accomplished that feat, they concentrated only on Roger's frequency. They captured and recorded every one of his calls.

"This opportunity cannot be passed up," Jim said while the technician packed up his gear. "Not only will we nail Ettinger in the act of being an accessory to murder, with luck we may find the location of lots of other missing people. The conversation Ettinger and Johnson had leads me to believe there is a burial ground out there filled with people who got in their way. This is our chance to find it."

Jim had played and replayed the message several times before this meeting.

"You want to use the remains of Lawrence Scarborough as bait. I don't know." Inspector Holland shook his head. He visualized the media storm he would have to contend with when this came to light. Did the ends justify the means? He believed this was seldom true.

"There are a lot of parents out there still waiting for information about their missing sons," Jim said. He played the empathy card. "This will give them closure. The sons may have been criminals but the parents are the ones suffering. They are innocent victims in most cases."

Inspector Holland nibbled at a breakfast bagel and sipped his coffee. The local Tim Horton's had been called into service to provide a quick breakfast for those present. He appeared to be considering Jim's argument.

"We can put a lot of open cases to rest," Jim offered. At the inspector level, statistics were an important consideration. Open cases didn't look good. Jim played the administrative card. He would play any card needed to get a favourable decision.

Holland set down his coffee. "This has to remain as quiet as possible. The first leak and it's over," the inspector said. "No one not taking part in the action knows what we are doing and even then, these people involved only know their own part."

*Great*, Kate thought. *Finally a break on our side.* She had been surprised that a man supposedly as smart as Roger Johnson had made such an amateur mistake.

Roger had contacted Big Willie by phone to return from Florida, carry out this one gruesome task of getting rid of Larry Scarborough's body and then return to his sunny hideaway. Willie reluctantly agreed to the job, but only after a great deal of discussion.

At first, Roger tried to persuade Willie to return and resume business where he had left off as number two man in the operation. Roger firmly had things back in control. Life was good again. Business boomed.

That avenue quickly proved to be a dead end. Willie had absolutely no interest in even considering returning. He threatened to hang up.

Roger rapidly grasped that Willie seriously intended to terminate the call. He changed course and instigated Plan B, a severely watered-down version of his Plan A. Willie would come in, clean up the Larry Scarborough mess and catch the next plane back to Florida. No meetings. No pressure to stay. A huge chunk of change in his bank account.

Even that took a great deal of persuasion on Roger's part.

"I don't need your fucking money," Willie had stormed into the phone. "You stupidly tied all your money up in real estate. I kept most of mine fluid." There was an obvious note of pride in his voice.

Roger knew Willie only partially told the truth. He knew about Willie's real-estate investments. That's how he tracked him down.

As a last resort, Roger drew on their long-time friendship. "You're the only one in the world I can trust to do this," Roger begged. "If anyone else could have handled it, I wouldn't have called you. You're the best man; you know that. Without your help, I'm sunk." Willie bought into the bullshit.

Kate checked her watch. The digital readout said eleven o'clock. The flight from Florida arrived at seven that night, giving Kate and Joe eight hours to fill.

Suddenly rain started falling from the sky. The overhead clouds held up long enough for them to find their body. It would shower the stench from them as they returned to their vehicles. They started to trot back up the road. Bosco's tail wagged like a flag in the wind. He thought the slow running indicated play time had arrived. He bounded joyously up and down the roadway.

After Kate thanked Ferguson and Bosco and hustled them on their way, she and Joe hunkered down to await the arrival of the forensic team. The drumming of the rain on the car's roof lessened. With luck it would end before the other team arrived. The plan required them to investigate, gather evidence, take photographs and then leave everything as they found it. They would return to the scene to do a more thorough job after Willie had done his part of the scenario.

When Willie arrived from Florida, gathered the body, and set out to stash it somewhere, Joe and Kate would follow him to wherever he led them. The arrest would then take place with Willie having his hand in the cookie jar, so to speak. A Canadian Forces helicopter stood by a few kilometres up the road at the airport waiting to be brought into service.

Corporal Scott Bowen, a local RCMP patrol officer very familiar with the area, had been seconded to do a fly along. He and Jim Mcdonald had a history of working together. Bowen could provide local knowledge to the team not available from the maps.

Securing a locator device on whatever vehicle Willie chose to carry out this gruesome task loomed as the most difficult part of the operation. Neither Kate nor Joe would even entertain the idea of losing track of him. Kate's face still burned with embarrassment if anyone dared to mention the Roger Johnson incident within her earshot

Losing Willie Ettinger and cargo would be a reason to never show her face at police headquarters again. She may as well get on the plane with Big Willie and fly down to Florida with him. Her services would never be required in Nova Scotia again. Only Kate and perhaps Joe harboured these feelings. Everyone else had moved on.

However, Kate intended to take no chances. Hiding a locator would be risky, but she considered it a necessity. Willie's work would take place under the cover of darkness and if the current weather continued, visibility might be further reduced. All of the techno toys available would be at their beck and call for this adventure. She intended to make use of them all.

# ≈33≈

DETECTIVE-SERGEANT Jim Mcdonald gazed out the fourth-floor window of the Law Courts Building. The morning fog rolling over the city restricted his view of the harbour. Already, the sister city of Dartmouth, across the narrow harbour, had disappeared from view. Soon the sight of the water itself would be gone. Only the peaks of the towers of the harbour bridges would be seen sticking out above the fog bank. Above them low, black clouds threatened to dump buckets of rain on the twin cities.

The policeman shared a cafeteria table with a distinguished member of the legal profession, Judge Harold Kendrall. Jim had been summoned when he had been meeting with the inspector. The judge wanted to discuss a recent case. Jim had little choice but to attend the meeting.

A story circulated throughout the judicial professions about a suspect who had failed to show up in court at a scheduled hearing in Judge Kendrall's courtroom. The judge, it was said, issued a bench warrant for the man's arrest. When the man finally appeared in court, Kendrall demanded that he account for his absence.

"I had a previous engagement," was the defendant's reply.

Judge Kendrall reportedly leaned over from his perch behind his desk and glared down at the man. He waved his forefinger in his face. "Sir, only an appointment with the Almighty pre-empts an appointment in my court," he declared. "Your presence here today indicates that was not the case. Failure to show up for any more hearings in this matter will earn you jail time for contempt of my court."

The man heeded the warning and met his burden of attendance for the rest of the trial.

Now it was Jim's turn to heed that warning.

"How's our drug case coming along?" Many people would feel this wording inappropriate coming from a judge. Kendrall did not. He saw his task as getting and keeping criminals off the street. He was involved. He viewed himself as part of the solution, not part of the problem.

Jim squirmed in his seat. He still felt uncomfortable talking to a judge like this. However, the ends justified the means.

"The evidence is piling up," he said. "We'll soon be looking for warrants. It's just a matter of time. We'll hit them harder and deeper than ever before."

Holland had stressed the importance of secrecy in their current operation. Jim concluded that informing a judge of what might be considered entrapment was in no one's best interest. He would allow events to play out in the natural course of time.

The judge nodded his head. His face maintained the sombre courtroom look. "I look forward to it. Something has come up that I'd like your views on. The lawyers in the DUI case against Roger Johnson have presented me with a brief suggesting the breathalyzer machine had not been calibrated on the day in question." The judge slid a copy of the report across the table to Jim.

Jim looked up. "How would they get this information?"

The judge shook his head. "They're entitled to it, but that's not important. The thing is they have it. Or, for that matter, it might simply be a wild guess to consume our time and resources. If we don't follow through with an investigation, their client may walk. What are your feelings on how we should proceed?"

Jim expressed surprise. He didn't think he was being invited here to offer a legal opinion, especially to a judge. "It's no big deal. Johnson faces a fine and loss of his licence for a few months. That's going to be the least of his problems. Right now we have him under secret surveillance. We're gathering lots of incriminating evidence. Let's let him think he's won this one."

Homicide detectives often scoffed at the lesser crimes. If Jim could nail him for murder, nothing else mattered much.

The judge nodded in agreement. "OK, we can do that. However, there is a spin-off result. We charged Leroy Leblanc at the same time. We put him in jail for his repeated DUI failures. If Mr. Johnson gets a bye, ipso facto, so does Mr. Leblanc.

"I can inform Mr. Johnson's lawyers that my calendar is crowded at the moment and I will take this matter under advisement and make a ruling at some unnamed date in the future. That's like a win for them. Delaying the outcome is to their advantage."

He rubbed his chin in a thoughtful manner. Jim had seen this move in court on many occasions before the judge made a ruling. "Mr. Leblanc would stay in jail until that time arrives. That presents a problem. There will be repercussions if it turns out that we've incarcerated someone deemed to be an innocent man for some length of time."

Jim nodded. "We sure don't need any more bad publicity on that front. Everyone still remembers Donald Marshall as if it happened yesterday. You've outlined one response. What is the other?"

The judge smiled. He had reached his intended destination. "I answer them this morning. Tell them they are right and Mr. Leblanc is a free man again."

Jim stroked his chin, mirroring the judge's move. "Which way do you think we should go?"

The judge sipped his coffee. "Unless you want to do an investigation on whether the machine had been properly calibrated and prove them wrong, Mr. Leblanc will walk at some point. In a month or so, he'll be back on the street anyway with time served."

Jim shook his head. "I don't have the manpower to spare right now for a DUI investigation."

"Exactly. Let's pick our battles judiciously. They win the little ones. We win the big ones." A rare smile filled the judge's face.

Jim picked up on the judge's intention. "Of course. If Leroy is in jail when we make our big sweep, we may miss him. Now that would be a crime."

Jim's cellphone vibrated in his pocket. He glanced down at the screen. He recognized Kate Irving's number. He hesitated briefly before holding up his phone.

"I should take this," he said.

"Go for it," Judge Kendrall said. "We're not in court."

Jim flipped open his phone as the rain started pounding on the outside of the window, leaving long silvery streaks from where it ran down the glass in the reflected glare from the overhead lights.

"Raining there yet?" he asked. He paused. "Get ready. It will be soon."

# ≈34≈

"ANOTHER HITCH. That Johnson guy has more luck than any three men," Detective-Sergeant Jim Mcdonald found himself explaining to Inspector Holland again. "It appears the breathalyzer machine we used when we arrested him hadn't been calibrated that day. The constable thinks he remembers doing it but nothing stands out in his mind to make this day any different from the rest so he's not prepared to swear under oath. There is always the possibility he overlooked it and the computer checklist hasn't got it noted."

The inspector stood behind his desk looking out the window at the traffic on Bayers Road. Rain swept in waves along the roadway. The wipers on the cars could hardly keep up with the deluge coming from the skies.

He turned and faced the detective. "Picking him up on that DUI was more a form of harassment than an attempt to keep him off the street. It won't greatly alter our plans."

"That could be, but it gets worse. Leroy Leblanc was charged on the basis of the readings from the same machine. They want to overturn his guilty plea claiming he should never have been arrested in the first place.

"Judge Kendrall is trying to give us all the benefit of the doubt but our agreement with him is that no one walks away free if they are guilty. It works both ways. If the machine's calibration was really off, well, he thinks there are bigger battles to fight. Leroy only blew point zero eight. That's cutting it pretty fine. Pushing this could come back to haunt us down the road when more serious offences are being questioned. As of this morning, Leroy Leblanc is once again a free man, another criminal turned loose on society."

The inspector shrugged his shoulders. "That's not such a big deal, either. Our plan is to disrupt their daily operations. We've done that for a couple of weeks. Bringing Leblanc back into a changed landscape might work in our favour. He's two weeks out of sync with who the bit-part players are and who has moved up in the operation. If we get him scrambling around stepping on toes, upsetting the apple cart again, we achieve our goals. Besides that, when we make our next big raid, he'll be part of it and we'll put him away for a lot longer than a simple DUI does."

"Ah, the old glass half-full theory," Jim said. "Judge Kendrall said the same thing. The whole gang will be reunited. Willie Ettinger is winging his way back from his southern retreat, giving up his life as a recluse, at least temporarily. Events we discussed at this morning's meeting are unfolding as we hoped. There should be some good news on that front before the day is out."

"Everything is being kept quiet, as I requested?"

"Everything. You and I are the only ones in this building who know what is going down. There will be no leaks, accidental or otherwise. The forensic team finished their investigation about an hour ago. They understand the need for secrecy. They'll keep their findings quiet for the time being."

Jim hesitated as if reluctant to bring up a new concern. "Occasionally someone misses the calibration check on their breathalyzer equipment, but I wonder. Might someone have changed the form? We have people infiltrating their organization, do you suppose they have done the same to us?"

The inspector walked across his office and closed the door.

"Our vetting protocols are a little more intense than theirs, but anything is possible."

"Would this information be on the computer or on a paper form?"

"Both, I would think. The paperless office is a myth. Someone with specialized training might be involved in that case. I'll have it checked out."

Jim was thoughtful for a moment. "Johnson has been in power for a little over four years now. Do you think he planted someone or did he inherit a plant? If it's the former, then our search field is narrowed by that time line." Jim examined all the possibilities in his mind and searched for the best approach.

"No offence, Sergeant, but you have other things to think about. This matter will be passed over to another department. I don't think we have an infiltrator, but no stone will be left unturned."

Jim gave the inspector a hard stare. The interpretation of that statement suggested no one was above suspicion, including his own crew. He started to argue the point but reconsidered. The inspector was right, he did have other things to worry about. Let internal affairs ask the unpopular questions. His staff was clean. Jim had nothing to worry about. He looked up at the big clock ticking off the minutes on the wall of the inspector's office. It was 5:30 p.m.

"I'm going to head out to the airport," he said. "Big Willie will be arriving soon and we can't have too many eyes on him. Since we are keeping the team in the know small, I'm an active part of it. What are you doing later this evening?" He gave the inspector a broad smile.

"I could still do it. I was staking out villains when you were still in diapers," the inspector said. He returned the smile. He could but he wouldn't. Jim went out the door and headed for the parking lot and his car.

The storm had blown over. He could still see the dark storm clouds to the east dumping lots and lots of rain on the eastern shore. For now the sky overhead displayed only a few high clouds. The sun cast long shadows across the parking lot.

He pulled out and drove along Bayers Road for a few blocks and then veered onto Veterans' Memorial Drive, the main provincial highway heading towards the airport. He still had lots of time to get there before Willie Ettinger landed. He wanted to pick a good watching spot and settle in.

The seat beside him held a casual shirt and jeans to replace the suit he had worn all day. Unknown events filled the night ahead making choice of clothing a challenge. That said, he didn't know Larry Scarborough well enough to feel compelled to wear a shirt and tie to his funeral. Besides, if this adventure led him over hill and dale on foot, he didn't want a piece of cloth clinched tightly around his neck. Changing at the airport would raise fewer questions than doing it in his office. There was no suspected security leak at the airport.

# ≈35≈

BIG WILLIE Ettinger had been sitting beside his pool in his large recliner enjoying the heat of the early morning sun when his phone rang. Slowly he opened his eyes and glanced over at the display to see who was calling him in his Florida hideaway. The phone came with the house; he expected no calls except for wrong numbers and telemarketers. He had no ambition to talk to either. A huge palm tree on the edge of his yard shaded him but the phone was out in the bright sunlight, making the readout impossible to read. Willie tried to ignore the ringing but it wasn't in his nature. Too bad for Willie.

He reached out without looking and knocked the receiver off the cradle.

"Damn," he said, sat forward and swung his feet onto the pool deck, leaned down and picked up the phone. He had a closer look at the display and saw that it read 'Long Distance Unknown Name.' He should have hung it back up and went back to doing nothing. Instead he brought it to his ear.

"Hello," he said, sounding distant and uninviting.

"Big Willie? Is that you? Man, you're a hard guy to get hold of," a jovial voice said.

"Whatdayawant?" Willie said. The voice on the line sent chills down his spine despite the heat in the air. He had no desire to talk to anyone from his past, especially this voice from his past. Hanging up crossed his mind.

"We miss you, man. When are you coming back?"

"Roger, you're supposed to be a smart person. Why do you think I walked out with no goodbyes, no forwarding address and no contact since? It's over, man. I've retired. I've hung up my colours. I'm never coming back, ever."

"Willie, don't talk foolish. I've shaken the cops. I'm back in control but I'll be honest. I need you, man. You're an indispensable part of the team. Get the hell home where you belong."

Willie said nothing. Several thoughts rumbled through his mind. His life as a youth working on a farm in Raymond's River in rural Nova Scotia, his move to the city and introduction to the underworld culture, his climb up that ladder to sit on the rung next to the top, all played on the screen behind his eyes. He thought of all the violence he had seen, been part of and ordered. He compared this to his life now, free from worry, free from any outside demands from others, especially free from Roger Johnson with his incessant desire to acquire more and more and more. Willie didn't need any more. The silence stretched out.

"Willie? Willie? Are you still there, man?" Agitation filled Roger's voice. Begging was foreign to him but he needed Big Willie, needed him badly.

"I'm hanging up, Roger. I'm not interested in any of that shit anymore."

"No, don't hang up. You don't have to make up your mind about coming back right away," Roger said, "but listen, I've got a job that has to be done now, today if possible."

There it was. The thing Willie had escaped from. Things needing to be done right now, drop everything and do this, NOW. His life no longer moved to the beat of that drum. He had disengaged from responding to someone else's insistent requirements.

"No," he said more emphatically than he had planned. His inner calm began to crumble.

"What do you mean, no? You didn't even ask what the job is."

"It doesn't matter, Roger. The answer is no." Willie was firm. He no longer cared.

The conversation continued in this vein for several more minutes. Willie threatened to break the connection when the demands became orders. Roger backed off and changed his tactics again. In the end, he appealed to Willie's ego. Of all the things from his former life he had shaken off when he crossed the international border, his ego clung to him for the trip south. That exaggerated sense of self-importance that everyone either secretly or overtly felt. Roger knew how to manipulate the feeling to the fullest.

"You're the only one who can do this, Willie. The job is too important to trust anyone else. If you don't do it, no one else can and the organization will go down the tubes." There it was. Something that no one in the world except Willie could do. How could he turn Roger down on this? Spending his days lying around in the warm sun had worn away at Willie's ego. He thought about it but refused to capitulate.

"And that will stop my company pension cheques?" Willie asked, sarcasm dripping from his voice. "Get Leroy, he can do it. Just spell out the steps one by one. He's not as stupid as you think."

"You're wrong. Leroy's in jail. Came up before a bad judge in a DUI."

"A DUI? Jesus man, don't you have any lawyers on your payroll anymore? No one goes to jail for driving under the influence."

"Leroy does. Sometimes I think he wouldn't be able to pour water from a boot if the instructions were written on the heel. I need you back here. The whole ball of yarn is coming unravelled without you. You gotta come back, man."

"No, Roger. I've given up that life. I'm not that person anymore."

Roger detected a weakening in Willie's resolve. The refusal wasn't as firm. Roger moved in for the kill. "Come back and get rid of Scarborough for me. I don't trust anyone else to do that. Then go back to wherever you're hiding. I won't call you again, but you think about coming back. Give it some serious thought, that's all I ask."

The ego hadn't quite been vanquished by the quiet, southern life. Willie could understand Roger's reluctance to trust anyone else. Willie had performed this task before.

When the previous version of The Boss mysteriously disappeared, never to be seen again, all hell had broken loose on the streets. Three lieutenants, each of whom believed they divinely had the right to rule the organization, showed no willingness to compromise. Logic told them to divide the territory, form a triad while the power struggle worked itself out, and keep the organization running smoothly.

Instead, beatings and killings became routine. Willie became Roger Johnson's undertaker.

Both of the opposing would-be crime mavens disappeared. The police considered them adult missing persons. No serious investigation ever took place. No remains ever surfaced.

It appeared to Willie, from talking to Roger, that history now repeated itself. The last time this senseless violence happened, Willie was poor and struggling to keep his life together. This time, he had no money worries and all his needs were taken care of. Perhaps he owed Roger this much.

"One thing. We don't meet. We don't talk. I'll find myself a new place to live when I come back, maybe in another state. You don't track me down and you never call me again."

"That's no way for friends to talk, buddy, but I promise, I'll wait for you to contact me. You don't have to give up your current digs. Can you get a flight out today? One leaves Tampa around three o'clock your time and gets here around seven local time. I'll book you a seat with an open-ended return ticket. You don't have to make any snap decisions about going back right away. One more thing, pal. I'll make this worth your while. Don't worry about money."

"I don't need your fucking money." Willie's voice erupted over the phone line. "You're the one who tied all your money up in real estate and now can't get at it, not me."

Roger immediately realized the error of his ways. "No offence, Willie. You know me. I always pay my own way. Pay what I owe. Just come up, take care of the job and be back home in Florida before the sun rises tomorrow. Do it your way. Everything's cool."

As quickly as Willie blew up, he calmed down. "Damn right, I'll do it my way. You stay our of it. I'll send you a bill, later."

"Right. Send me a bill." Roger laughed. They were friends again.

They continued talking over the open airwaves filling in the name the ticket would be booked in, where the body was hidden and all the other details necessary to play funeral director. In a van outside the hotel in Halifax, every word was recorded.

So when Big Willie came down the escalator to the international arrival's area of the Stanfield International Airport, Kate Irving served as the custom agent welcoming him to Canada. The other agents manipulated their passengers to make sure Willie ended up in Kate's line. Willie had only one small, blue canvas sports bag as carry-on luggage. Kate checked his documentation. It was flawless. This explained why Willie was able to slip away from their surveillance without a trace the previous month.

Kate opened the overnight bag and examined the contents while a fellow agent talked to Willie. Willie gave no thought to the extra attention. He expected it when dealing with authorities. Inside he was still a criminal.

"Must be hot in Florida this time of the year," the true agent said.

Willie smiled. "Canadians might think so. I love it. In fact, it's a little cold up here. I don't know how ya all can stand it here in the winter." He played the native Floridian to the hilt, even throwing in a little southern drawl. With his involvement in this by-play, he failed to notice the small tracking device Kate slipped into the lining of the bag. This was the backup monitor. Kate glanced across the cavernous room in the airport reception area to a man at the far wall. He gave Kate a thumbs-up. The signal worked. Kate acknowledged the sign and zipped up the bag.

"Sorry for the inconvenience, sir. Enjoy your stay in Canada," she said.

Meanwhile, Joe Davis battled the bugs on the opposite side of the road from the late Larry Scarborough. The principal tracking unit was snuggled safely in his pocket waiting to be snapped to the underside of Willie's car, truck or whatever. A magnet would hold it firmly in place. Joe figured he could attach it while the criminal was digging up the body. That task should hold Willie's full attention for a few moments. Even to a lowlife like Willie, this could not be considered a routine assignment.

Joe touched the button on his watch that caused the back light to shine. It was 7:48. Willie should be here soon. Joe had observed a plane coming over him at 6:55. The plane from Florida was right on time. He swatted at another mosquito whining around his head and watched the road. Not much longer, he told himself.

# ≈36≈

JOE DAVIS hugged the ground as tight as he could. The sound of the slosh of tires in the muddy tracks on the old, hauling road drifted up to him. The approaching vehicle had no lights on despite the fact that dusk hung heavily in the air. Full darkness lurked nearby. Joe lay in a small dip in the ground so as to be unseen from the roadway.

He wore the black uniform of the ERT team with all the white insignia removed. On his head, he substituted a black stocking cap for the helmet. Black paste covered his face. For now, he blended into the scenery like a shadow. Once darkness arrived, he would achieve invisibility.

He had cleared the path to the road of sticks, broken branches and anything else that might trip him or make a noise as he crawled across it. Fortunately, the wet leaves would cushion any walking sounds. He had chosen this spot carefully.

For his part, Willie Ettinger had his eyes focussed on the left-hand side of the road away from where Joe lay. He knew the object of his search should be hidden from sight, but sometimes you get lucky. This was not one of those times. After driving the three-tenths of a kilometre as prescribed by Roger Johnson, he stopped and got out. Somewhere close by rested the body of Larry Scarborough.

After almost a week of exposure to the elements, Willie's nose should be the principal organ used in the search. He sniffed the air and immediately expelled the breath.

"Jesus," he said under his breath. This first inhalation indicated he was in the right neighbourhood. Roger, as always, had given explicit instructions.

Willie took a small flashlight from his pocket and scoured the landscape. A mosquito bit him on the neck. He slapped and killed the annoying insect. A look at the red spot of blood on his hand told him the swing had been too late. *Great*, he thought, *I have to put up with these blood suckers as well*. Roger had painted an image of Larry as a money-hungry opportunist, a human blood sucker, someone who deserved to die.

A slight glint of metal reflected in the glare of Willie's flashlight. He started towards it and spotted a shell casing lying on the ground.

"Sloppy," he said to himself and reached down and snatched up the brass casing. He slipped it into his pocket to dispose of later.

"This has to be the right place," he said. Scarborough remained silent. Willie communicated with the dead or himself. It didn't matter which. He just wanted to wrap this up and get the hell out of here. He killed another mosquito.

His light swept a three hundred and sixty degree circle. Darkness had completely set in now. There was no giving up. Willie had to find Larry in this gruesome game of hide and seek. He spotted a second brass casing in the duff of leaves. The body should be close by somewhere to his left. Semi-automatics usually expended their spent shells to the right.

The beam of his light picked up a mound of leaves that was too neat to be natural. Two quick steps and he knelt down and prepared himself. The smell became so overpowering that he knew he had found his target without disturbing a single leaf. He brushed away a couple of scoops anyway and looked into the maggoty face of the late Larry Scarborough. He fought back a gag reflex and lurched back to his station wagon.

In the back, he found a neatly folded tarp provided by Roger Johnson. Roger arranged for one of his crew to steal the station wagon earlier in the day and equip it with everything Willie would need—tarps, picks, shovels—to cover any contingency. The man parked the car at the airport unlocked with the keys in the ashtray.

Stealing cars with keys, it turns out, is quite simple. Break in through the back door of someone's house. Take the keys from hook just inside the door, unlock the car and scoff at computer technology as you drive away.

When Willie arrived, a quick call to the bartender at the Foggy Night bar got him the required location and description of the vehicle. Roger avoided all contact with the car; Willie avoided talking to rental agents. He gave Roger full points for efficiency if nothing else.

Willie spread the plastic burial shroud out over the six-foot cavity in the wagon. Larry was too heavy to carry by himself, Willie figured. Throwing two hundred and fifty pounds plus of bug-infested dead weight over his shoulder and stumbling through the forest in the dark would be a fool's errand.

Instead, he would grab Larry's heels and drag him to the roadside and then muscle him into the back and wrap him up. With luck, all the maggots and any body fluids that would spill would remain in the forest and not find their way into his car. This was beyond optimistic, he knew. A smelly drive lay ahead for him.

As Willie headed back in to the bush to capture Larry Scarborough, Joe Davis stole from his location in the woods and, in a low crouch crept, up beside the car. Overhead a squirrel started an incessant chattering to warn Big Willie of what was taking place. Willie's mind concentrated on other things. The extra, natural forest sounds brought a smile to Joe's face. It would cover any unintended noise he might make.

He took the tracking device from his pocket and crawled under the car, making sure he found metal and not plastic to stick it to. This task completed, he slunk back into the woods again, being just as quiet on his return journey as he had on his initial trip. Planting the device didn't give him a licence to get careless. He burrowed down into his hiding place again and waited.

Meanwhile, Willie cursed his way back to the car, dragging Larry's body. Larry, it appeared, felt secure with his previous resting place. Although he had missed all his meals in the previous week, he had not missed many in the years before that. He easily weighed in at the two hundred and fifty pounds of dead weight that Willie had estimated.

When Roger had told him Larry came into town on his hog with plans to take over, Willie thought Roger referred to a motorcycle, not a travelling companion.

Every branch reached out and grabbed a piece of Larry's clothing and held on tight. This caused Willie to give an extra hard pull and caused him to tumble off balance when the offending obstruction released its grip. The higher branches insisted on slapping Willie across the face for having the audacity to desecrate Larry's burial grounds. The flies and mosquitoes multiplied exponentially in numbers when the body was exposed to the open air.

The Deep Woods Off provided by Roger had been washed away in the rivers of sweat running down Willie's back and chest. The perspiration pouring down his face became an open invitation to the bugs to come and feast on him. They accepted the offer with gusto.

*What the hell am I doing here?* Willie wondered. *I could be sitting in a bar, chatting up some young thing and enjoying a drink.* He filed away every bite, every scratch, every stumble in the depths of his mind. These would all be recalled if Roger Johnson ever had the audacity to solicit his services again, and the answer would be a resounding, go fuck yourself, no. In the meantime,

Willie struggled to breathe through his mouth while trying to get this task finished as fast as possible.

Across the road, Joe also had to put up with the biting insects. Listening to the struggles of Big Willie helped to ease the discomfort. To help him in the fight with the little Draculas, he had consumed several oranges during the afternoon. This built up an acidity in his system which repelled the mosquitoes, or so he believed. The information came from his mother so it must be true. All Joe knew for sure was it seemed to be working.

Meanwhile, two motorists appeared to be having car trouble out on the main highway. On one side of the road, Jim Mcdonald stood in front of the open engine bonnet of his big Ford. On the other and up a few hundred feet, Kate Irving's car, trunk up, sat on a jack while Kate knelt beside a fully inflated tire on the gutter side of the road. The jack had a quick release and the car could be dropped to the ground in less than five seconds. Passing motorists had the distressed pair in their view for less than a minute and took no notice of the fact that neither was making any progress at fixing their respective problems.

Several slowed down to offer Kate a hand. She waved them on. At any other time she would have appreciated this bit of chivalry. Not today.

The police were unsure of where the mobsters maintained their burial ground and had both directions covered. They too battled a few mosquitoes, but that was the cost of doing business outdoors in the early hours of dusk. A few drops of blood were worth the sacrifice for the expected returns on this adventure.

Both watched the turnoff for the approach of the green station wagon. One would immediately follow Willie; the other would whip up the side road, pick up Joe and catch up for the capture. Let's get this show on the road. All four participants shared this thought.

Back at the airport, a helicopter sat idling on the tarmac. Its pilot, Lieutenant Wyatt Samson, sat inside away from all biting bugs calmly sipping a cup of coffee and chatting with his travelling companion, RCMP Corporal Scott Bowen.

Scott was familiar with both Willie Ettinger and the area they might be flying over in the darkness. His task was to interpret and translate the hard data the machines collected.

A blinking red light on a GPS device flashed on the seat between them. The signal from Willie's carry-on luggage had been acquired. A blue signal would indicate Joe's success with his device under the car. They noticed when it came to life in counterpoint to the red flashing. They had their own little police car signalling in the darkness.

They used two devices in case Willie had brought no luggage at all. It would have been more of a challenge to plant something on his body and there was always the fear that he might not take any carry-on with him once he picked up the body.

Planting the device on the car should be an easy enough task for Joe. But this takedown was too important to take any chances.

The pilot had instructions to take off and track the second signal when it started moving. He had no idea who or what travelled in the car and didn't really care. Keep it in sight and relay the location back to following ground operatives were his instructions. As long as one of the devices worked, that would be a simple task to carry out. Otherwise he would have the challenge of a visual pursuit on a moonless night. That was where Scott entered the picture. Either way, he would be flying and flying trumped everything else.

Jim decided to use both cars and a chopper in case Willie decided to just dump the body someplace else and not bury it. It was important to have a car in the immediate vicinity to grab him if tried this manoeuvre. The copter could follow with ease but landing in a wooded area would present a challenge. All avenues were covered.

At long last Willie wrangled the body out of the woods and stood in front of his open hatchback. Roger had neglected to mention Larry's obesity problem. Getting him into the car would require Willie to get much more intimate with Larry and all his maggot friends than he ever would have in life. Success would necessitate Willie standing astride the body, reaching under Larry's arms, hugging him around the chest, staring him in the eyes and lifting. At least Larry had been out here long enough for rigor mortis to have passed.

Larry stood over the body reviewing that procedure in his mind. "Fuck this," Joe heard him say. "I don't give a shit who finds you." A car door opened and closed. The car engine sprang to life.

Joe waited. This scenario had not been in any of the planning. Should he grab Willie now or let him leave and have the other cops snatch him? Once Willie and the body became separated, it would become a battle of the lawyers in the courts. Right now, Joe had the two of them hand to hand so to speak. His hand crept down towards his nine-millimetre pistol strapped to his waist.

Then silence dominated the scene. Willie had shut down the car's engine. Was he having second thoughts? The car door opened and a string of expletives shattered the tranquillity of the forest. Joe could hear some heavy thumps. Willie's big boots hammered Larry's ribs, again and again.

"You stupid, fat, son of a bitch," Willie said and kicked Larry yet again. He took a few deep breaths and leaned on the open hatchway of the car. Again, Joe waited.

Willie leaned down and encircled Larry's bloated body and he heaved. Larry's ass landed on the bumper and started to slide towards the ground again.

"No you don't, you son of a fishmonger," Willie admonished him and leaned in to give another heave. Larry's head lolled forward and landed on Willie's shoulder, seeming to want to kiss him on the neck. A shudder passed through Willie's body.

This was too close, much too close. He had participated in the killing of a number of people, but he didn't dance with the corpse afterwards.

Again he exerted all his strength into a lift and slide. Larry rigid body landed in the back of the wagon on the unfurled tarpaulin with a swoosh. More body fluids exited the various orifices in the body. The previous unwelcome stench become overwhelming.

Willie backed out of the wagon, staggered to the opposite side of the road and retched. Joe hugged the ground even tighter, thankful he wore black clothing from the soles of his leather boots to the top of his head. He could barely discern Willie's outline in the darkness. Would Willie see him? Joe stopped breathing.

Willie's airplane meal hadn't been great, but he didn't want to deposit it here in this backwoods area of Nova Scotia. He took a handkerchief from his pocket and mopped the sweat from his face, soaking the piece of white material. He looked at it with disgust. In places it moved. The hanky contained more than sweat. He wretched again and threw the cloth into the ditch. He must wrap this body tightly if he was to survive the trip.

"Roger, you rotten pig-fucker," he exhaled, "you're going to pay for this, big time."

In the bushes, Joe heard this admonishment and suppressed a smile. Poor Willie. He would be even more upset when he found what awaited him at the end of this journey.

# ≈37≈

WALLY AND LEROY sat in The Bull and Bear sipping beer. Wally half listened to Leroy's tale of woe and half listened to the conversations going on in the room around him. He was working.

The Crime Stoppers TV spots broadcast this week talked about the missing money, which in turn brought the matter back to life in the bars again. Wally thought the actor driving the car looked a little on the dozy side, but it was better than someone who looked exactly like him. He wished Leroy would stop his whining and let him concentrate on the task at hand. He should tell him that.

"They'll never get me back in there again," Leroy was saying. "I'll shoot my way out first." He looked up at Wally. "Are you listening to me?"

"Yes, damn it, I'm listening," Wally said in a low hissing whisper. "Not because I want to. You're like a broken record going on and on and on about the same subject ever since we sat down. Give me a break here. I'm trying to pick up some leads on the missing money. Stop bitching and listen to what the people around us are saying. One of them might know something. It will get you back into the good graces of The Boss if we find it."

"I'm already in his good graces. He sprung me from jail, didn't he?"

Wally looked at him and considered telling him the truth. The Boss was protecting his driver's licence and couldn't care less about Leroy sitting in jail. Leroy being liberated was just a tag-along bit of luck. He would let his buddy continue his delusions.

"Right, he got you out of jail. He really cares about your welfare." If Leroy detected any sarcasm in Wally's voice, he said nothing. He preferred to believe the statement was true.

"Where is The Boss hiding out anyway? I've got to get in touch with him and get back to work. He didn't spring me so I could have a vacation. He must need me."

"Things have changed since you went inside," said Wally. "The Boss will contact us. We never, let me emphasize that, *never*, contact him. You just go about your business and when he wants you, he'll find you.

"Blow his cover and you'll be in deeper shit than you've ever been in your life, deeper than when you lost his money. He's free now and intends to stay that way. You should have seen the scheme we used to shake the cops off his tail. It was poetry in motion."

Wally described in detail the trip to Yarmouth. His part grew in importance with the telling. He gloated when he reached the part describing the impotent looks on the policemen's faces when he stepped from the car. Leroy was laughing out loud by the time the narrative finished.

"I wish I'd been there to see that," he said. "That would have been priceless. Those are the same cops we fooled when I dumped the money in the woods. What a bunch of jerks."

Wally became a more serious. "Watch your mouth." He looked around the room and lowered his voice. "We made them look like fools, there's no denying that. Now they are more anxious then ever to bring us in. It has given them a drive and determination we could live without. There's been a serious crackdown on the organization since it happened. Everybody who might know where

The Boss is hiding has been picked up and questioned. Mark and Louie are in jail."

"I know," said Leroy. "I've talked to them. They blame their arrest on The Boss. Claim he led the cops right to them. They have nothing good to say about him or his organization. The Boss hired them lawyers and they sent them packing. Let me assure you, no one inside is leaping to The Boss's defence in defiance of Mark and Louie."

"You included," said Wally. He had heard the tales out of school.

"Remember, at the time, his lawyers were too busy to come to my aid. I spent two long, miserable weeks inside. Sure I agreed with Mark and Louie."

"Now they're running TV spots on Crime Stoppers about us. Trying to get whoever found the money to turn it in, or if their neighbours know about it, squeal on their friends. We're up the creek without a paddle if that happens. We have to hope that greed wins out over the need to do the right thing."

"With what's in that bag, we don't have to worry about that. Nobody will feel any urge to be a hero with that much money involved. Hell, I'd keep it myself if I knew where it was."

Wally blanched. "Don't even say that man, not even in jest. Words like that will get you killed. You heard about Larry Scarborough?"

"That pinhead. No, what happened to him?"

"Thought it was time for him to be movin' on up. Hasn't been seen in about a week. Smart money says he's dead. His so-called gang have disappeared as well. They were seen packing suitcases and getting on trains, planes and buses, anything to get out of town. Seems they don't want to be even seen talking to the cops. Things have taken a nasty turn while you were inside. Half a dozen or so are in the hospital. Louie and Mark tell you about them? It was their handiwork"

Leroy sat quietly staring into his beer, watching the lines of golden bubbles make their way from the bottom of the glass to the top and turn into foam. He remembered the last time there was a power struggle of this proportion. He had been fortunate. He had grabbed the right coattail, but he had friends who chose the wrong horse. Some were dead, some disappeared. The lucky ones were just disfigured or walked with a permanent limp. *Not another pissing contest*, he thought. *Maybe he was better off in the can.*

Without Big Willie around to contain him, Roger Johnson's butchery knew no limits. He would do anything to maintain his power. During the last power war, the area became divided into three camps—peninsular Halifax; Dartmouth and suburbs; and Bedford, Sackville and the rest of the county. One hood ruled all three camps with an iron fist and maintained a heavy-handed peace among the three participants. When he mysteriously disappeared, all hell broke loose. Roger Johnson ruled the Bedford-Sackville area, but craved total power.

While the other two leaders made dire threats about what they would do to anyone who impinged on their territory and made overtures about taking over the entire operation, Roger arranged to have them removed from their own fiefdoms.

The others were hesitant to act. They had no idea of the whereabouts of their leader. They kept expecting him to return and clamp down on any and all offenders. Roger had no such fears. He made no threats. He simply acted.

At the time, Roger had no powerful connections in Upper Canada. He did his own wet work. Leroy took part in both takedowns and would never forget the swiftness and brutality of the events. He shuddered just thinking about it. Both opponents fell for the same ploy. Big Willie arranged meetings with both gangsters at separate times but on the same night. He promised to give up Roger Johnson to them in return for Willie getting to rule the western suburbs. He would only work out details in person.

Willie arrived at the meeting with one hundred thousand dollars cash in small bills and flopped it down on the table. The stack of money looked impressive. While the two body guards forgot their protective roles and counted the loot, Roger and Leroy sprang from an adjoining room, automatic pistols in hand. Roger did all the shooting. First, a blaze of body shots and then, whether they were needed or not, a series of head shots that spread grey matter all over the floor and walls. Despite being both armed and forewarned, Willie's gun had not cleared its holster before the killing had ended. He could only stand and watch, his own sidearm unfired, as Roger put the final bullets in the heads of his victims. Roger's eyes sparkled with intensity as he finished off the gruesome task.

Willie reholstered his weapon. The thundering in their ears rendered them all deaf for a few moments. The smell of cordite permeated the room and assaulted their nostrils. Willie gestured to Leroy to take care of loading the bodies into the back of the truck stolen for the occasion. He gathered up the seed money and left for his next appointment.

The second meeting played out as a duplicate of the first. If anything, the practice from the first made the second go smoother. Roger's gun barked as aggressively as it had in the first shooting. Overkill failed to describe the destruction.

The one slight difference in the second operation saw Big Willie helping load the victims' bodies into the back of the truck. He drove off, alone, six bodies lying stacked like cord wood under a loose tarp in the back.

Young Leroy, pumped with adrenalin, asked about the whereabouts of the body-dumping site. "Mind your own fucking business," Roger told him in no uncertain terms.

Before leaving, Willie assigned Leroy with the task of chauffeuring an overstimulated Roger Johnson who sat clutching the still hot Mac 10 pistol in his hands between his legs.

Leroy, duly reprimanded from his first question, remained silent for the entire trip back towards Halifax. Roger constantly chattered about what he had just done, reliving each shot with a relish that brought fear to the young Leroy Leblanc.

"Pop, pop, pop," Roger barked as he described each killing.

Thank goodness Leroy served on the same side with the shooter. At the centre of the Macdonald Bridge, Leroy brought the car to a halt. He summoned his courage.

"I think we should dump that," he said, speaking for the first time since being told to mind his own business. He pointed at the murder weapon.

Roger looked down at the gun in hands. Leroy felt his reluctance to give it up. Then, without a word, Roger opened the car door, stepped to the edge of the sidewalk and heaved the gun into the waters of the Halifax Harbour one hundred and seventy-seven feet below. From that height, you could hardly see the splash let alone hear it, but in his mind's ear, Leroy could hear the sizzle as the hot barrel sunk below the cold murky water. His mind's eye watched it waft back and forth as it made its way to the bottom of the second deepest harbour in the world. The water was deep enough for every ocean-going container ship in the world to pass through fully loaded. Tides flushed the harbour every six hours. The gun disappeared from existence.

Roger stood staring for several seconds until the lights of another vehicle approached where they were parked. He turned, jumped back into the car, slammed the door and now, he too was silent for the rest of the trip to their house in Sackville. The two never discussed the event again.

The police had all kinds of witnesses who heard the shooting, but nobody saw anything. Forensic evidence existed in abundance: DNA, bullet casings, angles of flight, blood and spatter patterns. Diligent searching failed to find the bodies which donated all this evidence. The gun which contributed all this evidence remained elusive. Officers passed over the resting place of the weapon of destruction every day but it would never be held in the hands of a man again, would never take another life.

Word on the street about the killings spread like wildfire and the lurid details expanded with each telling until the Valentine's Day massacre from Chicago of 1929 became a kids' picnic by comparison. Roger established himself as the new gang leader with no further opposition. Until now, that is.

Leroy unconsciously wiped his hands on the legs of his jeans. He could still feel the blood and God knows what else on his hands from wrestling the bodies out of the room, into the alley to a loading dock and onto the back of the truck. Of course, this was all in his mind, a too vivid memory. A memory he thought he had expunged from his brain. Now it was back, in full bloom. Without too much effort, he could still see Roger's pistol sitting on the bottom of Halifax Harbour right under the bridge.

He recalled one moment at the second house when he and Big Willie were manhandling one of the bodies out to the truck. This was the body of one of the followers, not the leader of the drug gang. It slipped from Leroy's blood-stained hands and fell to the floor. Willie said nothing but reached down and picked up the remains by the belt and hoisted it into the truck by himself. As he turned from the task, his eyes met Leroy's. Both men were thinking the same thing and read it in each other's eyes. If the other gang leader had made his move first, this would have been me. Now, it was all starting again, the beatings, the killings. Would he be as lucky this time?

"You can help me out while you're waiting to hear from The Boss." Wally brought Leroy out of his reverie. "Tomorrow we'll go door to door again, see if anyone remembers anything new now that they've seen it replayed on their TV sets."

"I don't think so," Leroy said. "That guy playing my part could be my twin brother. I should sue them for defamation of character. I show up on anyone's doorstep, they'll be calling the cops. I'll hang around the taverns and listen in to the conversations. There will be less scrutiny in those places."

Wally thought about this before agreeing. "You think that guy looks like you? In your dreams, buddy. He's much better looking than you ever were. But you're not the religious visitor on the doorstep type either. Pubs are more your speed. Remember, you're here to listen and not drink. And for God's sake, stay out of your car if you have too much beer. The cops weren't thrilled to see you walk and would jump at the chance to lock you up again."

"That's not going to happen," Leroy said. "I'm never going behind bars again. They can shoot me first." He patted his chest. "Guy from the lawyer's office got me a piece and stashed it in my car. As soon as they let me out, I was carrying, right under their stupid noses."

Wally shook his head. "Come on Leroy, don't do anything dumb and don't get yourself killed." Wally was a cerebral member of the gang and deplored violence in any form.

"Here's a cellphone. Stay in touch." Wally got up and walked out of the pub to seek another venue to listen in.

In a far corner a foursome of friends parted company, two leaving, two staying. It wasn't often they got to socialize while on surveillance duty.

"Was he talking about having a gun?" one cop asked the other.

"I'm not sure but we'll pass the information along as a possibility. No sense having someone get shot by this dirt bag."

# ≈38≈

DUSK HAD become a distant memory by the time Willie had finished securing the body of Larry Scarborough in the tarp. His original plan had called for him to be in and out in about ten minutes with enough daylight left to guide him. That idea had quickly gone to hell with Larry's lack of co-operation. The enveloping darkness only added to the time required to finish the task.

Willie checked his knot work. He pulled the ropes as tight as he could to reduce the smell to a bearable level. He had no concerns about cutting off Larry's circulation. Larry had done that to himself when he defied The Boss.

Willie slammed the rear hatch shut, opened the driver's door and jumped in. He started the car and simultaneously powered down both front windows. He looked back and watched the rear windows go down as far as they could. This guaranteed a continual supply of fresh, clean air as he drove.

Turning on this narrow road in the dark presented a problem, so Willie drove forward a few feet until he located a clear spot. Gently, he dropped the front wheels into the shallow ditch. The beams from the headlights lit up Detective Joe Davis as he lay hugging the ground and making himself one with the rock providing him shelter.

Willie's eyes were focused out the side window on the ground beside his front tire. He measured the distance between the bottom of his vehicle and the edge of the ditch on the uneven terrain. After going only about four feet into the underbrush, he stopped, reversed, and backed across the road before repeating the manoeuvre.

Again he lit up Joe. Again Joe willed himself into invisibility and went undetected.

One more cycle and Willie's car pointed out of the woods. He gunned the engine, creating a shower of mud from his spinning tires, leaving Joe behind, thanking his lucky stars.

In seconds, Willie sped beside the industrial park and back towards the Veterans' Memorial Highway. He chose the exit ramp taking him towards Truro and away from the city. He pushed the gas pedal to the floor and watched the speedometer needle climb to 130 kph before easing back. He didn't want to risk getting caught by the highway patrol but at the same time he wanted to end this ordeal as quickly as possible.

To his right, some poor slob had her car up on a jack and was in the process of changing the tire. It gave him a slight feeling of pleasure to see someone else having as bad, if not worse night as he. He had no thoughts of stopping to lend assistance. Under other circumstances he might have offered to help a damsel in distress, but tonight Willie had more pressing business..

Kate heard the helicopter lifting off from the nearby airport.

At the same time Joe's voice crackled in his ear. "He's on the move."

Joe triggered everyone into action. First he alerted the helicopter pilot and then made sure the chase cars were ready to start their pursuit.

He started running down the hauling road on foot towards the industrial park. He could cover the three hundred yards to the paved road in less than a minute if he didn't fall on his ass in the mud. He radioed the others to wait for him there if they got to the area first. Every minute counted at this point.

Out on the highway Irving received another message. This one was from Jim Macdonald. "That's him passing you now, Kate." From Jim's vantage point on the opposite side of the road, he had a better location to trace the path of the station wagon as it exited the forested area.

"10-4," Kate responded. She watched the vehicle go by before smacking the quick release on the jack and throwing it into her trunk.

The airport turnoff waited about three kilometres up the road. Kate was certain Willie would not turn off there. About five kilometres further down the road, the next exit turned towards Enfield or Oakfield. She might safely catch him by then but it would be better to rely on instructions from Lieutenant Sampson from his position safely above the traffic.

She flipped on the GPS tracking device on the seat beside her. Both cars were so equipped as well as the chopper. But at the speeds they would be travelling, it was easier to rely on the eyes of the pilot than to take her own off the road ahead.

This worry became academic as Willie continued past the next exit as well and continued deeper into the centre of the province. Within minutes, Kate had a visual on the long straight stretch of road ahead. She could see a set of tail lights in the passing lane speeding by everything on the road

As soon as the lights of the station wagon swung towards Truro, Sergeant Jim Mcdonald slammed his engine bonnet shut and dove in behind the wheel of his car. An "official vehicles only" turning point existed two kilometres down the road and he sped towards it. Gravel flew as he slid around the unpaved U-turn and headed back in the direction of the airport. Horns blared at him as he pulled onto the highway into the fast lane.

He flipped on his red and blue strobes situated in the rear windows and in the front grill. The horns stopped as the cars around him dropped down to the posted speed limit and were soon left behind. Jim slowed slightly as he raced up the ramp leading to the road into the industrial park where Joe waited for him.

He jumped into the passenger seat, strapped himself in and took a few deep breaths.

"So far, so good," he said as a welcome to his superior. "For one scary moment, I thought he was going to catch me. He chose my hiding spot as a turning area. It was dicey for a minute or two. Which way is he headed?"

"North towards Truro and making good time." Jim indicated the GPS unit on the seat between them. The small dot had moved slowly along the black line in the little screen of the electronic device. "Kate should be right behind him by now."

Joe picked up the unit and held it on his lap. "I think he will take the Milford exit and turn onto Route 14. He lived in the Raymond's River area when he was a kid." Joe had been doing his homework.

"His other option would be to take Exit 9 at Milford, but he would have to drive through Shubenacadie. Route 14 is less populated."

Joe was a technophile but he still believed in honest police work. Finding out as much as he could in advance prepared him for whatever twists and turns Willie might throw at them. Sure enough, the dot turned from the heavier black line to the lighter one and turned left.

"Turning west on Highway 14." The helicopter pilot's voice filled the car.

"Good call," Jim said. "Do you have a specific address?"

"No, his family owns a lot of land in the area. Willie, himself, owns about four separate parcels. Looks like he's preparing for life after crime. He's in for a disappointment when the state seizes it all as proceeds of criminal activity." The two cops shared a smile.

For her part, Kate Irving was still on the tail of the body-carrying station wagon. She hung back to be not quite in sight of him, relying on the helicopter to keep her informed. The speed had not dropped much on the twisty, windy provincial highway and Kate had to keep all her attention on her driving. Willie's obvious familiarity with these roads added to Kate's challenge. She just hoped no one pulled out of a driveway in front of her. Stopping was out of the question.

The pursuit continued for about twenty minutes, only slowing down for brief periods when another vehicle appeared on the road in front of them. Willie's first-hand knowledge of the roads got him quickly by; Kate relied on brief burst from her flashing red and blue lights to get by.

"Chase car one, slow down. The subject has pulled into a side road to your left." Pause. "You are coming up on it now." Kate could faintly hear the thrumming of the copter engine but she knew it was there. To anyone else it would be indiscernible. Wyatt must be flying quite high.

In the cabin of the helicopter, Wyatt took in the greenish glow from the night goggles he wore. Not only did he have the tracking device to assist him but infrared waves from the hot engines of the cars were visible to him, making both cars stand out. Cows lying in some of the pastures were also visible but to a lesser degree.

Corporal Bowen, also decked out with night-vision glasses, called out community names as they passed over them.

The second chase car remained a fair distance back but now started closing the gap. At the original speeds, it would never have caught up. The dot on the GPS indicated the subject's car floated in open space. This small road was not stored in the machine's memory.

"Can you see how far this road goes?" Kate asked the pilot.

"Sorry, it disappears into the trees," came back the answer. "The corporal advises there's a few farms up ahead and then it dissolves into a hauling road. Hang back and I'll keep you informed. You'll raise some concerns if you close up on him. He probably knows every car that comes in here."

"That's what I was thinking."

During the planning session, all the cops agreed this would be the trickiest part. At some point, Willie was going to be in an area where he expected to be alone. Any headlights would be spotted in the darkness from a considerable distance. This was where the helicopter entered the picture. But they still had to get close enough to make an arrest with the evidence in sight.

"Good news," Wyatt said. "He's reached an old farm house and is parking the car. I see the red signal moving while the blue one is sitting still. He must be taking his travel bag inside. Move in quickly and turn out your lights.

"Chase car two, you're still about five miles behind the action. There are no vehicles between you and the turnoff. Catch up."

"That's easy for him to say," Jim said to Joe. The implied message was to speed up. Jim was already driving faster than the road was constructed for in his opinion. Joe had a firm grip on the door arm rest with one hand and the tracking device with the other.

"Don't let him make you do anything foolish. Willie's not going anywhere. If he's reached his house, we have all night. Slow down." Joe may have been speaking out of turn to his sergeant, but his advice made good sense.

Jim slacked off on the gas petal. "You're right," he said. He picked up the microphone of his radio. "Hold back, Kate. We'll be there in about five minutes."

Kate had moved to the end of the driveway of the old farm house. She sat in the inky darkness of her car. No moon shone down to assist her, both a plus and a minus.

A yellow glow shone from one of the downstairs windows. They had hoped Willie would lead them directly to the other bodies, but without any lunar light, he might choose to wait until morning. It could be a long night.

"Chase car two, you are at the turnoff."

Jim slowed down and swung onto the side road. "What's your status, chase car one?" he asked Kate. The military pilot assisting them seemed to prefer coded language.

"I have the suspect's house in sight. He's inside. We are only about one kilometre from the main road. Proceed, but be prepared to turn your lights off if I give the command."

A shadow of a man appeared in the lighted window and stayed there. Kate figured Willie was standing at the kitchen sink washing his hands with the overhead light behind him. *Good*, she thought. *As long as he stands there, he can't see us. The window will act as a mirror with the light reflecting off it from behind.*

She glanced back in the direction he had come. A faint glow could be seen above the tree line moving up the road, getting closer by the second. Stay where you are, big boy, she mentally commanded. Willie failed to listen. Obeying the wishes of cops was not one of his strong points.

"Lights out, lights out," Kate whispered into her radio. The glow in the sky disappeared and at the same time a crack of light came from the house. Willie started to open the door, but for some reason stopped. Then the door opened all the way and a beam of light could be seen bobbing up and down with each step away from the house.

The light stopped moving and passed over the trees in the direction of the road. Kate could hear the faint sound of the engine of Jim's car in the silence of the countryside. The steady thrumming of the helicopter in the distance joined the symphony. Sounds carried a long way with no local background noises to cover them.

Willie then aimed his light into the sky which simply absorbed the rays a few feet up. Nevertheless, Kate's gaze went skyward as well. Suddenly, a sense of awe overwhelmed her. Thousands and thousands of yellow pinpoints of light covered the sky.

"Oh my god," she said. "I've been spending too much time in the bright lights of the city."

As far as the eye could see in every direction, right down to the horizon, were more stars than Kate ever remembered seeing at one time. She picked out the Big Dipper, Cassiopeia, Orion's Belt. Things she remembered from when when she was a kid.

High up in the darkness, the blinking lights from a passing jet caught her attention. Near the horizon, another set of flashing lights came into view. Off to her left she could see a third passing plane. Several feet behind the first set of lights, Kate could gradually hear the roar of a jet engine as the sound struggled unsuccessfully to catch up to its maker. This brought her back to the reality of why she was out here.

"Hold up for a minute," Kate whispered into her radio. Jim's car engine dropped out of the band.

Willie's light dropped from the sky and returned to ground level. A large barn slowly loomed into existence, red no doubt making it harder to see.

The beam of light disappeared through a door that had materialized and could be faintly seen at one of the dusty, dirty windows. It then disappeared. Kate assumed Willie had gone into the main part of the barn. A faint outline in the darkness exposed two big, wagon-sized doors without windows.

"Get your asses up here right now," Kate commanded into her radio. "I'm parked at the foot of the driveway. Don't run into me." She watched the glow behind her grow brighter. The barn stayed dark. Jim's black Ford eased up beside her. Jim cut the lights and the car disappeared in the gloom again.

All three cops disembarked from their vehicles and moved to the back of the cars. Time for a revised planning session to bring their strategy of attack up to date with the current circumstances.

"What's our status?" asked Jim. He struggled to perceive anything in the direction of the house, but could only detect the yellow glow from the kitchen window. His eyes still hadn't adjusted to the dark. That would come soon, he hoped.

"There's a barn to your right." Kate pointed. No one could see her finger but looked right anyway. "He went in there a couple of minutes ago. There's at least one man-sized door, a set of double doors and one window in the front." The others strained to see any of this.

As Kate finished her description, a roar of a diesel engine reverberated from the barn. It coughed a couple of times, then caught, running with a slight hitch threatening to quit at any moment. The double doors swung open, revealing two bright headlights shining across the field above them.

"Oh shit," said Kate. "I hope we're not too close."

"Unless he comes right at us, I think we're safe," the sergeant reassured her. The driveway ran downhill and they were parked at the bottom. The barn yard itself appeared quite level in the lights of the tractor, causing the beam to shine straight out into the night.

The engine revved up and the tractor slowly crawled out of the barn and headed towards the back of the station wagon.

"It looks like a late-night funeral," said Joe. "I wonder if the Reverend Willie will say any more prayers over the body. He certainly blessed it while getting it out of the woods."

"We'll let him lead us to the grave site and then we'll grab him," said the sergeant. "I don't want to spend forever looking for the other bodies. Hopefully they'll all be in the one spot."

Willie's eerie silhouette swung down from the tractor and opened the hatch in the back of the wagon. He had a rope in one hand with a hook attached to it. There would be no more intimate hugs. They had had their last dance. He hooked the rope between Larry's feet around the knot holding the tarp in place and then climbed back up onto the big red machine.

The tractor pulled away from the station wagon. The cops couldn't see what was happening but the thud of the body landing on the ground provided all the graphics they needed. This would not be a religious burial. Willie unhooked the rope, turned the machine around and scooped the body up into a bucket attached to the front of the unit and lifted the bucket high in the air so as not to impede his view. The tractor trundled off into the pasture behind the house.

"Helicopter One, what's your location?" Jim said into the microphone at the neck of his shirt.

"I'm standing by about ten kilometres away," came the reply from the pilot. "I no longer have a visual but the transponder indicates the subject is not moving. I should be too far away to be heard."

"You are," Jim confirmed. "What's the absolute fastest you could get here?"

"I didn't know you were looking for speed. I'd have brought the Griffin, but the Kiowa can boogie if it has to and it can hug the ground in the process."

Wyatt paused while he did some mental calculations. "Assuming you are at the same location as the subject, I could be there in three minutes, two and one-half if I really, really push it."

"When I give you the signal, really, really, really push it. There will be a tractor with a hot engine in the field. We're going in dark so we want you to light up the area as bright as day. Can you do that?"

"I can give you a sunburn, sergeant."

"That's what I want. Hold off on the light until you are right over the subject."

"Sergeant, Corporal Bowen here. My buddy at the controls and I have been discussing this while we were standing by. We can offer you a way to take the perp down without any gunfire if you're interested."

Although not officially in on what was going on, the two men in the copter didn't have to be rocket scientists to figure out that this was a late-night burial. All the elements were there. Scott and Wyatt had discussed Willie's life of crime and rise through the ranks. Scott knew other bodies were missing. He had spent time on the investigations without success.

Looking at the journey from a wooded location near the airport to an open field in the middle of nowhere with a tractor carrying some kind of cargo could mean a few possible scenarios. Scott's money was on a body disposal. Wyatt agreed.

"Always. Let's hear your plan," Jim said.

"It involves you guys playing ostrich for about ten seconds. First, we'll move closer. A kilometre will be safe if he's running a tractor. That'll put us about fifteen seconds out.

"At your command, we'll come roaring in from nowhere. We'll be dark, no lights. When we're right over the suspect Wyatt will flash his lights once. You guys bury your heads in the ground with your eyes closed as tight as you can. At that point, Ettinger will be looking up at us and we'll hit him with three million candle power for about ten seconds. It will blind him, the pilot guarantees it. He'll drop the light to an ordinary spot and you guys jump up and grab him. No shooting, no resistance. I can almost put that promise in writing."

"Good job, Scott. That's a plan any cop would love," the sergeant said. "We can always use someone with your talent in major crimes."

"Don't even go there, Sergeant. You know you're wasting your breath."

This was a standing battle between the two officers. Jim wanted Scott to join his department of detectives. Scott was more than happy in his present position, although he did enjoy working with the sergeant every once in a while.

"You're sure? You could be down here taking part in the action instead of sitting up there in the air as an observer."

A deep-throated laugh came across the airwaves. "Down there in that dark field? You have to be kidding. Who wants to trip over a prickly porcupine in the dark or step on a sleeping skunk? No thanks, pal. I'm happy up here in the sky looking down."

"What did he say?" Kate whispered loudly. "Are there animals roaming around this field with us? Porcupines? Skunks?" Her eyes swept the field around her.

"Don't listen to him," Jim said. "He's just jealous."

His voice turned serious.

"OK guys, let's follow that tractor. When he stops, we'll spread out, but stay in a row on this side of him. We don't want to be in each other's line of fire. If he wants to fight instead of surrender, I don't want any of us three to end up dead." He paused for a few seconds. "Everyone else is fair game."

The ground rules were laid. All three knew that the heads of the drug-dealing gangs didn't live by the same rules as everyone else. Larry Scarborough would testify to that. Without the slightest hesitation, Willie might try to shoot his way out. If that happened, your mind had to be in the right place before you got yourself into a kill or be killed situation. Waiting to make decisions at the time might get you dead. The fact that Willie couldn't see his attackers didn't guarantee he wouldn't be shooting wildly in all directions.

The three moved out across the open pasture, making good time. They felt no fear of being heard above the roar of the tractor. Occasional stumbles over humps of grass or ant hills protruding above the surface kept them on their toes, literally, but not enough to impede their passage as they closed the gap between themselves and Big Willie.

Kate stayed slightly behind the sergeant. He looked back at her tentative steps.

"What's wrong, Kate?" he asked in a low voice.

"Nothing," she answered, equally quiet.

In the dark he couldn't make out her facial features. "Are you still worried about skunks and porcupines?"

He could barely make out her white teeth in the glow from the tractor's lights. He knew she had smiled.

"Maybe, just a little."

Joe leaned in a little closer. "Don't worry about them, Kate. At this time of night, they're all lined up beside the road waiting to get run over."

The pitch of the tractor engine changed and the rumble got lower. This must be the burial ground. They had travelled about two hundred and fifty yards. They could faintly make out the tree line in the glow of the tractor's headlights. Willie had driven as far as conveniently possible from the farmhouse.

None of the officers were breathing hard, as the tractor's pace was just that of a good walk. About fifty feet from where Willie stopped, they spread out and crouched behind hummocks built by ants or slipped into a dip in the terrain. The tractor bucket tipped, dumping its cargo unceremoniously to the earth with another thud. Poor Larry, he was getting no respect.

Jim buried his head inside his jacket and whispered to the helicopter.

"OK, helicopter one. Let's put your plan into action."

"Good luck, Jim. Be safe," Scott said from the safety of the skies.

In seconds the wacka-wacka-wacka sound crackled through the still night air. A spot of blackness obscured part of the white band of stars making up the Milky Way. The image grew larger as it moved across the sky. Willie, who had just jumped down from the tractor, reached up for a shotgun lodged beneath the seat. This was intended to dissuade any skunks or other varmints who might take too much interest in his nocturnal actions and not to fight off people, especially airborne people. Willie could not believe anyone knew what he was up to, but as always was prepared to shoot first and ask questions later. He searched the night blackness, unsuccessfully. He was looking for some sort of glow in the sky. Then he saw it, right on top of him.

The helicopter lights flickered once. The three cops made like ostriches, eyes closed tight, palms tight against them, heads buried in the grass. Willie pointed the gun upwards and stared right at the noise over his head. Suddenly he was at centre field in Yankee Stadium, on stage at the Rose Bowl, the main attraction at Maple Leaf Gardens. A light, with so much intensity that he could actually feel the heat, lit up the night sky.

Willie squeezed the trigger of the gun, adding a thunderous boom to the show taking place in this out of the way pasture. A few pellets ricocheted off the Plexiglas of the chopper doing no harm. The gun carried No. 6 shot designed for shooting at small animals and not large machines of war.

The CH-136 Kiowa was not primarily a combat platform, but it did serve in areas of conflict. Willie's shotgun offered little threat.

Nevertheless, Wyatt pulled the stick to the left and moved from the location over Willie's head. He knew Willie's vision would not allow him to track the machine in the sky except by sound and he was so close, the noise would seem to be coming from all over. He killed the super bright spotlight and lit up Willie with a smaller spot.

"Go, go, go," Scott barked into his microphone connection to the police on the ground.

The detectives opened their eyes and sprang forward, all three ordering Willie to drop his weapon, all three aiming their own nine millimetre pistols at him. Willie, dazzled by the light, his hearing still suffering the effects of the shotgun blast, stood confused in front of them.

His first instinct was to aim at the sound of the voices and shoot but the voices seemed to be all around him. He was unsure of how many cops materialized out of nowhere in this pastoral setting where he and Larry Scarborough should be alone. Florida had never looked so good to him as it did now. Why had he ever left?

As ordered, Willie dropped the shotgun to the ground. Fighting unseen targets while blinded was futile. He thrust his hands into the air.

"Don't shoot. Don't shoot." It was over.

Over for these four people at any rate. The morning light would bring a team of forensic experts and searchers to start looking for the other bodies believed to be buried somewhere in this pasture as well. Probes would be forced into the ground. If a cavity was found, digging would start. Jim looked forward to the report landing on his desk, but he was content not to take part in the actual exhumation ceremony. He had worked all that day and night. He would beg off for tomorrow morning. Or was it this morning? He looked at his watch. No, it wasn't midnight yet.

"Cuff him," he said, as he waved away another squadron of black flies sent in to help Willie battle the cops. "Let's get the hell out of here."

# ≈39≈

THE LIGHTS were turned down in the home workshop. No whirr of machinery disturbed the tranquillity. No sounds of wood being sluiced off in long thin strips could be heard. John Lester sat in front of the open window breathing in the cool, night air. The time had come.

Tonight he would put his new plan into operation. A little more than two months ago, this was the farthest thing from his mind; now it seemed the natural thing to do. Finding the big bag of money had been a life-altering experience for him. The time had come to move on and stop playing games. The money had to be returned. His mind could conceive of no other option.

He remembered the day he gave his notice to quit his job and also announced he was starting his vacation right away. His supervisor went ballistic.

"You can't walk out on us. We chose you to stay when the company downsized. I went out on a limb for you. You are one of the chosen few."

"Am I?" John had asked. "Chosen to work longer hours for the same pay. Chosen to carry a beeper seven days a week, twenty-four hours a day. Chosen to do all the work alone in what had been a three-person department. How can I thank you for considering me for this honour?"

"Not by quitting, that's for sure." His supervisor missed the irony in John's statements. "You're the only one who can do this job."

John had thrown him the keys to his office. "Sorry, good buddy. I've just had a better offer. It includes no job security, but I guess my ex-fellow workers showed me I didn't have that anyway; longer hours, no, that can't be. 24-7 is the most you can work in a week.

"I'm my own boss and that means no corporate headquarters can tell me I have to fire a dedicated, loyal staff member for the sake of saving a few bucks on the bottom line. Did you think we were overstaffed with three people? No, you didn't and you know it, but you kept your mouth shut when the order came down.

"Au revoir, my friend. I know you truly believe you were doing me a favour and I hate to let you down. The truth is the company shafted me in the same way it shafted those who lost their jobs. It took me a little longer to see it. Don't take this personally, it's not worth it. You could be next. Toronto doesn't give a damn about you either."

With that, he had picked up his box of personal belongings and walked out of the office. The only difference between his exit and those of his former co-workers was that he didn't have a security escort to the front door.

No, there was one other difference, a big difference, he was not unemployed but free, free to start living his own life, his own way. Knowing he had a bag of money to fall back on made the decision easier at the time. Now he knew he didn't need the crutch anymore. Eric's announcement at supper the previous evening about securing guaranteed sales was the deciding factor. It was time to turn the money in.

Once the decision was made, John knew he had to act quickly. Putting off returning the loot would only add unnecessary stress to his life. He would start the wheels for his plan rolling without delay. This day had been inevitable. At some point, he knew the money would have to go back. He had spent a great deal of time deciding how to go about this task. Three things stood out in his mind.

One: don't get caught.

Two: catch the bad guys.

Three: don't get caught.

Really, one and three couldn't be stressed enough. He had no intentions of being caught.

He did have a plan.

Earlier in the evening, he and Danka had gone rambling through the wooded area along the deserted road. For over two months, his walking route excluded this part of the green belt. Now he felt confident enough to return.

Most of the underbrush was tramped down from hundreds of feet searching for thousands of dollars. Everyone in the subdivision had made at least one trip through this area.

John had no definite target in mind, but knew he would recognize if he saw it. His scheme involved moving the eventual discovery site of the money away from paths that led to his neighbourhood. This meant moving the money a couple hundred yards up the road.

He needed a big maple tree and a hiding place that could have been overlooked in the search. Danka ran back and forth among the trees, sniffing the rocks, peeking in holes, applying himself to the job at hand with a dedication which suggested he really understood the nature of the task. But it was John who found the perfect spot.

Two trees had fallen close together, leaving a small cavern between them. Most likely searchers had checked it out several times, but it created an ideal hiding spot. It would serve John's purposes. He made note of the location from the road. It could be reached with a good throw if the thrower's strength was infused with an adrenalin boost. The kind of boost one could get from having two cop cars chasing you through the night while you carried hundreds of thousands of dollars in drug money.

A big maple towered close by. The first traces of red were starting to show in its leaves as the summer season wound down. It could have been the marker John heard the voice talking about on the day he found the money. In fact, now it would be. John alone had the power to make that decision.

John listened to the silence in the house, not an absolute silence. He detected the ticking of the clock, the hum of the refrigerator, the gentle snoring of Marla in the upstairs bedroom. He opened the door to the area under the steps. There, untouched, lay the big bag of money under a couple of old lawn chairs. The Montreal Canadiens logo stood out in the dim light coming in through the open door.

This bag had revolutionized his life and yet it had never moved, never been opened for over two months. The contents were untouched since the day he dragged it into the house. John had no idea how much money was even in the bag. He wondered if he should count it. No, he decided. It was best to leave it untouched, not to disturb any fingerprints the paper might hold, definitely not to add his own.

With that thought in mind, he slipped on a pair of thin, brown leather driving gloves. He eased the lawn chairs aside, thinking it was a little late in the season to bother fixing them now. Maybe next year. The leather in the bag stuck to the cement floor, requiring a little tug from John before it released itself from its hiding place. It was as if the bag didn't want to return to its life of crime. It seem content to serve the purpose of supporting a fledgling business. The heaviness of the bag surprised John. The excitement of the discovery had given him extra strength last spring.

He reached down to pick it up when something touched him on the back. John froze. His blood ran cold. After all these weeks, had he finally been caught just when he decided to do the right thing? It wasn't fair. Then Danka's head moved in beside him to sniff at the bag. The dog turned towards his master. In John's bent position, they were face to face. "What's up?" Danka seemed to ask. The palpable relief John felt caused him to let go of the bag and hug the old dog beside him.

"I guess you are a part of this adventure, Danka," he whispered. "You've been in it right from the start. You may as well come along and see it end."

Danka wagged his tail in agreement. Maybe he understood John's words, maybe he didn't. One thing was certain in the dog's mind. They were going out somewhere together.

John checked his watch. One a.m. He picked up the bag and eased his way through the doors, trying not to bump into anything. This was no time to make a noise and wake up anyone else in the household.

He slipped out the back door and crossed the lawn to his driveway. It was a moonless night and the darkness enveloped him. Alfred Hitchcock could not have come up with a better setting for this final journey. He dumped the bag into the back seat, returned to the house, where he picked up a six-volt flashlight. Danka jumped in beside him ready to go wherever the car would take him.

John pulled out of his driveway and started winding through the streets of the subdivision heading for the back road. He opted to deliver the parcel by car instead of by foot so that no police dogs would be able to back track to his house, regardless of the distance needing to be covered to the new location. Perhaps he had watched too many episodes of the Littlest Hobo and gave the German shepherd dogs too much credit for their tracking ability. Be that as it may, John intended to take no chances.

As he drove along the street, a pair of headlights materialized in his rearview mirror. There was no mistaking the distinctive profile of the rack of red and blue lights mounted on the roof even in the darkness of the night. Instinctively he glanced down at his speedometer. Seventy in a fifty. The big bag of money lay on the back seat fully exposed. The same feeling of despair experienced when Danka snuck up behind him returned.

His foot slacked off the gas pedal, not touching the brake, while he watched the mirror to see if the roof lights started flashing. Nothing. The cop car pulled out, passed him and left him behind.

John had to pull over and stop. His hands shook in an uncontrollable fashion. Naturally, the only other cars on the road at this time of night would be the police doing their constant patrolling.

Was the Back Road on their nightly route? John doubted that. It would be a poor use of manpower to be on that desolate stretch of road. Still, this was one more thing not included in his plan, one more thing to worry about until the money was out of his hands and into those of the police.

He took several deep breaths and got himself under control again. He eased back onto the road. There were no other halos of light to be seen. It was just him, Danka and the bag of money.

He turned onto the Back Road and started watching for his maple tree. The criminal who said they all looked alike in the dark knew whereof he spoke. Everything looked eerily similar.

John knew where the path from his own house came out and knew his maple tree was just down the road from that. He proceeded to the intended location and stopped the car. He turned out the lights and sat in complete darkness.

He brought his hand from the steering wheel and up towards his face. His palm touched his nose. The hand remained invisible. Danka whimpered beside him.

"Why are we stopping here?" he wanted to know.

"Easy boy," John said. "You best wait in the car."

John opened the door and flooded the interior with light. Danka started bouncing around. He had no intentions of staying in the car. Adventure awaited him outside. He bounded across John's lap and into the blackness.

"Danka, get back here," John called. His voice sounded extra loud in the preternatural darkness of the forest.

"Just hide the money and get the hell out of there and back to bed before you're missed at home," he told himself. "Danka, you stupid dog, you're on your own."

The six-volt light cut a sharp beam into the trees. He swung it back and forth trying to locate the exact spot of the downed trees. Things looked different than they had earlier in the evening. Shadows from his light created huge many-handed, many-fingered creatures. The uneven ground made it difficult to walk without shining the light at his feet. When he did this he couldn't see far enough ahead to make forward progress. The bag of money increased in heaviness. His footing on the rain-soaked leaves gave way and toppled him off balance. Down John went into the bushes, scratching his face in the process.

The light fell from his hands and went out. He fought back the urge to panic. A slight glow from the open door of his car provided a small degree of light. Danka appeared beside him, concerned.

John took a couple of deep breaths before spotting a slight reflection from the lamp. Nearby he spotted the battery separated from the base. He picked up the two parts, slid them back together and instantly sat in the puddle of light produced by the conjoining of the parts. This had all seemed like such an easy plan when he sat in the comfort of his workshop formulating it in his mind. He gave the dog a reassuring pat. Having companionship made the endeavour a little less scary.

The opening in the trees lay just ahead of him. He made a superhuman effort to pick up the bag of money and throw it into the slot. Bingo, first try. He flashed the light back and forth across the results. It looked to him like it could have been thrown from the road.

He scrambled back up the embankment followed by Danka. He herded the dog into the car and jumped in behind him. He took one look back at his handiwork. He could see nothing in the darkness. It would have to be good enough. He started the engine and headed for home.

One-half mile down the road he pulled over and stopped. His body trembled uncontrollably. What had he done? How much money had he heaved into the darkness? He forced several deep breaths into his lungs.

"Smell the flowers; blow out the candle. Smell the flowers; blow out the candle."

Relaxation settled over him like a warm blanket on a cold, frosty night.

A weight lifted from his shoulders. As crazy as it seemed, he knew he had done the right thing.

With one strong throw into the abyss, the big bag of money had flown from his life forever.

# ≈40≈

AFTER THE heavy rains of the previous day, morning came in clear and sunny. Even this early, it was already warm. John, despite his late night adventure hiding the bag of money, had been on the street searching at eight o'clock. Now he had some success.

"Found you, sucker," he said to himself when he finally spotted Wally McIssac coming down the steps of a split-entry brown bungalow.

"Going down to the studio," he had told Marla earlier after he gulped down a quick orange juice. "Some guy's dropping by to check out some bowls."

She looked up from the breakfast dishes, surprised. "Does Eric know?" she asked. "Isn't that his department?"

"It is, but he's out of town. He letting me entertain the client with breakfast at his expense. I guess I'm moving on up. He gave me a Tim's card so maybe the guy isn't too important."

The flower bed in front of the house showed signs of the season winding down, but a bright red burning bush at the corner of the lot offset the diminished colour of the others. Two blue jays pecked at the seeds being dropped by the dying flowers, oblivious of the people in their vicinity.

In his hand, Wally held the Watch Tower magazines. They too were showing the signs of wear. He didn't seem to understand the concept of leaving the literature behind so people could read it and have their souls saved.

John sped down the street, parked his car and walked back in the direction Wally was travelling. A jogger trotted by in the same direction. John recognized him as the undercover cop keeping Wally under surveillance. Unlike Wally, who was a stranger in the neighbourhood, John knew who belonged and who didn't. The jogger showed up at the same time as Wally did and only did his workouts when the drug dealer was in the area. John noted that the cop had dropped a few pounds and was looking quite fit. He had developed a deep, bronze tan over the summer. The jury was still out on whether or not that was healthy but he did look good, John thought. The jogging allowed him to work off the beer consumed on the in-between days when his baby-sitting took him to the local taverns.

John hurried up behind Wally and then fell in step beside him.

"Nice day for being out and about," he said, trying to sound casual.

Wally looked at his new travelling companion. "This day the Lord hath giveth," he said in his best biblical voice. "Have you taken Christ as your saviour?"

"Yeah, sure. I guess." John had not expected to be converted. That was not in his plan.

"Give yourself unto the Lord and He will provide for you, my son." After a couple of months of doing this, Wally thought he was ready to be ordained. The words rolled off his tongue with ease.

*Provide for me,* this was the opening John was looking for. "Yeah, He could provide me with a big bag of money. That would take care of my needs. Some people have all the luck."

Wally stopped in mid-stride. The hairs on the back of his neck stood up. After spending the entire summer pounding the pavement in this subdivision, having door after door slammed in his face, having little, old ladies spill all their troubles on him, resisting the invitations of some frustrated housewives, was he was about to get some results?

"The Lord works in mysterious ways," Wally said, struggling to contain his own excitement. "Have you heard of someone receiving a bag of money?"

"As a matter of fact, I have," John said. "If I give myself to the Lord, do you suppose there is a bag of money in the cards for me?" He laughed to show his contempt at the thought.

"Wherefore I say unto you, all manner of sin and blasphemy shall be forgiven unto men. You mock the Lord but He will forgive you, my son. Tell me about this bag of money so I can spread the word of God's good works."

John got serious. "I have never seen it myself, but a friend of mine in the next subdivision over was telling me about it at a soccer game the other night. It seems some of the local kids have been flashing twenty dollar bills in the area." John looked around to make sure no one was listening and leaned in a little closer to Wally. "They claim they found a bag of money in the woods but I think the kids are dealing drugs myself. Who ever heard of a bag of money laying around like that?"

Wally took a few deep breaths and struggled to control his excitement. "I'd like to talk to your friend. If, indeed, his kids are involved in unscrupulous acts as you suggest, I might be able to bring them around to the path of righteousness."

*Oh, you're good,* John thought to himself. "Perhaps you could be of some assistance, but please don't be offended by this. Accusing his kids of breaking the law is bad enough, siccing a Jehovah's Witness on him could end our friendship."

"For Christ's sake man, what's his name?" The frustrations of two months were catching up to Wally. He quickly apologized. "I'm sorry, that didn't sound right. I've had training in this kind of counselling. I know I could help the boy. It's my mission in life to save sinners." The wheels in Wally's head were spinning double time. He was so close and this fool was holding out on him.

"I'll tell you what," John suggested, "you give me your telephone number and I'll have him call you if he's willing. That's the best I can do." He wanted to tell Wally where the money was but he didn't want the police to observe him doing it. He didn't want the authority's second stop to be at his door. Already he had been talking too long out in the open.

"Time is of the utmost importance in cases like this," Wally pleaded. "If we don't intervene early, often it is too late after that. Just tell me his name and I won't mention you. I don't even know who you are."

*You're damn right and let's keep it that way.* "Give me your number and I'll have him call you within the hour. Go wait at McDonalds or somewhere. That's the only way this plays out. Now that you've brought up the subject of intervention, I should recommend he seek professional help. Maybe get the police involved. They deal with this shit all the time." John started to turn away but Wally grabbed his arm.

"555-1723. That's my cell. I'll be waiting for the call. 555-1723. Stress the urgency. Keep the cops out of it. From my experience, they only make matters worse. They'll arrest the boy rather than help him. Call me."

John walked away as the undercover cop made another lap by them.

"Religious fanatics," John said to him. "The streets aren't safe anymore."

"You've got that right," the cop agreed and trotted away, leaving John walking back to his car. The policeman had observed citizens getting cornered all summer by Wally.

Some listened politely, some argued with him, others just walked away or slammed their doors. He should do a study on the different reactions of people. Whoa, he thought, this assignment has dragged on much too long. He had no interest in people's reactions and if he did, he was sure a government-funded university study existed somewhere. Government-funded useless studies abounded everywhere and people complained about their taxes paying his salary. He gave John no additional thought.

For John, phase one, hiding the big bag of money, and phase two, getting a contact number for the crooks, were completed. The next part of the plan required getting the cops and robbers to arrive at the bag of money at the same time. This would be the tricky part.

He drove into the city and went into one of the larger shopping malls. He fed a quarter into a pay phone and called the Crime Stoppers number. He looked around to make sure no one was watching and placed a felt pad from one of his face masks used in woodworking over the mouthpiece. He had experimented leaving messages on his answering machine. His voice was distorted but the words could still be made out.

"The police are looking for a bag of money in the woods near the Back Road. I saw the ad on TV last night," he said when the call was answered.

"Yes sir, do you have any information about this? The call is confidential and is not being recorded. If you have something over the mouth piece of the phone, that's not necessary." The operator had played this game before.

John ignored her advice. "Tell the police to keep a close eye on the people they are following. They will lead you to the money." He hung up. Phase three complete.

He dialled Wally's number. He answered before the first ring died away.

"Yes, yes, what can you tell me about the bag of money?"

John smiled into the phone. So much for saving souls. Should he tease him some more or just give him the information and get it over with? He chose the second option. He was as anxious as Wally to pass on this information and be done with it.

"What's he saying?" Wally had tracked down Leroy for the wait. They sat in their favourite drinking hole, The Bull and Bear.

Wally held up his hand for silence and scowled at Leroy's interruption.

"I don't think there is any money. I think the neighbour kids are into drugs and this is just a story. My kids tell me the money is about twenty feet off the Back Road near a maple tree. They think these bad kids stash their drug money there rather than taking it home and have their parents confiscate it. I really don't want to get involved."

"Wait. Wait," Wally demanded. "Where did you say they keep the money? It's important that you give me this information. Tell me and then you're out of it."

John gave a detailed description of how to find the exact spot. A description that even a kindergarten kid could follow. "You will check this out and if it's a scam and they are dealing drugs, I understand you have experience in helping troubled kids out."

Wally was caught off guard for a minute. Then, he remembered his cover story. "With the help of the Lord, I will bring these children back to the path of righteousness," he said.

Leroy rolled his eyes and shook his head. "Where's the fucking money?" he mouthed.

Wally slowly repeated the directions to the money to make sure he had them right while he scribbled on the back of one of the Watch Towers. John hung up.

There was no doubt in John's mind that both the good guys and bad guys were getting this information at the same time. He felt positive Wally's cellphone must be monitored. Phase four complete. Exit stage right. He was finished with the big bag of money.

# ≈41≈

B-E-E-E-E-P, B-E-E-E-E-P, b-e-e-e-e-p, the electronic whining of
the phone dragged Jim Mcdonald back to consciousness.
Yesterday had started at 6 a.m. and wound up at 3 a.m. this
morning. Willie's arrest took place around 11 p.m. He then had to
be transported back to the city and the never-ending paperwork
mill started grinding to make the arrest a reality. Questioning had
been minimal. Willie had nothing to say and the policemen
wanted to wait to see what they located in the burial field before
getting serious about the interrogation. Other cops started
working at that joyful task at first light.

"Mcdonald," Jim mumbled into the phone. Light streamed in
his bedroom window making him squint as he studied the face of
his watch. It was 11 a.m. already. He had fallen asleep around five
after reliving the events of the night and the arrest over and over
in his mind as he struggled to fall asleep. He thought he had set his
alarm for nine but the button was in the off position. Either he had
failed to set it or he shut it off without waking up. It didn't matter,
he was awake now.

"Ah, to be able to sleep-in all morning; you sergeants get all
the perks," Inspector Holland sounded uncharacteristically jovial.

"Good news all around. The team at the farm has had success in digging up more remains, six in a mass grave so far, and they're still looking."

"Great, the risk has paid off. No flak from anybody yet about how we did it?"

"Only William Ettinger's lawyer, but no one is taking him seriously. Same shylock used by Roger Johnson, Leroy Leblanc and those two thugs. I love it when they all tie themselves together."

Jim rubbed the sleep from his eyes and looked around the window blind in his bedroom. Another sunny day in paradise. "Thanks for the call; I'll get dressed and be right in and start interviewing Ettinger." He swung his feet onto the floor and started to stand up.

"That's not the good news. Sorry, I got distracted. I wouldn't have bothered calling you to tell you that. I saw the times on your arrest report and know how late you left here this morning. However, we have more arrests imminent and I'm sure you and your team want to be in on them. We have found your bag of money."

Jim snapped to complete alert. "The missing drug money? When? Where?" He leapt to his feet, his heart racing. This had been a goal for the entire summer and he wouldn't miss it for anything. "Who are we arresting?"

Holland chuckled. "Everybody. The tails on Wally McIssac, Leroy Leblanc and Roger Johnson all report their subjects are heading for the money. McIssac and Leblanc are waiting for Johnson at a local tavern near the site. How fast can you be there?"

Again, Jim looked at his watch although the time of day would have no bearing on how long it took him to get dressed and out the door. "Fifteen minutes, tops," he said. "I'll come in my pyjamas if I have to. Should I call Kate and Joe?"

"That's being taken care of as we speak. The Emergency Response Team has been assembled and final details worked out.

We are going to meet at the end of the Back Road on the opposite side from the way the druggies will be coming. That end of the road will be blocked right away. As soon as Johnson and his gang go by, their end will be closed off as well. Members of the ERT are heading for the subdivision to cut off any exit from there and to dissuade any dog walkers and keep them out of the area."

"You've been busy," Jim was impressed with the amount of planning already done.

"We were tipped off from the Crime Stoppers line that something was about to happen. It seems you were right about stirring up the publicity again. It generated results. Somewhere out there is a citizen who knows more about this than we do. The plan is partially his. He called us to be on the alert and then we monitored his call to McIssac filling in all the details.

"We'll worry about him later. We might want to use him as a strategic planner." Holland was enjoying all of this. Years spent sitting behind a desk only allowed him a vicarious enjoyment of the big takedowns. He had to settle for seeing his plans come together and culminate in arrests and bad guys being taken off the streets. This would be in Jim's future as he got too old for street work. He was unsure how he felt about this.

With the tip-off, the cops were operating on the same time schedule as the criminals instead of playing catch-up. It was not often they got to be out in front of the action, but they seized the opportunities when they arose. If they could eliminate any innocent bystanders from the area, they could make a more aggressive, and thus a safer for themselves, takedown. Jim skipped his planned shower, jumped in his car and sped off to the meeting site.

The black van of the ERT had taken its position before he arrived. Kate Irving had passed him coming along the road, lights and siren. Kate was not going to miss this for anything. Joe pulled in two minutes later.

The detectives were assembled, all present and accounted for. Jim reported to the officer in charge. Kate and Joe had worked with ERT during the previous arrest of Louie and Mark. They knew their own roles would be insignificant, but giving up an hour or two of sleep to be present for this arrest superseded everything in their schedule.

The ERT officer had a map spread out on the engine bonnet of one of the marked patrol cars being used for traffic control. The edges fluttered in the wind and he placed a night stick on one side and an automatic pistol on the other to hold it in place. A red X marked the known location of the money. A red circle was drawn around this a little farther out.

"We already have men planted in the woods, here, here and here," he pointed out to Jim indicating the perimeter defined by the red line. "They have verified the exact site of the money, here."

He tapped the red X with his forefinger.

"We want the perps to have the bag in their hands when we arrest them. It will make your job easier as you wrangle the case through the courts."

"Perfect," Jim said. "They'll probably try the old finders-keepers defence anyway. Were just innocently walking in the woods and *voila*, look what they stumbled across."

Joe leaned in and looked at the area marked with the X. "That's further up the road than our primary search area but I'm sure we must have looked there."

Kate looked at the map a little closer. "We covered that whole area with a fine-toothed comb. Us, the K-9 unit, search and rescue, cadets. I can't believe we missed it."

"The men at the scene say it's lodged between two trees and out of sight. They think it had to be one shot in a million to hit that location from the road in the dark." He looked back at the map.

"At this point," he indicated the entrance to the Back Road from the tavern end of the subdivision, "we have a squad car waiting to block the road as soon as the perps go by and a team waiting to follow them in, staying just out of sight. They'll give us the word as soon as the road is sealed, and we'll move in closer, and then all three groups will attack at the same time."

He brought his hands together in a silent clap.

"You and your men can come in when the capture is complete. The inspector said you would like to personally make the arrest."

This last step caught Jim by surprise. He had not been forewarned. "Detective Irving should get that honour."

"Right on." Kate shot a fist into the air. "Let's get them."

"But," the ERT man continued, "let me stress you don't come in until it's over. My team are trained to work together. As the situation evolves, so do their assignments. If it escalates to live gun fire, we all know how not to shoot each other. Strangers can upset the flow. Our reports show at least one of them may be armed, possibly two." He smiled, trying to soften his words to these long-serving, trained policemen. He wondered if they had ever actually fired their guns in the line of duty.

"No problem," Jim said. "You do your job, we'll do ours."

The radio in the black van crackled to life. "We have a light grey Ford Explorer in the area. Three males inside. Fit the descriptions of our suspects." Everyone became alert at once. "We are proceeding in behind it. Stand by."

"Mount up," the officer in charge said. "Cock your weapons."

Click, click, click, click. Metal against metal sounded all around them. The guns had to be ready when they hit the ground running. They didn't want this extra warning noise to alert the perpetrators of their arrival. The van moved out.

Wally consulted his notes as he slowly drove down the dirt road. "Here's where we looked the last time," he said as they drove by the previous search site. "The guy on the phone indicated the money should be up here a ways further. Look for a big maple tree."

Roger rolled his eyes. "Not this big maple tree crap again."

"That's right," said Leroy, "I told Big Willie it was near a big maple and he laughed at me. This proves I was right."

Roger scowled at him. "It's about fucking time."

Wally pulled the car over to the shoulder and all three disembarked.

"Look for a couple of fallen trees lying close together." All three scanned the area. Dead trees lay everywhere. Wally consulted his notes. "He said it would be easy to spot."

"So did Leroy the last time," Roger mumbled, "but we don't have anything to show for it."

Wally followed the shoulder of the road for a few feet, changing his angle. "There. Over there. That's got to be it." He pointed to two downed, overlapping trees.

Leroy jumped into the ditch, slipped, caught his balance and scrambled out to the spot indicated by his friend. He crawled up on the first tree and looked into the crevice. "It's here," he shouted. "The fucking bag of money is here." His hand made a repeated pointing motion between the two downed trees.

"For Christ's sake, keep your voice down," snapped Roger. He didn't want it advertised he had found the money being shown on TV every night for the last week. He was surprised it was still here and the place wasn't crawling with searchers. His view swept the surrounding trees. He thought he spotted a movement.

One of the ERT members hiding in Roger's line of sight spoke one word into his neck mike.

"Now."

From one direction of the road, a black van skidded to a halt in the loose gravel. Six men in black body armour jumped out, fully armed, guns aimed at the three surprised men. From the other direction at the exact same moment, a black souped-up, four-door Ford roared in. Each door produced another copy of the attack team. They too, had their weapons pointed at Roger, Wally and Leroy. In the forest, three more black-clad men popped up like jack-in-the-boxes, armed like the others.

"Get down on the ground and spread your legs," one of the arriving men yelled. "Now. Get on the ground."

Wally dropped at once. He hit the ground and covered his head with his arms like a mistreated puppy waiting to be beaten.

"Spread out your arms," the cop closest to him ordered as he prodded him with his foot. Wally spread his arms and looked up into the barrel of the gun pointed at him. He closed his eyes and waited.

"A fucking trap. You stupid, goddamn idiots," Roger said as he also kneeled to the ground and then assumed the spread-eagle position. Resistance never entered his mind in light of the overwhelming force surrounding him. He would do his fighting in the courts. "This is entrapment. I won't even spend the night in jail."

The cop standing over him smiled. "Save it for the judge, pal. That's not our part of the job."

A shiver passed through Roger's body. He had not had a whole lot of luck with judges lately. He got off with the DUI, but somehow he thought this will be a bigger fight.

Leroy did not come to the same conclusion. He reached under his jacket and pulled out his new pistol, firing as he brought it out. One of the ERT members let out a startled yell and fell to the ground. Gunfire cracked through the air from all directions. Bang, bang. Six shots sounded like two as one member of each of the three attacking components put two shots into Leroy's chest. His body flew from atop the broken tree and landed in the scramble of underbrush ten feet away. There was no further movement.

One of the three men from the wooded location came forward and aimed his gun at Leroy's head. Leroy's gun lay beside the money bag where he dropped it the instant he was shot. A second team member recovered it. A third member came forward and checked for a carotid pulse.

Four spots, the colour of the leaves in the maple tree overhead, formed a tight group in the centre of Leroy's chest. There would be two more in the centre of the back if he rolled him over. This was an officer-involved shooting and would require an investigation so he left the body untouched where it lie.

No exit wounds showed from any of the shots. These three shooters carried a medium load in their cartridges, enough to take a man down but not enough to penetrate the body through and through. In crowded situations like this, no one needed extra bullets ricocheting around.

The man checking the pulse shook his head and got up and returned to the side of the road. The first man stood down from his firing position.

A loud, piercing wail came from Wally when he saw the cop shake his head. "Oh, Leroy, you crazy bastard, what have you done?"

Wally had few friends in the organization. With his quiet, plodding manner, he didn't fit in. Leroy accepted him anyway. Now that was over. There was nothing Wally could do to help him. A big burly cop stood over him with a rifle held three inches from his head. Wally lowered his head again and wept.

Roger lay in a similar position. There were no tears in his eyes. "You idiot, Leroy," he mumbled.

"Get on your feet and put your hands on the top of the car as far apart as you can reach," the cop ordered them both. A hand in the belt and at the collar lifted them from the ground before pushing them towards separate vehicles. The rifles followed their heads. A quick search showed Wally carried no weapons.

"I have a gun on my belt," Roger volunteered. He didn't want anyone getting antsy when they found it during the search. The cop opened his jacket and removed a semi-automatic Glock. They withdrew a Swiss Army knife from his pocket.

"That's everything," Roger said. The cop patted him down anyway.

A paddy wagon pulled up along with Jim's car. Jim, Kate and Joe jumped out and took in the scene. They hadn't really expected any shooting considering the manpower disadvantage the drug dealers were at.

The ERT member who was shot pushed back those examining him and stood up. His body armour had served its purpose, but he would still have a bruise where the bullet hit. A bruise was better by far than a hole.

Kate Irving stepped up to Roger Johnson and placed a hand on his shoulder.

"My friend," she said, "you are under arrest for..." Kate paused. "There are so many charges I don't know where to begin." The smile couldn't be pried off Kate's face.

# ≈42≈

SMILES ABOUNDED at what was dubbed the wrap-up meeting for Operation Enduring Success. A little more than three months had passed since the other police forces had made their initial arrests but that didn't make this occasion any less sweet. Detective-Sergeant Jim Mcdonald, detective constables Kate Irving and Joe Davis sat in Inspector Garry Holland's office, each with a celebratory mug of coffee in their hands. A week had passed since the arrests and the report lay on the inspector's desk between them.

Jim Mcdonald spoke. "A hockey bag held the missing money, \$432,150. It bulged at the seams it was crammed in there so tight."

The inspector gave a low whistle. "Four hundred and thirty-two thousand. I expected a big haul, but..." He paused, at a loss for words. "No wonder Johnson was so eager to get it back. That would go a long way towards covering our operational expenses."

"That's the good part," Joe Davis jumped into the conversation unable to contain his zeal. "Some of the loot was from our operational budget. We found stacks of money used by our undercover operatives to make drug purchases, all with the serial numbers duly recorded. And," a dramatic pause, "with the fingerprints of Johnson and McIssac as clear as could be. We've got them, big time."

"Wally McIssac served as the accountant; Johnson just couldn't keep his hands off the cash," Jim explained. "Along with the fingerprints, the lab boys have found Roger's DNA on every tenth bill in some of the stacks of hundreds. Seems he wet his thumb, counted out a thousand dollars, wet his thumb, counted out another thousand, and so on. The hundreds were ours. Corporal Randy Carroll made the buy. The drugs were to go to the west end of the province. They were uncut. We still have them and can now marry the money and the drugs together for trial. We even have pictures."

A slight frown crossed the inspector's face. "The money was missing for over three months. Is that going to cause a problem?"

"None at all," Jim said. He picked up a walnut cruller from the box on the table. "We pursued Leblanc and McIsaac into the area on the night of the bust. We know they stopped and dumped it. We caught them with their hands in the cookie jar in the same location. We can tie it all together." He bit into the pastry.

"What about whoever had the money in between?"

"Who was that?" Jim asked with mock surprise. "We never found anyone and it wasn't for lack of trying.

"The evidence shows we searched the wrong location. If someone out there had the money, we would have tracked them down regardless of where the loot was thrown. Their lawyers won't have any more luck than we did." He licked some of the frosting from his fingers.

"Johnson worked harder at finding the loot than we did. He scoured the neighbourhood all summer. He had at least one person talking to the locals full time.

"It appears the money lay there in the woods, undiscovered all summer, until some kids stumbled across it last week. They didn't move it but told their parents, one of whom tipped us off through Crime Stoppers.

"That ensures their anonymity. The chain of custody is intact as far as we are concerned."

He sipped his coffee.

"So somewhere out there the citizen who gave us the big break is breathing a sigh of relief," the inspector said.

"I doubt that. He or she doesn't know we've stopped looking for them. Let 'em sweat."

The sergeant's face took on a serious demeanour. "That man or woman is no hero. They cost us hundreds of man hours that could have been better utilized, thousands of dollars in expenses for unnecessary surveillance and even contributed to the death of Larry Scarborough."

"No great loss there," Joe Davis said in a low voice intended only for his partner, Kate Irving.

The sergeant wheeled on him. "Larry's mother won't agree with that assessment. No mother wants to attend the funeral of one of her children, no matter how misguided their lives were."

Joe did not back down. "Yeah, I know, he bought her her smokes."

Jim struggled, then gave way to a smile and then laughter. "See. Everyone has one redeeming quality."

The others joined in, not because a man had been killed, but because they had all been under a great deal of pressure all summer. They needed a relief valve. Larry Scarborough provided it.

"Anyway, I hope the so-called hero shakes in his boots every time he sees a cop car in his rearview mirror or if we happen to patrol down his street. It's the least they deserve."

"You've got a mean streak running through you, Sergeant," the inspector laughed. "Did they take any of the money for themselves, sort of a reward or finder's fee?"

Jim took another bite of his cruller, chewed, swallowed and shook his head. "We have no way of knowing, but it doesn't seem likely. That bag was jammed so full of money that it spilled out every time the zipper slid open. As a bonus, buried beneath the money we found loads of drugs. It seems the druggies just threw anything incriminating that was in the house into the bag and took off with it. We can add another charge of possession for the purpose of trafficking to the already long list of charges. We'll bury their lawyers in paperwork."

Joe sorted through the donut box and fished out a blueberry fritter. "Didn't we nail a spy in our operation, as well?"

Jim nodded. "We've arrested a young IT employee here at headquarters. We can tie her into the operation as well. She altered some records for them like the breathalyzer report, but wasn't really a spy, per se. She didn't know that we had everyone under surveillance.

"Leroy Leblanc would have been better off if he had stayed in jail. Faking that breathalyzer report backfired on him big time."

"Aren't we leading the list of charges off with murder?" Kate Irving asked. "All this other stuff seems unnecessary if we can send them away for life. Any other sentences will just be served concurrently. Seems like a waste of time. The Americans have it right when they sentence someone. Let all the prison time stretch out in a consecutive string. Send them away for a hundred years."

Joe gestured with his fritter and laughed out loud. "Heard a case on the news last week. Man was found guilty of two counts of murder and sentenced to two life sentences without parole to be served consecutively and then, the judge, in a fit of whimsy, added another five years for good measure."

Jim understood where his detective was coming from. He too was frustrated with a system that sentenced someone to ten years in jail for a total of five different crimes only to have it boil down to two years when they were all lumped together to be served at the same time. To him, that made any crime after the first one a freebie. It encouraged criminals to keep offending.

"We're going to hold off on those murder charges until we are sure we can make them stick. There were a total of eight bodies plus Larry Scarborough found in the field. William Ettinger will be charged with illegal disposal of the dead. That will hold him for a while, but we want to build a solid case tying the actual killings to Johnson.

"We know he was responsible. The courts require us to provide a little inconvenience in the form of proof beyond a reasonable doubt. As long as we get him into jail on the drug charges, we will know where he is. If the investigation drags out until he serves his full time and is released on those charges, we'll arrest him again and hit him with the murder indictment then, and he can start from scratch with his new sentence. The bodies have been there for years, there's no rush in convicting someone." Jim smiled.

The inspector's smile faded. "Speaking of bodies, tell me about the lad who got shot by the Emergency Response Team. What went wrong there?"

Jim refreshed his coffee cup and offered the pot to the others. Joe accepted; the others declined. "We weren't present so I can only tell you what they told us at the time. Leblanc got off a wild shot as he pulled out his gun. Hit one of their team. He has the bruises to prove it so there is no doubting that. In true ERT style, as the report says, they took the shooter out. Seems they shot him six times.

"Nothing we wouldn't have done if he pulled a gun and fired at any of us. It looks like a clean shoot to me. Wally McIssac told me when I interviewed him that Leroy didn't want to go back inside. It was his choice. Maybe even suicide by cop."

Jim took another sip of coffee.

"He was rumoured to be bipolar. Must have been in a depressed state. He didn't take his medications on a regular basis. When I talked to Leroy after his DUI, he told me he would never go back to jail."

The inspector slowly shook his head. "Unfortunate, but sick or not we have to defend ourselves when someone starts shooting."

"No arguments here." Jim held up a stack of pictures. "Joe went to his funeral and got lots of pictures of his friends and associates."

"Good," said the inspector and reached out for the pile of photos and started looking through them. "Next week, as you know, Jim, we are going to make another province-wide bust. We've had a great summer collecting new evidence and we're ready to roll. We think we can just about shut them down for a little while with this raid on the heels of the one at the beginning of the summer, especially here in the Metro area where everything is in chaos with Johnson's arrest."

He paused at some of the pictures, recognizing the faces as known criminals, but mostly they were just strangers standing around attending a funeral. He stopped at a photo of the funeral urn.

"One last picture of Leroy?" he asked showing the selected photo to Joe.

"Yeah," Joe said. "That's a beautiful piece of work, solid maple. Some mom and pop wood-turning business in the local area made it. Seems they couldn't crack the market in the city so they ship all their stuff to the states. Too bad because they do great work. A friend of Leroy's mother, some old guy connected to the business, gave this to her for Leroy's ashes. See the mark on the front, they call it a flaw, a little like Leroy himself, I guess, so they can't sell it. I think it adds personality to the thing."

The inspector took off his glasses and held the picture close to his eyes. "What's the inscription say?"

Joe smiled. "Leroy's mother's idea. *There shall be joy in heaven over one sinner that repenteth.* Can't beat a mother's blind love."

# ≈43≈

"OH, I GET religion when you do that to me." Marla was lying on top of John. Her hair hung down around her face and tickled John's nose. It was 7:30 on Sunday morning. They had been awake for a little over half an hour. John was fulfilling the terms laid down by Marla when she agreed to let John go into business with Eric Sanderson. Sunday morning was their time together.

"You know life was good before now..." She let the sentence trail off. She pulled her knees up on each side of John's hips and sat up straight. She rubbed her hands over his chest, massaging the muscles being formed by the manual work of holding a chisel all day. "I have to be honest with you. I never thought you'd ever quit the security of a steady pay cheque and set out on your own. I'm proud of you."

John remained silent enjoying the feel of the fingers digging into these newfound muscles. He adjusted his hips a little to accommodate Marla's sitting position a little better. She responded with a little wiggle of her own.

"Life is still good," John said, his breath coming a little harder. He ran his hands up the sides of her rib cage and then slid his hands around until his thumbs touched. Marla leaned forward to let him take her weight. John brought his head up to meet her and they shared a kiss. He let his head fall back to his pillow.

What she was saying was true. If it hadn't been for the bag of money that lived under their basement steps all summer, none of this would have happened. It was ironic in a way. John had never touched the money after the first week. It was like a sooky blanket carried by little kids until it wears away to a rag and then is disposed of. The money had served no real purpose. He could have done the same thing at any time in his life.

"Yeah, I know," he said. "Somehow this just seemed like the right time to try something new. It was a moment in time. The planets were properly aligned or something like that, but I couldn't have done it without your support. Let's face it, without you, I'd have been easy pickings for Eric Sanderson."

She took his chin in her hand and squeezed. "Eric is just a pussycat. You would have learned to handle him in time."

John pushed her hand aside. "Don't sell yourself short. Basically I'm a coward who would still be working for someone else. Your getting involved in the operation is what made the whole thing possible. Without you, it wouldn't have happened."

Marla leaned back again, picking up the tempo of her gyrating hips. "Poor Eric," she said. "I don't know why you have such a low opinion of him. He's been a great help, but you and me, we're a team. Together anything is possible."

John arched up and hung on tight.

"Right," he agreed. "Anything." After a few seconds he collapsed back onto the mattress, Marla coming down on top of him.

Any thoughts of the bag of money disappeared from his mind. Gone forever from his new life. He had never really needed it anyway.

# *Author's Note*

Many of you will disagree with this ending where John returns the money. Others, myself among them, believe honesty is always the best policy; two wrongs don't make a right, and other such clichés.

That is my theoretical belief. Like most things in life, we don't really know how we would act in any circumstance until the actual event occurs. We would have to factor in the size of the find and the location, and so on and so on and so on.

Now you know the genesis of this book idea.

I am still looking forward to finding my first bag of money to test my reactions.

Regardless of which school you fall into, I hope you enjoyed the story as presented and will look forward to picking up a copy of my next book.

# ABOUT THE AUTHOR

Art Burton lives in Latties Brook, Nova Scotia, Canada with his wife, Flame and dog, Charley.

He took an early retirement from The Halifax Herald at the end of 2002 where he had been a printer for 26 years before joining the IT Department. When he left the hustle and bustle of life in the big city for the more relaxed, laid-back lifestyle of rural Nova Scotia, he decided it was time to move up from printing to writing.

This is his fourth mystery novel. He is also the author of two books of related-short stories about the hobos who passed through Central Nova Scotia during the Great Depression.

For more information on these books, visit his web page at users.eastlink.ca/~artburton.